IT TAKES
TWO

IT TAKES TWO

Mindy Hall

CITIOFBOOKS, INC.
3736 Eubank NE Suite A1
Albuquerque, NM 87111-3579
www.citiofbooks.com
Hotline: 1 (877) 389-2759
Fax: 1 (505) 930-7244

Ordering Information:
Quantity sales. Special discounts are available on quantity purchases by corporations, associations, and others. For details, contact the publisher at the address above.

Printed in the United States of America.

ISBN-13:	Softcover	979-8-89391-195-4
	eBook	979-8-89391-196-1

Library of Congress Control Number: 2024914306

Table of Contents

CHAPTER 1

Emily Kristich was on a mission. Considering the circumstances, she drove the car at a reasonable speed through the two-lane highway, but when those lanes were narrowed to one lane by the cement barrier, the traffic slowed to a foot-by-foot pace. Hoping the chaos was less on the side roads, she took an earlier exit than she normally would have, approached the checkpoint and was waved through by the army of uniforms holding their walkie-talkies. Although the uniforms directed the caravan of weary vehicles to proceed, the line only grew longer and slower as time eked by.

The first intersection presented a gaping mortar hole, so she, along with her other escaping compatriots, gingerly skirted the ditch with their vehicles. To take the place of the inoperable traffic lights, portable stop signs, looking like they had been riddled with bullet holes, were anchored by sand bags. Cement barriers lined the edges of the rutted lane while the sand of the street kicked up by the wheels passing over it formed a hazy cloud making throats dry and eyes water. It was only mid-morning, yet the hot sun gave the surroundings a yellow cast that made the day seem hotter than it was. Because of some ruckus at the intersection, traffic was almost at a standstill. The heat, the dust and the confusion made tempers short and blasts on horns long. The wait to proceed through the barriers to her destination tore at Emily's nerves, so that by the time the convoy of traffic began moving, she began to question her resolve to proceed to her destination.

After all, it was only to get year-end gifts for her kids' teachers.

The traffic construction, which in Northern California begins in April with the end of the rainy season and concludes in November with the new onslaught of rain, was only going to get more intense. It was better to forget her incipient headache, move on with the not-so-flowing traffic and get the errand done. Onward, full speed ahead.

However, fifteen miles per hour was hardly full speed.

The kids' teachers put their all into their profession; they deserved some token of thanks. Better to get it over with, get the gifts and not have to deal with the traffic construction that was scheduled for the entire summer. Better to get it over with and be able to think of one less item on her schedule. Better to get it over with and…

But it was looking tentative as to whether she'd accomplish something so seemingly minor as picking up a couple of gifts. Emily had not set off on a National Geographic expedition, but that's what this trip was becoming–explore torn up streets and rout her schedule. Now, as she appraised the parking lot—now, she was going to have to defeat an overwhelming snarl that was quickly escalating to road rage in the parking area. She had set out early in the morning just to avoid the morass of shoppers searching for bargains; instead of buzzing into a space close to the department store, Emily was to wait in line while bored road repair people directed her to the few areas left to park cars. Not only had the city streets been gutted to increase lanes, the parking lot of Del Oro Plaza was being decreased in size to allow the space for the extra lanes of streets. That unavailability of parking lot space plus the massive construction equipment parked in the mall's lot had put parking spaces at a premium.

Emily's dog, Byte, had spent the trip to the shopping plaza hopping between the front and middle seats of the minivan. Perhaps the heat of the day and the traffic congestion of the construction had agitated her as much as it had Emily. Even in her air-conditioned car, sweat was beginning to mold her chestnut hair to Emily's head. No telling what the heat was doing to the double fur coat Byte was wearing. When she wasn't concentrating on the pitfalls of the road, Emily was watching Byte's ears as they alternately flattened and peaked in response to the myriad of construction sounds besieging her dog's hearing.

Reaching over to the passenger side of the van, Emily patted the German Shepherd's head and rubbed her ears. "Is it giving you a headache, too?"

Byte gave her a quick glance, hung her tongue out the side of her mouth and panted.

"I told you it was too hot for you to come with me. Even if we park in our regular spot, you're going to be too warm."

Byte looked at her again and panted some more.

During the next stop to allow the oncoming traffic to exit the mall's parking lot into the lone lane bounded by orange cones, Emily said to Byte, "You know our errand days are coming to a close."

A withering glance from Byte made her continue with an explanation. "With summer all but here, the weather's getting too warm to keep you in a car. You'd end up looking like melted lard if you had to stay in the hot car too long. Now, I know you're smart, and you know you're smart, but you're not smart enough to run an air conditioner, and you sure can't shop in the stores with me."

A snort at the window was the only response from Byte. No look of acknowledgement this time. The sleek, black and tan face ignored Emily.

Emily, certainly not a stranger to the mall and its parking facilities, had long ago discovered an area no one seemed to know about. It was almost always empty as it was recessed in the lot far from the shopping area, and few people felt the obligation to expend energy walking to the shopping center from an inconvenient parking spot when they could use that same energy for their actual shopping. She escaped the line of cars being directed in a circle by the crews and headed for the dumpster area, her private parking space. Hurriedly, she rounded the dumpster and aimed her car for one of the two spots between it and the retaining wall that held a hill from encroaching onto the shopping center. There was a car in the spot she had long ago designated as her own, but she didn't see it until she was almost upon it. As she suddenly braked her car while swinging the half circle to park, she flung her right hand to prevent the dog from going through the windshield. Her arm broke Byte's slide into the dashboard, but just barely.

"Sorry, Byte. I didn't expect that car to be there. Looks like someone else found our spot."

Emily angled her car into the adjoining space, cracked each window a couple inches, got out and locked the doors. The heat of the day intensified the odor of the dumpster, so that it stifled the air which should have been cool and fairly refreshing.

"I'll be back in a jif, so you won't have to stay around that odor long. That's terrible."

Holding her breath so she wouldn't have to smell the dumpster, she hustled to the department store side of the mall and glanced at the car next to hers. It didn't register at first, and she was already in the main area of the parking lot before she sensed her uneasiness. Emily reached to open the glass door of the department store but stayed her hand in midair as she became aware of distant barking that sounded much like Byte.

Knowing her dog had better manners than to incessantly bark, Emily retraced her steps back to the car. As she, intent on discovering Byte's trouble, approached the right side of her minivan, she made another discovery. It was one of those findings one would never really want to see, and she didn't actually see it. She felt it. She felt it like a herd of snails crawling her back leaving a trail of mucoid slime that would never wash off. She shivered as she watched Byte bark at her. She shivered again but didn't want to move. Byte quieted her barking and looked questioningly at Emily who wasn't responding to her although she continued to stare at the dog. Emily's green eyes gazed at the dog and wondered how long she could stay in this position, stock-still, muscles taut with adrenaline, watching her dog bark at an empty car.

Only the car wasn't empty. Emily had known that even before she had made it to the busy area of the parking lot in her rush to get to the department store. She even knew what was in the car. She had known that also; she had smelled it, she realized. And she even knew why it was disturbing Byte. But she didn't have to look, did she? She didn't have to turn in that spot where she had welcomed the dimness for its cool shade and now dreaded that cold umbrage for what it was hiding, did she? She could back herself out, turn to the left side of her car, and the minivan, which was higher than most vehicles, would protect her from seeing the contents of the car next to her. She could back out and look straight ahead and not down into the car next to hers.

No one would know either. She would never tell anyone what she saw one day in the very darkest and remotest corner of the Del Oro Shopping Plaza. Just she and Byte would know, Byte who was waiting for her to move. The dog wasn't even barking now, just whimpering and looking for guidance from Emily.

Emily, certain of what she would see, slowly turned to the car and bent slightly to look in the driver's side window. At first, her brain didn't allow her eyes to focus, so she presented herself with the false hope that she was truly peering into an empty vehicle. Almost relieved, she straightened up quickly, too quickly, because the bullet hole in the back of the head that was lying on the steering wheel registered, and even though she was prepared for her find, a sharp gasp still jostled itself out of her body. The adrenaline, which had pumped her into steadiness so readily, now seemed to desert her as her muscles quivered, and her body wavered. If she had moved more slowly, would the bullet hole have melded invisibly into the tableau presented allowing her to move forward?

Odd, how that little hole, not even half an inch in diameter, could command so much attention. She gazed intently at the little hole, a little hole that punched the life out of this man. Such a little hole for so much bulk; the proportions were all wrong. To kill an adult human being with such a little hole seemed impossible. Emily had studied the hole in the back of the head leaning over the steering wheel so long, but she doubted she could describe the host of the bullet hole to the police, and she knew she'd have to. She knew she'd have to call them and report her discovery. She commanded her body, rubbery muscles tottering, to move. She commanded her arm to reach into her purse to take her cell phone and call the police.

When she had completed her call and promised to wait for the police to show up, she started walking to smooth out some of the quivering her body had begun. The shock cycle she permitted her body to complete sent tears of frustration down her face. In her walk to steady herself, she located a drinking fountain, and, leaning her height down to the spigot, she depressed the button. After taking a quick drink, she laid her face into the spurt of frigid water. That washed away her tears and jolted her brain into some sensibility. She wiped her eyes with her hands and slapped her face with more cold water. The person behind her loudly emitted a huff of disgust. Emily turned to face him, but he sneered at her unconventional use of the drinking fountain.

"Sorry," Emily apologized to the retreating individual.

She hurried out to meet the first wave of authorities, the uniformed police officers.

The crime reports in the local paper of Pleasant Creek are both droll and reassuring. Droll because many of the reported police calls were for situations that could be in a comedy—the caller forgot why he called, a woman saw a naked man in her yard and realized it was her husband when she put on her glasses, a woman's toe was stuck in the bathtub faucet. There were the more serious reports of domestic violence, thefts, a few assaults, some arrests for driving under the influence, but for the thousands of people who inhabited the area, they were proportionally few. In that regard, people reading the crime watch reports were reassured because violence and lack of safety seemed to be minimal in Pleasant Creek. Murder, however, changed the equation. Murder in one's living proximity sullied the area with a corrupted filth that no amount of decontamination could obliterate. Murder decreased the comfortable safety factor too much.

Seeing turmoil ransacking Emily's face, the woman in police blue calmed her by asking questions in a professionally decent manner to elicit Emily's account of discovering the body. After the policewoman, Officer Sandoval, had finished transcribing Emily's report, she said, "Now, we're going to need to keep your car. When you drove into the area, you became part of the crime scene."

"My car? I can't have my car? I need my car."

"I know you do," consoled Officer Sandoval. "Unfortunately, so will the crime scene investigators. I'm sorry. Maybe I can get someone to take you home."

"Wait. My dog. Do you need my dog, too? She just barked. She didn't do anything. She didn't mean to become part of a crime scene."

"No, you can have your dog. It's the car we need."

"For how long? I need to do errands." Emily put her hand to her head and rubbed her forehead. "Look, I'm sorry. I'm being insensitive. Here's this poor man who doesn't even get to decide if he needs his car or not. I'm just, well, I'm just…"

"Understandable. This isn't something you encounter very frequently. It's okay." Officer Sandoval looked—really looked—at Byte for the first time. She cleared her throat, "Hmmm, is your dog going to be nice if we take him out of the car?"

Emily looked at all ninety pounds of Byte and smiled. "Would you like me to do it? She's very well mannered."

Again, Officer Sandoval cleared her throat. "Let's do it together. Be very careful about where you walk; I'll lead."

As the two women extricated the dog from the new addition to the crime scene, several non-uniformed personnel pulled up in their cars.

They and the policeman who came in with Officer Sandoval barricaded the area with yellow caution tape and began taking pictures of the parking area with disposable cameras. Officer Sandoval guided Emily and Byte to the passenger side of the automobile of the last car to arrive.

A very tall man, sparse hair askew where he habitually riffled his hand through it, unbent himself out of the car. He peered intently through his glasses at the darkened area where the parked car still sat with its burden, and he visibly sniffed the air before he looked at the officer standing by his car. Nodding his head at her, he slowly walked the area around the car, bending down periodically to examine small items on the ground.

"Too much of that smell could make you sick," he said as he acknowledged the presence of Officer Sandoval patiently waiting to introduce him to Emily.

"Detective Washburn, this is Mrs. Emily…"

Bob Washburn looked from the officer to the woman she presented.

"Kristich. Emily, how did you get here?" Detective Washburn explained to the policewoman, "Officer Sandoval, I know Mrs. Kristich quite well. Her mother is a very good friend of mine."

"She's the one who made the original call to the department," Officer Sandoval began.

"You are? So how did you get here?"

"This is my parking spot when I come to the shopping center. Not very many people know about this area. Even the Christmas shoppers, when the lot is overflowing, don't know this spot well. If Byte is with me, I'll come here because it's shady, and the car doesn't get hot. It surprised me there was a car here when I drove in; I don't think I've ever seen another car here. It's too far for the people to walk, so why should they park here? When Byte barked so much, I came back to see what was bothering her." Pointing to the car, she said, "And that's what I saw. Do you know him?"

"Who, Byte? Yeah, I know him, but I thought he was a she," Detective Washburn said as he continued to survey the area more intently than listen to Emily.

"She is, but that's not the 'he' I meant. Do you know who died? Did the officers find anything to tell you who he is?"

"No, I have no idea. They haven't even opened the car yet. Probably isn't even his car. Bet we can't find a serial number on it either." Stepping carefully toward the car, he looked in with a flashlight. "The bullet hole looks like a single .32 caliber bullet to the back of his head. Someone knew what he was doing. There's not much in the way of saying he was even killed in this car. Haven't checked any missing persons reports, yet."

Stepping back toward Emily, Bob said, "I'm sorry, Emily, you had to find that. Are you all right?"

"Sure, after the shock wore off; I'm fine. Officer Sandoval was quite helpful."

Officer Sandoval accepted Emily's appreciation with a smile and said to Detective Washburn, "I've got Mrs. Kristich's statement. We have the area cordoned off. We need to keep her car, so she doesn't have a way to get home. I'll see what I can do. Anything else you need us to do besides keeping away the gawkers?"

"No, I'll look around, and the crime scene investigators will continue fingerprinting and searching for clues. I want to sketch this out and take some pictures to add to the ones the officers took initially." He produced from a bag a throw-away camera. With that he started snapping the car and the surrounding area at various angles. He asked Emily and Officer Sandoval a few more questions and finally said to the policewoman, "Don't worry about Mrs. Kristich. I think we can take care of getting her home. Thanks for your help."

To Emily he said, "Just because you're you, Detective Yoshiwara and I'll get you home, along with Byte. Did you finish your shopping?"

Emily shook her head.

"Tell you what. This is going to take time, so, if you feel up to it, go shop."

"But Byte. Byte can't go with me. I'll wait here."

"Officer Sandoval," Bob Washburn called, "do me a favor, please."

She walked over to the detective, saw him holding Byte's leash to her and swallowed noticeably. "Sir?" she squeaked.

"Hold this leash, please."

Emily heard her clear her throat a second time. Hastening to reassure the policewoman, Emily said, "She'll be okay. She knows you now. I won't be long." Turning to Bob Washburn, Emily offered, "Maybe I should just stay here with my dog. Then, Officer Sandoval won't have to hang on to her."

"No," said the detective. "You need to get your errands done. The dog will be fine with the officer here, won't she?" He directed the last question to the woman in blue.

"If you say so." Officer Sandoval stood the full length of the six-foot leash and held the end gingerly. Panting as she edged closer to the officer, Byte sat next to her.

"Go shopping," Bob said gently.

With the nod of an automaton, Emily headed in the direction of the shopping plaza. Looking straight ahead and ignoring the activity of the police crew and the bystanders that activity had garnered, she walked into the department store and robotically picked out some miscellany to serve as gifts. She left the store, mechanically retrieved her keys from her purse as she walked toward her car, saw the police cruisers and stopped. She opened the shopping bag to remind herself what she had just done, looked again at the police cruisers and then remembered with a sharp flash the body lying in the car next to hers. Dropping the bag of gifts on the asphalt, she leaned against a concrete pillar supporting the garage floor and cried with quiet, stringy sobs.

When she recovered her composure, she continued to lean against the pillar. Slowly a wry smile touched her face because she realized what

Bob had slyly done. Sometimes routine is the best medicine for shock. Maybe that's why Bob sent her to finish the errand. Not allowing her to stay with her dog and certainly not allowing her to voice dismay, he had sent her on an inconsequential errand while he orchestrated the whitewashing of the murder scene. He got her out of the way as deftly as could be done. She had gone shopping while a man lay in a disheveled death. The murdered man's situation wasn't fair, and there was something irreverently imbalanced in her shopping and his death. Yet, Bob had used her need to complete her mission to shield her from an unnatural occurrence, kind of a topsy-turvy respect for death.

Emily knelt down to pick up the bag holding the teachers' gifts. Third time's charm and on Emily's third attempt to get into the stores, she had made it to the department store and picked out her gifts–a victory over obstacles as great as any encountered in a battle.

CHAPTER 2

Joan Chavez enjoyed every working day of her career, and because she had enjoyed the workdays, she was pleased with her life that was defined by her career. There were several reasons for the contentment she felt. She liked the crisp cleanliness of the hospital, her hospital, because it was a cleanliness that was palpable, one she could see and smell. Having an environment so ordered and clean provided the consistency to her life that gave it the structure she needed.

She had worked hard for her position in her profession. As she had nursed her widowed father through a debilitating cancer, she had learned much about medicine and the psychology of illness. When her father died, money wasn't available for long-term schooling, so she supplemented her income with several jobs and meager scholarships to get through undergraduate and nursing schools. Since the scholarships wouldn't stretch the wages enough to let her complete medical school, she opted to work toward a degree as a physician's assistant.

The disappointment in not being able to obtain a full medical degree was an insecurity that followed her throughout schooling. It caused her to study all that much harder to graduate at the top of her class. She understood she would always be under a physician's scrutiny and not able to make major medical treatment decisions herself, but she rationalized that was a small price to pay to be in a healing field. She found a few years of working at the county hospital had given her position an aspect of longevity that other hospital employees respected enough to seek her advice on patient management. By working so closely with physicians, she continually learned new solutions to caring for the ill. At this point in her life she felt she had achieved it all. She enjoyed her work, she had the respect of her peers, and she liked her working environment.

That's why she hated doing what she was about to do. She hated being put in the position of having to use her accessibility to steal when she knew it would jeopardize all the goals toward which she had worked so hard. Her small boned face was glum as she approached the closet where the pharmaceuticals were warehoused. She became more depressed as she filled her large tote bag with the small boxes of medications. No one had caught her yet, and she didn't think anyone suspected what she was doing, but she knew it was only a matter of time before they did. And the crime she was committing was akin to that of being a common drug pusher on the streets of San Francisco.

CHAPTER 3

The detectives made good on Bob's promise to take Emily to her house. Emily finished her shopping just as the sheriff/coroner's van was leaving the area, so she had only to wait a short while for them to complete their work, but she was running roughshod on her day. As Emily entered the detective's car, she looked up just as a mechanic was hooking her minivan to a tow truck. She felt a pang of guilt watching her reliable old automobile being slung around like an old nag. An old nag that had become an integral part of her life since the arrival of her second child, Lulie. She probably spent more time with her minivan than she did with her children and husband. It wasn't difficult to understand how riders became overly attached to their horses in pre-automobile days. She considered her minivan her faithful steed in charging through the perils and pitfalls of her quest to keep her family on a smooth and gratifying journey through life. Together she and her car had beat the clock to almost missed appointments for music lessons, dentists, Brownies, swim team and various kids' doings. They had carried heavy burdens of foodstuffs, household items, office equipment and yard equipment. They had purveyed children to class field trips, sports events and birthday parties. Now, simply because it was in the wrong place in the wrong time, her loyal vehicle was being sent to the ignominy of an impound lot, kind of like punishing the wrong child for a misdeed.

With the day and her energy all but spent, Emily banished her errands to the bottom of her to-do list and welcomed the chauffeured ride home. Sitting quietly in the backseat she placed her hand on Byte and rubbed her behind the ears, but it was more to reassure herself than to keep Byte calm.

Because Detective Yoshiwara exited the Plaza at a location different than the one that she had entered, Emily thought he might avoid some of the traffic that began her day so frenetically. It was not to be. Same story; different location. Slow traffic. Stopped traffic. No traffic lights. Temporary traffic lanes. General chaos. Sensing that the men didn't want to talk—Emily was certainly not in the mood for conversation— woman and dog remained quiet in the backseat. Perhaps if there had been less disorder on the streets, the detectives could have kept their silence throughout the stop-and-go traffic, but they didn't. It began with one innocuous statement from Detective Yoshiwara.

"Did you see any media there?"

"Not yet," replied his partner.

"They're going to be on this like stink on garbage, like the last one."

Detective Washburn nodded. "You got that right. At least, we didn't have to deal with it. You think it's the same?"

"Crime scene guys will tell us. Same type of killing; same type of dumping. Looks like it."

Emily coughed slightly and sat upright. "You mean this isn't the, I mean, this happened before? A murder? In another car? This isn't the first time?"

Emily didn't see Detective Yoshiwara grimace, but she did see Detective Washburn throw an unappreciative glance at him. "Look, Emily, murders happen frequently. We're just supposing, thinking out loud. It could be anything."

"Not here. Murders don't happen in Pleasant Creek all the time. They happen like never, well, almost never. What are you talking about?"

Bob Washburn pushed out a deep breath. "There was a similar murder in another jurisdiction. We're just monitoring the happenings. Look, it would really help us if you didn't say anything just yet about all this. When it comes out in the newspapers, then you can talk about it if you wish. Let us have as much time as we can, please."

Emily nodded silently, but she was thinking very loudly. Don't tell anyone Bob had advised. Don't tell anyone about a dead body that happened to show up in somewhere as mundane as a parking space. How can one not tell a husband or a mother or a best friend about something this shocking and frightening? A dead body. It wasn't even a fair dead body. This guy's life was taken from him; he hadn't lost it as the result of the natural cycle of life. Chances are he hadn't given his life for a noble cause. If he had, he wouldn't have been dumped in the forgotten corner of a shopping mall. His life had just been yanked from him, and he had lain in that hot, stinking car before he was found by a stranger. Not a fair way to die. But Bob told her, don't say anything. That might be a tough one, but for the sake of her mother who had a thing for this guy, she would try to honor it.

She knew she was thinking loudly when Bob turned around to admonish her again, "Try to keep it as quiet as possible. Certainly, don't tell your mother. If she knew you'd seen that body…"

Emily wrinkled her nose as she stared at Bob and said, "I have two daughters and a husband. I run a household and my husband's business, and my mother still worries."

Detective Yoshiwara grinned, "Yeah, but you gotta love 'em. Doesn't matter how well you do with life, they've got a wart the size of Alaska that does nothing but worry."

Bob looked askance at him. "A wart?"

"Yeah, you know, as in worry wart."

"Right. I got that part. It's just that…oh, well, you're right. Mothers are universal, I guess. Worrying about their kids is their job in life, doesn't matter how old they are."

"The kids or the mothers?" asked Emily.

"Either one. So keep it under wraps, okay?"

"I'll try. I won't tell Mom. It'll be harder not to tell David. I mean, there's going to be no car in the garage."

"You'll figure it out," Bob reassured her.

When Detective Yoshiwara stopped the car in front of Emily's house, Detective Washburn got out of the passenger's seat, came around and opened the door for Emily and Byte. He walked them to the door and waited while Emily fished for keys in her purse. Again, he apologized for the exigencies of life, "I'm sorry you had to see that."

She paused in the process of unlocking her house. "Yes, but having you there made it easier. That man will be in my thoughts for quite a while. Thank you for your courtesy."

Bob smiled as he exited the porch. "We public servants aim to serve the public."

Emily wasn't smiling when she walked into her house, however. She released Byte from the leash, let her out the French door into the backyard, watched as the dog sniffed and ambled back toward the house. Emily shivered in the heat that edged into the room when she opened the door for Byte. Locating a blanket, she wrapped it around her and huddled on the sofa in the family room until the carpool dropped her kids from school.

David walked into the kitchen from the garage later that evening and asked, "Emily, where's the van?"

"The van?"

"Your car. It's not in the garage."

"Oh, yeah. A flat tire."

"So why didn't you call me? I would've come and changed it; there's a spare, you know."

Don't tell anyone Bob had said. He also said I'd figure it out. Can't lie to my husband. Why should I lie to my husband? Emily, face contorted in confusion, looked at David.

"No, that's not it. I saw this dead body, and then I saw Bob Washburn. He told me not to tell, but I can't not tell you. So, here's the deal." After she finished the rundown of the day, she said, "I'll use the car-in-the-shop story for everybody else, but I don't want not to tell you. Okay?"

David pulled Emily into an embrace. "Sure, that's okay. That's a horrible thing to see. So sorry, honey."

Emily slumped into the hug, and the comfort of David's body checked any tears of emotion that might have come. "Yes, but I'm going to be okay, now."

CHAPTER 4

However, Emily wasn't okay during the night. She slept poorly throughout the deepest parts of the night. As soon as her body had settled itself into that deep, healing slumber, her mind jolted it awake with a surrealistic angle of the dead body in the car. Two times Emily felt David reach out and gently pull her toward him. Drowsily murmuring, "It's going to be okay," he absent-mindedly patted her until he fell deeply into the sleep she would have liked to enjoy.

It surprised her when she awoke to the brightness of morning sunshine because she didn't think she would sleep at all. It surprised her even more when she awoke to David standing at the side of the bed with a cup of coffee in his hand. "This is for you. I know you didn't sleep well, so I got the girls off to school. If you dress quickly, you can take me to the office and use my car for the day. That way, we can keep the car-in-the-shop story alive."

"You didn't have to do that. I could've gotten a ride. I'm only going to Miriam's house for a PTA meeting. She would've come for me." She sipped the coffee gratefully. "Thank you; it tastes so good."

"Uh-uh."

"Yes, it does. It tastes very good. You're a good coffee chef." She smiled at him.

"I know that. Uh-uh is for the meeting you have to go to. You don't have one. You have two. I looked at your calendar because I was going to ask you to go to a movie with me tonight."

Emily fell back against her pillow and spilled the coffee on the sheet. "No. I don't have two meetings. Just the one. Don't I?"

"Apparently not. You've got that one tonight."

She looked at him blankly and then said as she remembered, "Oh, yes. Sustain and Shelter. If I hadn't just started with that group, I'd skip it. The meeting last month was that really long one. It made me so mad because it seemed like overkill. They could have completed the business in half the time. I'll go tonight, though. Just to see if that one last month was a fluke. Now I'll probably get mad just thinking about it. Going to a meeting when I could have a date with my husband."

David bent down to kiss her forehead as he said, "I know those meetings accomplish something, and someday I'll figure it out. I do miss you in the evening, though."

Emily nodded thoughtfully. "I know. It's just that we've got so much good going for us in life, it seems we can do some little something to help out."

"Ah, spoken like the daughter of a social worker. If Louisa could hear you now, she'd know she raised you up in the way she should." David chuckled.

"I know. It's only time I'm giving. If that time helps someone in the world, maybe it'll be a better place, don't you think? Like that murdered man. Maybe if someone had done something good for him, he wouldn't be dead like that."

"Save the world; salve your conscience?"

"Maybe. I hope there's more altruism to it than that. Just seems like...I don't know."

"I do. You're a mom, a wife, a comptroller for my company, a volunteer for what three, four boards. You must be the modern twenty-first century woman. There aren't twenty-four hours in your day because you've added ten more hours. I don't know about the man in the car. That might be a stretch, but maybe you're right. If someone had done something positive, maybe he wouldn't be dead.

"All I know is this week of hot nights we've been having is about to do me in. It would've been nice to go with you and relax tonight in that cool movie theater. I guess I'll just have to wait until tomorrow night. That'll work. I'll be waiting with baited breath for a date with you."

"You got it. I'll call Mom today and see if she'll play Gramma for the girls and baby-sit." Emily threw off the coffee stained sheet and hopped out of the bed. "Let me get a bath; I'll be fast. I can change all this later. Do you need me to pick you up early or late tonight?"

"Early. I'll get the kids to bed and read to them. You get their homework started, please."

Miriam had left the burglar alarm off, so Emily could walk into the travertine-marbled foyer without waiting for her friend to make the journey through her house to answer the door. Shouting her way through the large house, Emily began the search for Miriam. She peeked into the off-white living room with its brown and white wide stripped sofas standing at right angles to the fireplace. White leather French chairs were placed around the sleek pecan wood furniture. African masks and South American primitive artifacts decorated walls and shelves, but there was no Miriam. Moving herself into the family room where red checked fabrics played hide and seek with bold yellow and red abstract upholstery on overstuffed sofas and armchairs, she didn't find Miriam either. Not in the library, the breakfast room or the kitchen. A look in the wine cellar found Miriam and brought a sigh of relief from Emily because she wouldn't have to traipse through the upstairs sleeping quarters.

"Your house is too big," Emily groused.

"Hi, babe. Goes with the territory. We've got to entertain to keep the job, and the man does like the job. Here. Hold this." Miriam handed Emily two bottles of Chenin Blanc. "I'll serve this with the canapés to the ladies."

"Oh, that's right. Have you found out anything yet? Did he get department head at the hospital? Have you heard anything definite?"

"He got it. He's thrilled. Head doc of the emergency room at Mercy Hospital," Miriam said with repressed excitement.

Emily grabbed her friend and swept her up in a gleeful hug of congratulations. "Wow! Dr. Harold Rose, head physician of emergency room. You need to get him a plaque or something to commemorate this."

As excited as Miriam was about her husband's promotion, she didn't miss a beat. "So where's your car? Why do you have David's?"

"In the shop. Tune-up."

"How're you going to get those four little bodies in that little bitty car and get them home this afternoon? Your carpool kids are going to look like they were rototilled by the time they get home. Better let me drive. After our lunch." Miriam raised her eyebrows in anticipation.

Emily nodded agreement. "Speaking of school, I have the list of board members for next year. Some will be here today; some can't make it."

Miriam took the list from Emily and studied it. After a few minutes of waiting, Emily said, "It's just a list, Miriam. It's not the *Bible*."

"Shoot, girl, this list looks like the United Nations."

"What do you mean?"

"Have you looked at these names and thought about them? Akiko Watanabe, Partha Puri, Betty Chan, Rosalinda Rodriguez, Shamin Farhid—those don't sound like representatives to the U.N. to you?"

"I suppose so, but there's my name, Emily Kristich, and your name, Miriam Rose. Those sound like run of the mill American names."

"Who do you think you're kidding? Your name sounds like you're FOB German, and anyone who knows me or my kids knows I ain't quite what the name seems." She laughed, and when Miriam laughed, the long braids swayed back and forth. Whenever Miriam was at the top end of an emotional crest, she went colorful. Today she wore a sunshine bright orange, yellow and brown sarong type dress with burnished gold earrings the size of small dessert plates and an arm's worth of gold and orange heavy bangles. Her jewelry set her up for sonar tracking; she'd never get lost because all one had to do was listen for the pleasant clank of her bracelets.

"But it looks like a strong board, and they'll do their jobs responsibly. As secretary, you can help Akiko keep them in line."

Emily had taken the list from her and was verifying Miriam's observation when she said, "You missed one, Miriam. Rochelle Emory is in charge of volunteers. I don't think I know her, though."

"Oh, yes, you do," she whooped. "If you can get her off the list, do it now. She'll show up for a couple meetings, maybe, if you're lucky, and you'll never have volunteers. She was in our playgroup when Eli and Scott were toddlers. Never came. The baby came with the nanny, but she never did. I bet you've never seen the woman around."

Emily's puzzled look confirmed Miriam's supposition.

"Come on, Em. She looks like a very sophisticated, expensively dressed old punk rocker. You know, the gal with the spiked platinum hair, matte make up as white as I am black, red lips that look like they're bleeding all the time. She has a girl in fifth grade and Scott in Eli and Jojo's class."

"I still don't think I know her. Her kid is in our kids' class? What's his name? Scott? Scott Emory. Scott," she muttered trying to recall a child she should know from volunteering in the classroom.

"Scott. Wait." she exclaimed as recognition flashed. "I remember him. That's Rochelle Emory's kid? That's an unusual kid. He does seventh grade math, including algebra, and can't read one sentence. That's her little boy? I still don't think I've met her though."

"Believe me, you'd remember her if you did. You probably haven't met her because she's never around the school."

"You don't think she'll do a good job." The last statement came out as a question.

Miriam looked at Emily and slowly shook her head from side to side. "Sorry, you really should fill the job with someone else."

Brows frowning and perplexity on her face, Emily said, "Miriam, you know how hard it is to get officers for the PTA. So many parents work full time; they'd never see their kids when they came home from work if they had to go to these night meetings."

Emily continued trying to convince the implacable Miriam, "Akiko Watanabe told me Rochelle was dying to get on the board. She said she'd take any job, and since no one likes to organize volunteers, Akiko suggested this job for her. Akiko's going to be Prez, so I guess she'll have to put up with her."

Miriam shrugged and said, "Suit yourself, but you've been warned. Akiko doesn't have the whole story though. It's Rochelle's husband who wants her on all this volunteer stuff. He needs to keep his profile high in the community, so he makes sure she has her name on all kinds of boards. She doesn't mind having her name on the lists. She does mind doing the work."

Emily paused and finally said, "You know what?"

"No, give me a hint."

"I think she's on the Sustain and Shelter Board also. They went through the list last time I was there, and I think her name was on it. I have a meeting tonight. I'll have to see if I'm remembering the name correctly."

"Bet she didn't show up at the meeting, did she?"

Emily shook her head. "No, I don't think she ever did. That was my first meeting though, and it was disorganized, so I may have missed her. I can't recall anyone like that on the board. Maybe David's right. I must be on too many boards because, after a while, the board members kind of run together."

"There's no way this gal will run together with anyone. You've got a double chance to meet her. If you didn't know her before, you sure will now. If she ever shows up."

The doorbell announcing the arrival of the PTA cut off any more conversation. Board members arrived, meeting was held, business was done, meeting was over, quickly, to the delight of all, and the women left.

"Lunchtime!" announced Miriam as she shut the door on the last of the women. "Let's go now and miss the crowd."

During their weekly luncheon outings sans children, they made the rounds to over-decorated charcuteries that served undersized portions of non-substantial, but picturesque, salads and compotes. Their dose of sophistication imbibed, they capped off their afternoon with a huge sundae at the local ice cream parlor to appease their insatiated appetite. Pretty food, good company, relaxed afternoon.

CHAPTER 5

By the time the late afternoon arrived, Emily's aggravation at attending Sustain and Shelter and missing a date with her husband because of it had built to the point that she became churlish with the children. Altruism was just fine when it was in the future; it was very easy to agree to sit on a board of directors when one's calendar was white space. Now, her altruistic motives that were so pure were getting a little muddied as she thought about missing time to cozy up with her husband and, instead, being obligated to cozy up to a bunch of strangers in a disorganized venue. Even Byte avoided her, preferring to spend the afternoon outside lying among the carnations and gardenias Emily carefully cultivated. It was just as well Emily didn't check on Byte, or her irritation could have intensified by geometric proportions.

"Mom?" asked Lulie.

"What?" snapped Emily.

The tone of voice made Lulie back out of the room without finishing her request.

"What, I said," Emily repeated trying to play down the annoyance in her voice as she followed her daughter into the hallway.

"Nothing."

"Lulie, I wasn't mad. I just was thinking hard. What would you like?"

Lulie read her mother's face for a few seconds, decided it was safe to ask and said, "I just wanted to know if Jojo and me could watch some television."

"Oh. Sure. Sure you can."

Emily followed Lulie into the family room and absent-mindedly watched her daughters select wholesome viewing fare. Even though Emily stared at the television, her mind replayed the first meeting she'd attended at Sustain and Shelter.

It had been so much of a fiasco that the agenda hadn't been completed by the time she left at 11:30 PM. Between trying to find the key to open the conference room door and locating the plug to provide power for the portable laptop computer that no one had charged, the meeting started forty-five minutes behind schedule. The executive director showed up twenty minutes after that, but the remaining two people needed for a quorum didn't arrive until 8:45. The president of the board who had set the agenda listed committee reports to be heard first. Fortunately, only three committee chair people showed up, so the long reports that alternated between bellyaching and bragging were kept to a minimum. The treasurer's report was the most exciting aspect of the meeting when Ms. McIvey reported a $5000.00 deficit for the month. Startled faces were replaced by a din of backtracking as key board members tried to pinpoint the error in her fiscal reports. Actually there were no formal, written reports; she just stated there was a deficit. The executive director had just begun to be questioned when Emily decided she could better serve herself with a good night's sleep rather than listening to verbose excuses. If it had been a morning meeting, or even an afternoon meeting, she might have chuckled at the adults conducting more slapstick than business. She didn't know anyone currently on the board, and she wasn't sure what the organization did with its money. A few times prior to acceptance of the position, she had requested the balance sheets and financial reports from the non-profit's office, but she'd yet to receive them.

After saying good night to her family after dinner, Emily took off to her second board meeting with Sustain and Shelter. In the car, she dialed Louisa Daniel's number on her cell phone because she had spent most of her afternoon dwelling on the upcoming meeting and not, as she had promised David, checking with her mother about babysitting.

"Mom."

"What's wrong?"

I knew it. How does she do that? She always knows when something's wrong. "What makes you think something's wrong, Louisa?"

"I'm your mother. That's my job to know when something's wrong. You always know when something's wrong with your own girls."

"That's different."

"You have a different explanation than the last time we had this conversation?"

"Not really. Mom, they're only six and eight. I'm in my thirties. That's the difference."

"No, honey. That doesn't cut it. You're my child."

"I'm your daughter, but I'm hardly a child."

"Sorry, the equation hasn't changed. So what's wrong?"\

Emily gripped the steering wheel in aggravation and then said evenly, "I'm on my way to a board meeting."

"You mean for that organization you just started with? What is it? Food and Home or something."

"Sustain and Shelter," Emily corrected her mother. "That's it, but that's not why I called."

"I heard about that organization from another of your board members. She says they're very capable in providing food and help for the homeless."

"Yeah, well, that person must be going to different board meetings than I've gone to."

"Not good, huh?"

"Very disorganized. It's a wonder they can get anything done. Who's the board member?"

"Joan Chavez. She sits on our board at Community Action Group."

"Describe her to me. I'm not sure I know who she is."

"Intent on what she's doing and very intense about doing it. Blond, petite. A nurse or something in real life."

"I think I know her, but that's not why I called."

"So, what's wrong?"

"I just told you, Louisa. That meeting I'm going to tonight."

"You've sat on awful boards before, and it hasn't bothered you. You've always said it was a way of helping the community because you were able to do it, and you've got a good life. Sounds reasonable to me."

"I know that. It's still true. It's just that I had a chance to go on a real date with my husband tonight except for this meeting."

"And my responsible daughter chose duty over fun first. You're a good woman, Charlene Brown. So, go to the movie tomorrow night. I'll take care of the little dolls."

Emily rolled her eyes and shook her head and laughed inwardly. How does she know that? She always knows what's wrong. "Oh, Mom, that's why I called—to ask you that very thing."

"I'm psychic, Em."

"No, you're a mom, Mom. Talk to you tomorrow; come for dinner if you want."

"Better yet. Why don't you and David go out for dinner and a movie?"

"Yes, ma'am. See you around 5:00?"

"Yes, ma'am. Have a good time tonight doing good deeds. Say hello to Joan for me."

CHAPTER 6

The Board of Directors of Sustain and Shelter had bought the house that became its office cheaply before its residents realized developers were willing to pay top dollar to cut a swath through their neighborhood for a series of high-rise buildings. Although the conversion from family home to office building had been tastefully but inexpensively done, there was no masking the fact it had once been a house and was now out of league with its monolithic neighbors.

Originally the conference room where the board meeting was now being held had been two bedrooms. The kitchen was left intact as was one of the bathrooms. The living room was ringed with file cabinets to become a combination waiting room and business office. A fish tank capable of holding a small porpoise had been set up in front of the copy machine to divide the line of royal blue stacking chairs from the cream-colored file cabinets and receptionist's desk. The master bedroom and bath was now the executive director's office, and the fourth bedroom was set up as an unoccupied office. Unlike many grass roots non-profit organizations, this one did not have to make do with mismatched office furniture that was donated because colors were out of style or drawer handles were missing. When the stock plunge of 2000 inundated the dot-coms, not every organization drowned. Some actually swam to the top and benefited from the losses of those high tech companies. For a few cents on the dollar Sustain and Shelter was able to buy all its office furnishings in almost brand new condition. Therefore, all the furniture sitting on the blue and cream carpet was coordinated. Because of that, the office had the neat and ordered appearance of any thriving business. Who said a shoestring budget couldn't tie up things nicely?

A few founders still sat on the board, and they occasionally showed up at the meetings. That night the most heavily moneyed one was relishing his capacity as president of the board by droning on about his recent donation, and how it was to be used to partially fund the salary of the executive director, Chad Woodley. Rudyard Millup's gray pin striped suit had been as meticulously tailored to complement his massive body as his silver hair had been meticulously cut to complement his handsome face. Purple lines had been etched in his nose either by very cold winds or very warm spirits. Northern California, however, is hardly near the Arctic Circle.

"By contributing as I have, we are now able to raise Chad's salary to the cost of living index and add fifteen percent per year on top of that for the fiscal year coming up on July 1. I am very aware, as I am sure you are all aware, of how important Chad's presence is to the organization. His travels have brought much awareness of the homeless situation in our community. I've also provided a small stipend for our new low income clinic," he said with affected modesty and a self-effacing smile.

"I feel we should give a round of applause to show Chad how much we appreciate what he has done. I know you would all agree with me just as I know Chad is very grateful for what I and some of our other benefactors have done." Mr. Millup began clapping.

He had chosen to ignore Ida McIvey, the treasurer, who had blanched as soon as she heard fifteen percent. Ida was frantically flapping her hand, but because she sat off to Mr. Millup's side, the hand flapping was ineffectual.

To the rhythmic background of applause, Ida sputtered almost like a rap rocker, "Mr. Millup, as treasurer, I must protest. The budget won't allow…You can't possibly mean…fifteen percent…" Futility flashed across the poor woman's face as she turned a new point on her mechanical pencil like a nurse readying a hypodermic needle and began furiously writing.

Chad Woodley was about forty-five years old with his full head of graying brown hair blown dry off his strong boned face. His lips lacked any definition when he wasn't smiling his conviviality at his audience, and the welcoming warmth of his being was tempered only by the furtive slant of his puffy eyes. The pink, yellow and green striped golf shirt didn't do much to hide his paunchy stomach, but it neatly matched the pink slacks he had chosen to wear on this balmy late May evening.

He had learned his thank you speech technique from watching the last Academy Awards. As he dramatically rose from his chair he said, "Mr. Millup, from the bottom of my heart, I can't tell you how much I appreciate your approbation of my work here. All of you are aware how much effort I have put into feeding our homeless community. I will be reporting the figures shortly in my report, and you will be delighted to hear the number of people I have enabled to be fed and sheltered. This project is invaluable for our community of Pleasant Creek."

A quiet hum diverted Emily's attention to Chad's droning of back up figures establishing his good works. She looked around the conference table to see from where the buzzing emanated and caught the eye of the older lady sitting across from her. As Emily tried an understanding smile, the woman looked away from her guiltily and tried to inconspicuously jab her sleeping husband in the rib cage. An intake of breath at her discreet prod resulted in a snort. Again, Emily smiled what she thought would be a sympathetic smile. The little woman, blue-gray hair neatly curled, looked away embarrassed. Her husband, brown toupee askew as the result of his nap, smiled back at her. However, and Emily hoped it was the result of not being alertly awake, his smile was more of a leer. Must be some of the founders, she decided.

Emily looked away from him to the man next to them. Just as she hadn't remembered the older couple present at the last meeting, she hadn't remembered this man either. With eyes averted from them, he stared at Chad, either giving the speaker his undivided attention or locked in a state of catatonia. The youngish looking man appeared to be entranced with Chad's oration. As she studied him more closely, Emily realized his young man looks came from his compulsive neatness. Thin brown hair was cut in a boyish cap, round framed glasses provided a childlike innocence, and his bow tie gave him a spiffy look like his mother had dressed him in long, big-boys pants for the first time.

However, he wasn't young. She observed fallen flesh in the cheek areas, little arrows of lines radiating from his eyes and an immutable unhappy downturn of his lips as if life had provided very few upturns. A straightening of his shoulders indicated he sensed someone staring at him, but he never turned his eyes to glance at her. He wouldn't even allow himself the satisfaction of knowing who was studying him.

Emily was brought out of her scrutiny of the man by a sheaf of papers shoved under her nose. Deciding it must be the corroborating information for Chad's commentary on how wonderfully productive Sustain and Shelter under his leadership had been, she went from people study to report study. Except the report didn't require much study as it was only two paragraphs long and outlined the floor plan of two soup kitchens and one medical clinic and provided the addresses for each.

She turned her gaze to Chad as he started to bend into his chair. Straightening himself, he said, "Oh, and I mustn't forget our volunteers. It goes without saying they are important to my task here."

In the middle of reseating himself, he remembered something and took the floor again.

"Mr. Millup has an announcement to make," he said as he sat down.

Mr. Millup was vexed. "Mr. Woodley, I thought you were going to tell them."

"No, remember, we decided you would do it because you're president," said Chad in an exasperated stage whisper.

"But I don't want to," loudly whispered Mr. Millup.

Through clenched teeth, Chad said, "But we already decided."

"Oh, all right."

Mr. Millup put on his best funereal look and said, "It is with great regret we announce the passing of our fellow board member, Ralph Watkins. As some of you may have heard, a body was found at Del Oro Plaza. The body was identified today as Ralph Watkins."

He paused allowing the eleven people in the room to be suitably shocked that one of their own board members had died. Emily sat up straight and swallowed hard. "You mean…wait, what do you mean? The Del Oro Plaza. A body?" She cupped her hands on her face and dragged them down. "Del Oro Plaza? The man was a board member? Here?"

Joan Chavez turned her pale face with her dour, thin-lipped mouth in a perfect frown, and said, "Did you know him, Emily? Are you all right? Was he a friend?"

"No, this is only my second board meeting. I can't place him. I don't think he was even at the last meeting. Did he have a family?"

Concentration settled on Joan's face as she thought about Ralph Watkins. "I think he had a wife. He might've been divorced. There must be grown children somewhere. He was the age to have them. He was a husky, dark haired man. Looked like he drank a lot. You know, he had the big, red nose, and he smelled like garlic all the time. He looked like he ate enough of it along with his other food. Maybe that's what killed him.

"He was one of the big money men for the organization. I remember one time talking to him about how important the service this agency offered was, and he was low-key and wanted to help. It's too bad he died that way. You sure you're all right. You're really pale."

Emily nodded slowly. "Have you heard anymore about what happened?"

"No, this is the first I've heard of it. I wonder if there are any details. Guess he died of a heart attack or stroke. That's what people seem to die of when they're his age."

"Did you know him, Bo?" Joan had turned to the young man, hair tied in a ponytail, on the other side of her.

"Sure, I worked with him in the kitchens," he said. "We both served, and then, sometimes, we'd switch. Makes the time go faster if you share the jobs. Doesn't get boring that way. Then he'd do the dish washing while I brought in the trays of dishes. Kind of a quiet guy, but he watched everything going on, so he was like, man, you know, a supervisor."

Because he had slouched down into his chair, Bo's long legs poked out from under the table causing anyone who walked by to either walk around them or to step over them to avoid tripping. Bo didn't seem to mind, but he didn't bother sitting up to move his legs back either.

"So do you know how he died?" asked Joan.

Bo shook his head. "Maybe he was in a car accident. You know, they're doing all that construction out there. Maybe something freaky happened. Ask Rudyard. He might know; he made the announcement."

Emily's condolences fell to the middle of the room as Mr. Millup called the group to attend to the business of the meeting. As a way of closing the subject of Ralph Watkins, he said, "There is a memorial service to be held sometime this week. Please check your newspaper obituary section for details."

Joan caught Rudyard's attention. "Do we know how he died?" "Who?"

"Ralph?" Joan replied impatiently.

"No, no details. Just that they found him at the Plaza."

Catching Chad's signal, Mr. Millup said, "What, what?"

Chad was mouthing, "Tell them. Tell them."

"Oh yes. Yes, there is something else. Mr. Woodley is reminding me. As you know, Mr. Watkins was a computer wiz and had been inputting data into our computers. Since he is unavailable…" An uncomfortable snicker followed the last phrase. "Since he is unavailable, we would appreciate a volunteer to complete the input. There is no hurry, but we would like to have it completed before autumn. Would anyone like to volunteer?"

As if the cue had been given, all eyes turned to Emily. She couldn't decide if this were an initiation to the 'group', or if they concluded her husband's computer business would somehow give her mega-knowledge of computers and equate her with Ralph Watkins. It wouldn't, but she did understand computers some, and input was not that difficult. Besides, if it could be done over the summer, she would have the time, and it would provide a break for her in her summer routine.

"I'll do it," volunteered Emily.

Chad said pointing to a young woman, "Thank you. All you need to do is check in with Shannon over there, and she'll show you the ropes. Any day you can be here will be fine."

"Now, that's settled," said a pleased Mr. Millup who acted as though he wished to put his thumbs in his suspenders to acknowledge a job well done.

The young woman to whom Chad had pointed and called Shannon had been busily processing words on her computer as the meeting progressed. At the mention of her name, she poised her fingers on the keyboard and looked up adoringly at Chad when he got up to speak. Her smiling glow almost hid her acne flare up, but it did nothing to improve the honey blond hair that should have been washed three days ago. When he sat down, her fingers began frolicking from key to key renewed by the words of the speaker. Shannon happened to glance up from her keyboard at the woman who had just arrived and placed herself in the seat next to Chad. The woman moved in very closely to him when he regained his chair. As she gave him a pat on the arm and a just-between-us smile, the young woman gave the older one a hateful glare. In return she received a smug smirk.

Miriam had been right on the button. If Emily had ever in her life come in contact with Rochelle Emory, she would have remembered. She did, indeed, display platinum hair spiked at right angles to her head, facial make up as white as a kabuki dancer, lips that looked like they had just smacked up a ketchup cocktail and rings on every finger. They were not cubic zirconia either. The varied stones flashed their facets of color with each light ray that hit her hands just as the nail art on her stiletto fingernails sparkled. Nor were the diamond studs crawling up her ear cartilage like segments of an earthworm cubic zirconia. She wore a red knit off the shoulder blouse which framed the small snake tattoo on her back scapula nicely. Tight white knit pants were tucked into laced short black boots. The bored air in which she wrapped herself and her unsmiling face made her as approachable as if she were Vlad the Impaler. As Emily covertly watched Rochelle stare into a corner of the room oblivious to the proceedings of the meeting and restlessly drum her fingers on the conference table, she herself became aware of the argument going on between the treasurer and president.

Mr. Millup, his distinguished carriage broken by his pointed forefinger jabbing at the air in Ms. McIvey's direction, was saying, "Because we want it that way."

Ms. McIvey, her strands of graying brown hair made more out of order by her hand constantly running over her head in worry, the anxiety in her eyes magnified by her thick-lensed glasses responded, "But you have no money to do it that way."

Mr. Millup said, "Of course, we do. I just gave $10,000.00."

Ms. McIvey responded, "We paid off the creditors and then put the remaining into capital reserve for emergency."

Mr. Millup said, "Then use that."

Ms. McIvey, desperation floating around her like potent dollar perfume, responded, "But that doesn't cover fifteen percent and a pay raise."

Emily continued to watch Rochelle as she took in the scene between Ms. McIvey and Mr. Millup. As the fracas between the two died down,

Rochelle caught Ida's eye and raised her eyebrows. Quickly, Ida dropped her eyes. Rochelle shrugged and sat back in her chair.

Mr. Millup, his face made florid by the interference in his plans, said, "So what? Give Chad the money."

Ms. McIvey looked at Rudyard and repeated, "We can't. We don't have that much money."

And so it went. Like an old eight track tape, first one loop, then the second loop, until it rewound itself to start on the same track.

"Excuse me," interjected Emily. "Could we have copies of the financials? Perhaps, we could develop some sort of compromise to take care of both issues. That is, if we had tangible information to work from."

It stopped the argument but only to table the discussion to the next meeting. Mr. Millup, with an ingratiating smile sent in Emily's direction, said, "Mr. Woodley and Ms. McIvey and I will have had a chance to meet and develop a plan of action. A splendid idea, Mrs. Kristich. That is your name, is it not?"

"Yes, that's my name. Same one I had last month. I'll be happy to sit in on the discussion with you."

"No, that won't be necessary. We don't want to worry your pretty little head about this nasty old money, do we?" asked Mr. Millup who was making it obvious he did not have a thorough understanding of gender equity.

Emily, giving him the benefit of the doubt by chalking this misunderstanding to Mr. Millup's generation, said with gritted teeth, "I'm anxious to do a creditable job here, and it would help immensely if I could see the monthly financial statements and the yearly profit and loss statements. Could I have copies of those, please? I've requested them of Shannon, but she's been unable to locate them, I guess."

It was Emily's turn to receive Shannon's glare, although it was not as hateful as the one directed earlier toward Rochelle Emory.

Mr. Millup cleared his throat once, twice, and then again and said, "Yes, um, well, yes, Ms. McIvey will try to have them available for you next month, won't you, Ida?"

Bewildered, Ms. McIvey just nodded her head.

Mr. Millup said, "Mrs. Kristich, you really wouldn't understand them. It's awfully complicated for women, you know. Even poor Ms. McIvey has difficulty understanding her own statements, don't you, dear?"

Ida blustered, "No, well, hardly, after all I am, well, I'm good at this job. You really can't say that. I do know numbers."

"Yes, yes, dear," Rudyard placated.

At that point Mr. Millup was relegated to Emily's graveyard of male chauvinists, but she said in her low quiet voice that her children would recognize quickly as the one that sprang them to action, "You are aware, Mr. Millup, that my husband has his own business in which I play a somewhat, no, make that extremely, active role by doing accounts payable and receivables and banking and other money matters. You are aware of that, I presume?"

As he slowly shook his head to the negative, Emily proceeded, "Then, please remember that, Mr. Millup, and do not, I repeat, do not insult me or any of the other women on this board again by telling us that women do not understand something because you must by now be cognizant of the fact that these women are here for a purpose, and it is not tokenism." She tried to be gracious about the dressing down, and it probably would have worked if she had not spit out 'tokenism'.

A snickering nervousness from Mr. Millup accompanied Mr. Woodley's getting out of his chair and walking over to her chair to put his hand consolingly on Emily's shoulder while he said, "We understand."

The meeting adjourned at the reasonable hour of 10:00, thankfully. As Emily gathered her binder and purse, she watched the man dressed in brown who had listened so intently dash out of the conference room. He spoke to no one in his rush to exit. Emily turned to Joan Chavez and said, "Do you think he was offended?"

"Who?" asked Joan as she looked in the direction Emily was staring. "You mean Thomas? No, he's just so shy, he doesn't feel comfortable with people, so he leaves immediately. He's a hard worker; he just doesn't talk much. He's a researcher of some type, so I guess he reads and doesn't talk much. Bye."

"Bye," said Emily as she moved her chair from the table in tandem with the well-dressed woman who had been sitting to the left of her. They walked almost in step with each other to the parking lot. As they headed out the back door to the parking lot, they watched Bo get into his Volkswagen van. Bumper stickers calling for halts to various wars, rights for various animals, and election of various candidates, many of whom were now long forgotten, covered much of the bright orange finish. Tattered window curtains could be glimpsed among the decals of at least forty-five of the fifty states frosting the windows.

"You can always recognize Bo's car," smiled the woman. "He doesn't drive it that often, usually takes his bike. Saves the world's energy that way. Guess he had somewhere else to go, so he needed his car."

"Does he ride his bike everyday? To work even?" asked Emily.

"I think so. He doesn't have a job that I know of. He goes to school and is getting pretty close to completing a PhD in sociology. When he's not studying, he's out helping people. I see him in the kitchens. At night I see him rounding up people to go to the shelters. He takes 'love thy neighbor' seriously."

She changed the subject. "That was quite a delivery you gave to Rudyard in there."

Probably not her natural color, reddish-gold hair achieved an arresting effect combined with her fair skin showing freckles peeking through her light makeup. The orange and gold flowered blouse matched the gold collarless blazer and slacks perfectly. Gold leather pumps and varied gold chains completed her outfit.

Emily smiled. "Too much, do you think?"

"Rudyard needs something like that. Rochelle, when she bothers to come, doesn't much care what goes on with the board, so it was about time someone set him straight about women. Joan will step in every once in a while to give him a talking to. Mrs. Gridley is too busy trying to keep Mr. Gridley awake, so she doesn't pay much attention to what's going on. Anyway, they don't even come often enough to know what's going on. That's the first time I've seen them in months."

Emily held out her hand as she turned slightly to face the lady, "Emily Kristich. What's your name?"

"Mine is Blythe Oberstein. Is that true about your husband? Do you work with him?"

"Believe it. When he started business, I told him I'd help him any way I could. We've lived and breathed that business so long, our daughters even talk it."

Interestedly, she said, "Daughters? How many?"

"Two—six and eight."

"No sons?"

"No sons."

"What're they like?"

"My children? I imagine by any standard they're like any other children, but because they're mine, God threw away the mold when He made them because they're so special."

Blythe indulged Emily's parental chauvinism with a smile.

"That's good training for them. When you discuss your business in front of them, I mean. They'll understand a lot that way. They'll be able to make it on their own and won't have to rely on anyone to do it for them"

"I hope so," said Emily. "Do you have children?"

"No, my husband was afraid to bring kids into this world. He said it'd be all wrong because there's so much bad happening all the time. I used to tell him every parent took that chance, and most every generation came out just fine. I even asked him to adopt, but he wouldn't. He just didn't like kids. It turned out he didn't like very many people. I wanted children so badly. I think I would have done anything to get them."

"Yes, they're worth it. They make you think about your own values because they ask many, many questions.

"Do you live in Pleasant Creek?" asked Emily as they approached Blythe's blue, twenty year old Oldsmobile sedan.

"No, I live here." She pointed in the direction of the car.

Puzzled, Emily asked, "You mean in Oakland?"

"No." She paused before explaining further. "I mean in this car. I have no home. I'm one of those referred to as homeless."

Now Emily paused. Rather than muddle through and make the situation embarrassing, Emily headed it off with, "I'm not quite sure what to say. I'm at a loss for words."

Blythe wasn't exactly defensive, but she was discomfited. "It's okay. Most people are surprised when they find out I have no home. I don't dress how they think a homeless person should dress. That's why I'm on this board of directors. I'm supposed to speak for the homeless. They, the board members, don't listen to me though. I have very little credibility with them because they equate homelessness with ineptitude. They look at me and realize it could be they who are in my position. People aren't happy to be reminded of that. I don't say much anymore in the board meetings. I used to, but I don't anymore. That's why I was impressed when you spoke as you did to Rudyard. Tokenism was a good term; that's what I am, a token—token woman, token homeless person."

As she started to unlock the car, Emily couldn't resist the obvious. "Not to be nosy, but I am. How did you get where you are? You're dressed beautifully. You don't appear to have been aimlessly driving around. What do you do all day?"

"The inevitable question. My husband divorced me when he decided he didn't like me anymore. Actually I didn't really like him either, but I never learned any skills or profession, and I depended on him to provide everything for me. My parents died a long while ago, and they never taught me how to deal with money. I spent my divorce settlement before I realized how badly I was managing it. No one had taught me how to handle any money. Then I didn't have anyplace to go. I have no family, and friends drop off rapidly when a person looks to be in a hopeless situation. I have clothes. I use makeup and perfume from department store samples. There are plenty of places to shower—health clubs, public parks; I work out every couple days.

"But, hey, this is the Bay Area. The housing I could qualify for isn't even decent, and if it is, it goes to people with families. I can get a job making a few dollars an hour, but it won't pay for much, so I don't work. That way I can qualify for MediCal. I even rent a motel room every couple weeks. Sometimes I housesit for people out of town. Cell phones keep me in touch with the world. I manage." Blythe smiled an unsure smile. "Anyway, good luck on this board. You'll probably need it."

"But what about those programs that teach job skills? You could do that."

"Oh, I have. I've even taken classes at the local junior college. But you know what?"

Emily shook her head.

"Those jobs that one can enter into after the skills' class is over are only as good as their funding. When that runs out, the job is gone, or it goes to a person who's got more experience. Sometimes those programs work; most of the time they don't. Welfare to work; they sound like such a good idea. They sound like they should work. You just never know. Bye."

Emily stood at her car as she watched Blythe drive out of the parking lot. It was an interesting close to the evening even if it was discouraging.

CHAPTER 7

The next morning Emily switched carpool days with Miriam, and she skipped going into David's office to do accounts payable, so the lack-of-car situation was covered. When Detective Washburn called to inform her her car could be released, she was there to take the call.

"I'll come and pick you up later this morning, if that's all right. Then you'll have a ride to the impound lot, and you can complete the paperwork and have your car back," he offered.

"Is that standard procedure?"

"Only for our best customers. Like I told you, we aim to serve. Besides which, it's hard to be without your car, and I feel badly about your not having it these few days."

"Yeah, well, Mr. Service-With-A-Smile, I have a question to ask you."

"Can it wait until I get there? I've got to meet with someone right now."

Before Emily could tell him it was important, he announced his leave-taking and hung up the phone.

She wasn't smiling when she answered the door and saw Detective Washburn who was practicing the utmost in courtesy. She dived right into her question.

"Why didn't you tell me?"

"Tell you what?"

"You told me not to tell anyone, and I haven't. Well, except for David, I did tell him. But he's the only one I've told. I kept that secret just like you requested. I didn't tell one soul, except David, about Ralph Watkins."

Bob nodded his head and smiled. "Thank you. The department appreciates…wait, how did you know his name?"

Exasperated, Emily said, "That's what I'm asking you. How come you asked me not to tell anyone about that body, and everyone else seems to know about it?"

Stopping in their progress down the walk to Bob's car, Bob laid a hand on Emily's arm and asked, "What do you mean?"

"I went to my Sustain and Shelter meeting last night, and it was announced the body of Ralph Watkins had been found, and there should be some funeral arrangements, and we had to look for them in the paper."

Bob looked her in the eye and slightly shook his head. "Wait. Who made the announcement?'

"Rudyard Millup, the president of the board. No details, just that they announced he had died. Some people speculated he died of a heart attack or stroke. You told me no one else would know. That you would release the information to the paper when it was appropriate, and then I could tell Louisa and my friends if I wanted. I've been very good about keeping my part of the request. What happened to your part?" Emily stood with her hands on her hips.

"Look, I apologize. I'm sorry. That information was going to be released tomorrow; no one that I know of has given it out." Bob asked again as he took out a little notebook and pen to begin writing. "Who did you say let it out?"

"Rudyard Millup."

"What meeting?"

"Look, this is what happened." Emily related the previous evening's incident at Sustain and Shelter.

"And who all was present?"

By the time Emily had finished the list of attendees, Louisa drove up. She gave Bob a shy, giggly kiss on the cheek and Emily an engulfing hug.

"What are you doing here?" she asked Bob.

"A little community service. I'm taking Emily to get her car back."

Stepping back to look at her daughter, she remarked, "Still not doing well, huh? Your meeting didn't go well last night?"

Emily looked at Bob who shrugged.

"Were you at the meeting also, Bob? You two are keeping a secret from me, aren't you? Whose car, did you say? Yours, Emily? See, you are keeping secrets from me. Spill it, both of you."

Emily stared at Bob. "See what I mean? You can't keep it from her. She's going to find out just by osmosis."

Bob said grimly, "Emily saw a body a few days ago. A murdered body. In a car. It's supposed to be kept under wraps, but, apparently, that isn't happening."

Louisa glared a few small daggers at Emily. "I told you something was wrong. Why do you think I don't know when something is wrong? Go ahead, give me the details."

Louisa put on her professional mien and listened carefully as Emily finished the story. She reached out her arm and put it around her daughter. "Why do you think you have to do these hard situations by yourself? Don't you know I'm here to help? If only to listen? That's not a normal thing to go through. Thank heavens you have David. At least, you told one person."

Turning to Bob, she asked, "How long was he dead?"

"Maybe a day or so. Not all information is in."

"Was he actually killed in the car Emily saw him?"

Bob shrugged his shoulders. "Don't know. Evidence indicates probably not."

"Meaning there wasn't a lot of body debris in the car?"

Again, Bob shrugged to which Louisa said, "My, my, we are being a bit vague, aren't we?"

Bob smiled slightly. "It's an ongoing investigation. It's not appropriate to give out details that I don't really have. If this person were your relative, you wouldn't want the whole town to know that kind of information."

"True," agreed Louisa to which Emily nodded.

"So are we going to go?" asked Louisa.

"To where?"

"To get Emily's car. Isn't that what you meant? Emily's car is missing, and we're going to pick it up? Where are we going?"

With a sigh, Emily said, "Come on, Mom. Since your timing is so astute, you might as well go with us. Then, I'll take you out to lunch, both of you if you want."

Louisa placed herself between Emily and Bob and grabbed each of their arms. "Let's go."

CHAPTER 8

Emily called ahead to verify her coming into the office of Sustain and Shelter for computer input.

"What time," said the voice, presumably Shannon's, at the other end of the line.

"After I drop my children, around 8:30."

"Too early. Make it 10:00."

"Are you not open at 8:30? I thought someone told me the office opened at 8:30."

"Yes, but not for you. I need that time," Shannon said.

"Oh, I don't mind coming in early. I'll be out of your way."

"No you won't. I have to show you what to do, and I don't have time then."

"I'll be there at 10:00," said Emily resignedly, but Shannon had already hung up the phone.

Unlike Emily, Joan Chavez hadn't called to set up an appointment time. She just stormed into the office of Sustain and Shelter and whisked past Shannon sitting at the receptionist's desk picking at the dirt under her nails with the point of a letter opener.

"Wait, you can't go in there." Shannon bounced out of her chair, letter opener thrown behind her. "You can't go in there." She followed Joan as the older woman stalked down the hall toward the executive director's office. Shannon had caught up with Joan and reached out to grab her shoulders to halt her progress.

"Get away from me, you twerp. I can go in here, and he better be here. I'm sick of being waylaid by you every time I try to call this jerk." She grasped the doorknob of Chad's office to throw open the door but was stopped in her intent by its being locked.

Joan turned to Shannon who looked down at the petite woman and said, "I know he's in here. I saw him come in, and I want to talk to him now. Now. Do you hear me?"

"But you can't. Mr. Woodley gave orders to never, never interrupt him. You can't see him. He's too busy."

"Like hell he is. He just sits on his butt watching that paunch grow to a full-fledged beer gut. Let me in."

At that moment, the door opened, and Chad said innocently, "Is there a problem?"

Joan pushed her way passed him into his office while Shannon said, desperation in her voice and tears in her eyes, "I'm sorry, Mr. Woodley. I tried. She just came in. I told her how busy you are, and how important your work is. I told her you couldn't be interrupted. I'm sorry."

In his most practiced manner, he soothed, "It's okay, Shannon. I know you do your best. I'll take care of it. Ms. Chavez is just a little upset." He deftly eased her out of his office. "Go back to your work. It's very important you keep things running so smoothly for me. You are a treasure."

As Shannon floated back to the reception area, Chad closed the door, and Joan said, "Boy, you've sure got her buffaloed. You make me sick leading that young kid on like that."

Chad's eyes hardened when he turned to her. "Jealous, are you? You're past forty, you know. Past forty, and no one to curl up with at night. You jealous of that sweet, young lady? Nobody wants an old broad like you."

"Shut up. I want to talk to you."

"Did you get the medicine? At the next board meeting you will deliver it."

"Do you really think this is smart? Someone will find out about it. Then we'll all be in trouble. You said one time, and I could justify it. It only had to be taken from the hospital one time. Get the clinic going; I could see that. Even the second time I could see that, but it's getting out of hand. Those people need medicine; the state isn't going to pay for it. Half of them are undocumented, so how are they going to get medical care? We need to figure out how to get meds for that clinic. What happened to your supplier? You told me we just needed to fill in until your supplier could get us more medications. There has to be a pharmaceutical company that'll let us buy that stuff at discount. You need to look into that. We all have a lot to lose if we don't get this stuff legally."

"No, sugar. You have a lot to lose," he smiled cheerfully. "You're the one who's stealing it. I have nothing to do with it. You're in charge of the clinic, and I don't know how you do business. If you're doing something illegal, you're in for a world of hurt. If I were you, I wouldn't tell anybody how you got those drugs, but, now that the clinic is thriving, you've got to keep it filled with medications, or someone's going to wonder how you got them in the first place."

Joan stepped back from Chad's desk. "You sneak. You did this on purpose. What happened to your supplier? The one you said would help us out? You set me up; you made me risk my livelihood. I can't even stop now. What have you got me in to? I've worked hard all my life, and, now, you're going to ruin it."

Chad laughed at her realization of her situation.

Joan blanched and fled the room.

CHAPTER 9

At 9:45 Emily was sitting in her car in the parking lot of Sustain and Shelter watching the second hand on her watch creep up to 10:00. At 9:47, Joan Chavez rushed out the door of Sustain and Shelter. Emily hailed her, but Joan was in such a twitch, she didn't acknowledge the greeting.

If Joan can go in early, I should be able to do so Emily decided.

It was absolutely absurd to let a twenty year old rudely intimidate her, so she got out of her car and stalked into the office. When Emily opened the door, it banged into a cardboard box. As there were several of said boxes scattered on the floor, Emily stepped through them to Shannon's desk.

"I told you not to come until 10:00. What if I wasn't here? You couldn't get in." Emily jumped back as crumbs spit out of Shannon's mouth in Emily's direction.

"That's true. But I figured, if Joan can come in, why can't I? I came anyway because I wanted to get started. I didn't have much to do today, but I do have a busy week. It is, after all, only a few weeks until school is out, and I'm clearing my schedule to enjoy the time with my daughters this summer. Except for this computer input, summer will be family time. So that's why I'm here now."

Her mouth cleared of whatever she was chewing, Shannon turned back to the crate, slammed the lids together and shoved it off the desk where it fell to the floor with a plop.

Emily asked, "What were you doing?"

With dignity straightening her carriage, the secretary turned to Emily and said, "I was having a snack."

"Out of that box? It looked like you were eating the packing material. Is that packing material in all these boxes?"

Shannon looked away from Emily.

"You know, Styrofoam doesn't biodegrade. You may be doing yourself great harm by eating it."

Haughtily Shannon said, "That was not Styrofoam. That was water and starch pellets, and they are made to protect the environment. The water and starch melts easily, so landfills aren't full of Styrofoam. Obviously, you didn't know that. Those pellets taste like rice cakes. And they're low in fat."

"Oh." Emily surveyed the floor strewn with large packing boxes.

After a pause to allow Emily to digest the scene she had seen and Shannon to digest the snack she had just eaten, Emily said, "So, where did these boxes come from? Are they all empty? Well, I mean except for the rice cake packing material stuff you were eating."

"So what?"

"Do you eat all of these pellets in all of these boxes? That's a lot of snacking, low fat or not. Bet you could get very bloated."

"These boxes are none of your business. Chad left them here for me to break down and get rid of. There was a delivery last night."

"What kind of delivery?"

"I just told you. This is none of your business. You're supposed to input or something."

"How about if I help you break these down and get them to the dumpster? I'm not hungry, so I won't enjoy your snack, but I can help you unload and clean up the mess."

"No I don't need your help." Shannon started closing up the boxes and stacked two of them on top of each other.

Emily watched silently as Shannon went through her machinations of straightening the office and ignoring Emily. After she stacked the boxes, Shannon stood by them, fingertip in her mouth, trying to find some other way in which to banish Emily from her world.

"Could you show me the computer you wish me to use? And the data? I'll get started."

Shannon, posture aligned to display the greatest of stateliness, carried herself to a file cabinet behind her desk, slowly pulled out a drawer and extricated a file about two inches thick.

"This is a list of donors. Use that computer," she said pointing to the second desk in the room on which there was a covered keyboard, monitor and disk drive.

"Is there anything I should know about this computer?"

"I thought you were such a wiz at these things."

"My husband is the wiz. I'm afraid husbands and wives have only so much kindred spirit, and I haven't found it extends to computers," said Emily smiling at Shannon.

Shannon didn't return the smile to show the appreciation of humor, but she said, "I wouldn't know. I'm not married."

"What does that matter? You're young and single. There's so much women your age can do nowadays with their lives. You don't have to be married."

"That's what you think," she said as she turned her attention to her desk in an unmistakable sign of rebuff.

Emily waited a few minutes and then went to the desk to uncloak the computer. The mist of dust that arose when Emily uncovered the computer indicated Ralph Watkins hadn't used it anytime in the recent past. Mr. Millup wasn't kidding when he had said there was no hurry to get this information onto a database. Flipping through the file, Emily was again struck by the lack of urgency to complete the input. Ralph Watkins had a paperclip marking the paper that appeared to be about the middle of the 'd' section of names.

"How long had Mr. Watkins been working on this, Shannon?"

"Why do you want to know?"

"It doesn't appear he got very far."

"Of course, he did. He's worked on it for the past year. You shouldn't say bad things about the dead," Shannon said.

"I didn't. It just doesn't seem like he got through the list very quickly."

"He was very particular about how things were to be entered. He made sure it was done right," Shannon said with the implication Emily would not come up to those high standards of input.

"Did you know Ralph Watkins very well?'

"What do you mean?" the young woman asked sharply.

"Well, you know, he'd come in while you were working, so you must've talked to him and gotten to know him while he was here."

"I don't talk to volunteers while they're here. It takes up my time."

"I see. So Ralph didn't ever say anything while he was here?"

"He didn't come when I was here, at least, not very often. He had his own keys, so he could work whenever he wanted. I just told you. I don't talk to people in the office. It's like an invasion of my privacy, you know?"

Emily gave Shannon a look of perplexity. "Frankly, I hadn't ever thought of it that way. Just figured helping is helping."

Shannon turned her back to Emily and bent over to begin closing the flaps on some of the boxes.

"Is there a file designation for this, or do I start over?"

"Look in the file. It's there." Shannon said without looking up at Emily.

"Do you know where?"

A grunt of displeasure accompanied Shannon's plodding in scuffed loafers with broken backs over to Emily's desk where she grabbed the file from her, looked at it and exaggeratedly pointed to the file name. "There."

"Gee, I'm sorry I bothered you," said Emily.

Shannon missed the sarcasm in Emily's apology when she said, "This one time is okay."

As Emily's fingers flicked along the keyboard, she watched Shannon staring at the cartons still on the floor.

"How did you find out Ralph had died?" asked Emily.

Shannon jumped at Emily's voice and looked at her with a startled face. "What? What did you say?"

"How did you find out about Ralph?"

"The same way you did, last night. That announcement."

Emily nodded. "How did he die?"

"You know, like they said last night. He was shot."

Shot?" Emily adopted a façade of great surprise. "Oh. I don't remember that. That's terrible."

"You didn't remember? How could you not—oh, yeah, you…"

"I thought he had a heart attack or something. I mean, Joan said he was a man who enjoyed eating and drinking. I just thought a natural occurrence." Emily paused her typing as she thought of the body of Ralph Watkins lying in a heap across a steering wheel. "Who told you?"

"Told me what?"

"That Ralph was shot."

"Don't know." Shannon waved her hand in the air as if she could sweep Emily away.

"Someone must've told you. I didn't hear that at the meeting. Did the police call?"

"Yeah, yes, that was it. The police called. I took the call."

"Do you remember who it was? The person who called?" Emily continued typing as she continued drilling Shannon.

"How would I know that? No, I don't remember. Quit bugging me."

In an exasperated huff, she marched into the bathroom, slammed the door and locked it.

Emily was just completing the 'e' section of the list when Thomas, carrying an oversized briefcase, came into the office. She looked up and welcomed him brightly, "Hi, Thomas. How are you?"

"Oh. Well, hello, hi. I mean, how are you? Yes, I've got to go." He stumbled his return greeting and hurried down the hall to Chad's office.

Emily got through the 'f' section that day.

Shannon still hadn't exited the restroom when Emily left the office of Sustain and Shelter.

CHAPTER 10

It was time to set aside Ralph Watkins, the work on the new board and the end of the year school activities, if only for an hour or so. Emily decided she'd better get her sorry butt to the gym, or her butt wasn't going to be the only sorry thing about her body. Pilates is the exercise designed to feel no pain but lots of gain. What begins as a mere whisper of energy drain develops into a whine of exertion until an apex of struggle is achieved, all within one mere hour. And in that hour, one could think to one's heart's content. Or not, depending on one's desire to concentrate on the body or the mind. Picking up her equipment in the exercise studio, Emily arranged it in the corner farthest away from the warped mirrors that not only graphically displayed perspiring bodies, but also discouragingly distorted them like the funhouse at a circus.

Her choice of a moderate pace of exercise was wise because, even at that, halfway through the hour, her body was begging to stop while her mind cajoled her to go on. All her rationalizations about missing workouts lost as much ground as her body had during those sessions missed because life got in the way. Her adductors were stretched, her glutei were quivering, her deltoids and lats were taut and her heart was hustling blood through her body. Her mind, thankfully, didn't dwell on Ralph and board meetings and miscellaneous activities. The workout made her feel so beat down, it invigorated her enough to work on the machines for another half hour. By the time Emily finished the second part of her workout, the women in her Pilates class were clearing out of the locker room having made the transition from bedraggled sweat to perfumed freshness. Emily had the locker room to herself and had just completed dressing when Rochelle Emory walked in.

Surprised at first, Emily greeted her with a welcoming smile, "Hi, Rochelle."

Dressed in matching bicycle shorts and sports bra of red, black and gold and red workout shoes, Rochelle slowly looked from Emily's feet up to her face and said indifferently, "Do I know you?"

Rochelle's lack of recognizing her was not quite the welcome she expected, but it didn't deter Emily, so she widened her smile and said, "Sure you do. We sat near each other at the Sustain and Shelter board meeting. I think our children are in the same class, so we've probably seen each other at their class functions."

"No. Until recently I've been able to avoid school functions, so I haven't ever seen you. Until last week that is. You're the one who gave Rudyard a talking down, aren't you?" She cackled. "He needed it."

Then she asked, "Which child?"

"Beg your pardon?"

"Which child is in the same class as your child?"

"Scott, I think."

"Oh, that one. He's kind of stupid, you know. They say he has a learning disability, but I think they're trying to make excuses for him. It doesn't make sense he can't read. That's what my husband says, and I agree with him. My husband is very upset about it; he's ready to take him out of that school. I don't want to because then I'd have to drive the kids to some other school, and I don't have that kind of time. I thought about boarding school, but his sister seems to like having him around. Now they walk to school, so I don't want a different school for them. I think the brat is just lazy."

Emily's smile was replaced by dismay at the thought of Scott's mother dismissing her child's struggle so insensitively. Their talking paused while each woman dealt with the direction the conversation had taken.

"I just don't know what to say about him, so I don't even discuss it. Why waste time on stupidity?"

"I've worked with him when I volunteer in the classroom. He seems to have good thinking abilities," said Emily.

"But he can't read."

"He can do above grade level math though."

"But he can't read."

"Doesn't he get special help?"

"I suppose so. I sign something every year, and the school says he's in special help. He still can't read though. He's just stupid."

Changing the topic, Emily said, "We'll also be sitting on the PTA board together next year."

"I suppose so. I guess you're one of those do-gooder mothers. Probably go to all the meetings and do all the half-baked carnivals and bake sales. My husband's family considers itself one of the seven hills of San Francisco, and he insists we must uphold that name by being active in the community. So both of us sit on all kinds of boards and trusts. You have heard of us, haven't you?"

Emily shrugged in a manner that could be taken as a yes even if she meant the opposite.

"Everyone knows our name. I find the meetings so boring, don't you? Especially out here in the 'burbs. I mean, who cares? We're only furthering our own ends, all these wannabe philanthropists. We don't do anything, just go to stupid meetings with stupid people."

Not giving Emily much chance to answer, she continued with a half smile, "But we do what we must, don't we? I mean, someone has to help these poor agencies out. Might as well be the people who have the money. Do you come here often?"

Emily, sorting through Rochelle's responses, took a few seconds before responding to the switch in conversation. "What? Oh, yes. I do. I try to come about three times a week. I've been loose about coming the last few weeks because the end of the school year gets extremely busy for me. Do you come here much?"

"Usually late at night when the brats are asleep. That way they don't know I've left them, and they can't whine about my not being there. I hate listening to them complain," she said as she headed out the door dressed and ready to slink her way through her day.

Emily, on the other hand, was off to the kitchen that Sustain and Shelter maintained for the homeless of Pleasant Creek. Mom Louisa had agreed to meet her at the kitchen and put in some volunteer time herself. Located in a soft industrial area, the kitchen had been outfitted with used restaurant equipment, long tables and mismatched folding chairs. From what Emily had gathered in her research of Sustain and Shelter, much of the food came from the daily overages of orders that restaurants had placed. Rather than throw out food still in unopened packages, the restaurants would hold the food for the kitchen to pick up and use to feed those who couldn't afford daily meals. It was a nice recycling of food—nothing would go to waste. People ate, restaurants reduced their garbage, and the kitchen reduced its cost in feeding the homeless.

Working at soup kitchens is probably one of the easiest volunteer outlets because all one has to do is show up. Just show up, and someone will gladly point the volunteer in the direction of some task that requires minimal instruction and no training. The work gets done, the jobs are easier for all because there are many people to do the job, and the volunteer feels good about helping his community and fellow man. So that's what Emily and Louisa did. They showed up about 10:30; Emily passed out napkins, and Louisa passed out silverware, all the while smiling pleasantly at the patrons and the other volunteers. Like being in the Tower of Babel, the women listened to the various languages people spoke to one another. The language picked out most easily was Spanish, both because there were more people speaking it, and it was one of the few languages they could understand. But the women knew from the dress these people were wearing and the cultural make-up of Pleasant Creek that the other languages heard were Farsi, Tongan, Russian, Arabic, Hmong, and Chinese. There must have been other cultures represented, but who was to know? And it wasn't a need-to-know situation because these were hungry people; they didn't come to socialize with Louisa and Emily, they came to eat.

"Em, do you know who the guy schlepping food is; the one with the pony-tail? The young guy."

"Yes, that's Bo. He sits on the board of directors at Sustain and Shelter. Come on, let's go meet him."

After Emily stepped over and introduced her mother to him, Bo acknowledged the ladies as he dished out food onto a child's plate addressing the child by name and speaking to the mother in Spanish. Fluent Spanish as far as Emily could tell. Continuing to chat with Bo, the women watched him address another family in an Oriental language, possibly Chinese. Fluent Chinese as far as Emily could tell. When he did the same thing with an Arabic family, Emily looked at him and asked, "Just how many languages do you know?"

Bo shrugged as he continued to plop food onto plates. "Spanish, French and Italian fluently; Chinese okay and just learning Arabic; some German."

"Well, you can travel just about anywhere in the world. It sure looked like you knew all three quite well," remarked Louisa.

"Hey, man, when you're talking about food almost everyday, it's real easy to pick up the words. Plus, hunger speaks to everyone. Nothing hard about learning the vocab of the place you're working."

"Sure, makes sense. So how come you know all those languages?" Emily asked.

"My family spent most of my growing up years in Europe. Dad's a big wig in a pharmaceutical company. Mom made sure we traveled and learned languages. She always hired native speaking nannies for me. That way I had to learn the languages. Then I picked up some of the others at school. I use my Spanish most here in the kitchens."

"This is California; it would follow that Spanish would be the language of use. Do you come here everyday? I heard you were going to school." Emily asked.

"Yeah to both. I go to school; I come here everyday."

"And in school? What do you work on there?"

"I'm getting a PhD in sociology. This kitchen is kind of a field training for me. Social programs should help people, right?"

"Right," agreed Louisa, "and, sometimes that's what they actually do. Other times you wonder why you even learned to read and write because that's all you're doing—reading and writing reports, and then you wonder what you're helping. Certainly not the environment. All that paper has to come from somewhere."

"Mom's a social worker. Could you tell?"

Bo chuckled and shrugged. "I've heard those stories. Do you like it?"

"I must. I've been doing it for almost forty years now. Do you work another job in addition to all that?"

"Nah. Just go to school. Right now I'm supposed to be working on a dissertation. I work here to keep my languages fluent."

After a short lull in the conversation, Emily asked, "Bo, is this the kitchen Ralph worked in? Did you know him very well?"

"Yeah, this was his kitchen. Didn't know him like a best friend, but well enough. He was pretty regular here. Seemed a nice enough dude. I mean he was regular here, you know, like he cared about helping people."

"Do you know how he died?"

Bo averted his gaze from Emily, picked up an empty tray and turned to get another one to replace it from the kitchen. He muttered something, but, with the clang of dishes and talk of the eating public, Emily couldn't make out what he said. She turned to Louisa with a questioning look on her face. Louisa returned a blank look.

Louisa and Emily returned to watching the patrons of the kitchen and passing out eating paraphernalia, but the lunch rush had ebbed. They waited a few more minutes and turned in their silverware trays before leaving.

"You know, your boy is a drug user," Louisa remarked as she and Emily headed to their cars.

"What do you mean?"

"Bo is an addict, coke I would think. This is probably where he gets his supply."

"In three hours you got all that information? Man, you must've really bonded with the guy. Do you know the rest of his life story?"

Louisa shook her head. "Nope, only what he told both of us. Look at his eyes and his movements. Pupils dilated, jerky movements, restless."

"If you didn't talk to him, how do you know this is his 'store'?"

"I watched him. After we talked to him, I watched him pick something up from one of the trays he was serving. Made it look like he had spilled some food and was wiping the tray, but there was money left when he quit cleaning. Pretty quickly done, so most people wouldn't be aware of what had happened. Then, a few minutes later, he was off to the back. Are the restrooms around there?" Louisa pointed to an area away from the kitchens.

"Got me. This is the first time I've been here. Shall we go look?"

"If you want, but I don't think it's necessary. I may be way off base."

"Or right on target. You truly have eyes in the back of your head, along with your psychic powers. No wonder we couldn't get away with anything when we were young."

Louisa laughed. "Human nature is human nature. Study it long enough, and you can sometimes anticipate the next move, especially in your own children." She put her arm around her daughter in a quick hug and a kiss and was off with a wave.

CHAPTER 11

Emily was still thinking about her day as she waited for the final school bell to ring outside her daughters' school. More specifically, she was thinking about the parts of her day involving Bo and Rochelle. The mission of Sustain and Shelter might be pretty straightforward, but it was certain that the members of the board of directors weren't.

The school Jojo and Lulie attended had been built with a roundabout to be used as a bus turn-around for before and after school pick up of students. It would have been effective for the bus if it hadn't been for all the parents picking up their children in individual cars and using the roundabout as a spillover parking lot. Emily joined the throng of parents in that parking lot and sat among the conglomeration of alloys and wheels. While she half-heartedly sorted through the mail she had grabbed from the mailbox, Byte sat in the front seat and looked for Jojo and Lulie to emerge from their school.

A few families had tried to beat the odds of having their cars being destroyed by their children's journey from babyhood to teen driving by making Jaguars, Mercedes and Cadillacs their family vehicles, and those automobiles dotted the line of minivans and SUV's. But most families had chosen the practical side of family cars and purchased multi-passengered vehicles. Most had elected to make the minivan the sacrificial hack in hauling children, bicycles and groceries. Just like Emily and her minivan, her faithful warhorse. Now rescued from the impound lot, it was still raring to go. Like an old warhorse, the old minivan wore its battle scars proudly. There was the crack in the taillight where another parent had backed into Emily's car at the last birthday party Jojo attended. There was the dent on the passenger's side where Emily had maneuvered just a little too closely to a shopping cart at the grocery store. There was the gash of paint where one of Lulie's friends had scarred the finish with her bicycle. Inside the van red and purple juice stains had bled onto the carpet as reminders of all the snacks eaten on the run. The dagger slash in the seat had been caused by a youth's toy truck, but it had mended with plastic glue. The sliding drink tray hung at an angle much like a broken arm no longer usable but still a part of the body of the car.

The final bell of the day rang, and children burst out of the building like calves running out of their chutes in a rodeo. Guided by the crossing guard, Lulie skipped through the crosswalk looking like a mini-Quasimodo with her multi-colored backpack. A big old smile full of first grade innocence and happiness at being in school greeted her mother.

"Have a good day, Lulie?"

"Mrs. Ohura said I can read just like Jojo did when she was in first grade."

"You must be a good reader then."

"Yes. Yes, I am." Her response radiated self-confidence.

As her daughters began to tell Mom about their school-wide assembly, she interrupted to say, "Look, girls. I think those are the Emory kids. That looks like Scott, so that must be his sister. What's her name? Maybe they'd like a ride."

"No, Mom," said Jojo desperately. "You can't give them a ride. Samantha's one of the big girls at school. She'll laugh at me. It will be embarrassing."

"It's also hot," said Emily. "Would you like to be walking home today?"

"No."

"Mommy, he's a boy," Lulie, trying to back up her sister, said. "We don't want a boy in the car."

"Lulie, would you want to walk home today?"

"No, I don't think so."

"Then we have a unanimous decision. None of us wishes to walk home today," said Emily brightly as she pulled the car to the curb of the sidewalk on which the children were walking.

"Kids, would you like a ride home?" To Samantha she said, "I don't think you know me, but I know your brother. I work with him in the classroom sometimes. My name is Mrs. Kristich. I'd be happy to take you home because it's so hot."

Relief in her eyes and a shadow of a smile on her clear skinned face, Samantha said, "I know who you are. I see you at school a lot. And I know Jojo. It's okay, and it's nice of you to do this. Scott is so hot, and I have too much homework tonight to help him carry his books the whole way. Thank you."

She took Scott by the hand and helped him into the side door of the minivan, then took both backpacks and placed them carefully out of the way of any of the occupants of the car and, finally, seated herself in the seat Lulie had moved out of to make room for her.

"This is very nice, isn't it, Scott?" repeated Samantha.

Scott looked up as much as his downcast face would allow and shook his head.

"What do you say, Scott?"

A hushed 'thank you' was heard from the handsome young boy dressed in an oversized black tee shirt with wizards on it.

"You are more than welcome," said Emily. "Tell me how to get to your house, Samantha."

"We live on Bluebird Hill at the top. If you just follow the main entrance all the way up, you'll come to our driveway. Do you know how to get there?"

"Sure, I do. Can you get me in the gate?"

"Yes, I have the code."

Jojo said, "We have friends on Bluebird. Do you know the Roses? Dr. and Mrs. Rose have Eli and Tenandra. Do you know them?"

"Scott use to play with Eli. He liked him a lot."

Emily, ears perked and probing for bits of information, asked, "Do you not play with Eli anymore, Scott?" In the rearview mirror, she could see him shake his head no.

"Mother told him he couldn't go over there anymore."

"Oh, that's too bad." said Emily hoping for more information.

"Yes ma'am, it was," was all Samantha had to say.

By then they had arrived at the monster of a house. Emily knew this house well as Miriam and she had spent many a lunch dissecting the architectural blunders as they looked up and watched the house take shape from Miriam's back porch. The question of style had never been resolved, for the owners seemed to be unable to make up their minds about the architecture of their dream home. Their lack of decision had created a mansion composed of a Tudor facade, Mediterranean balconies, a Swiss chalet roof, black marble entry porch and Roman pillars.

Samantha, again, made a point of helping her brother exit the car. She took both the backpacks and reached for her brother's hand.

"I'll wait until your mother lets you in," said Emily.

"You don't have to do that. Mother isn't home. I have a key."

"Would you like to come home with us until she gets home? I can bring you back, or she can come to our home and get you."

"No, she's never here when we get home from school. We're used to being by ourselves. We get our homework done in the afternoon."

"Maybe your dad will be home?" asked Lulie.

Emily, not wanting to miss the answer, held her breath.

"No," said Samantha, "not tonight. He travels a lot and doesn't get to see us very often. Bye, we have to go."

They walked rapidly up the front walkway, opened the solid walnut front door and were enveloped by the house.

"Nice kids," said Emily as she drove to Miriam's house. "Let's go see Mrs. Rose for awhile."

It intrigued Emily that the Emory family had been in her family's sphere without either of them realizing it. Parallel lives will intersect only when an action or word strikes one life causing it to bounce toward another life in its vicinity. Rochelle had succeeded in making the lives of the two women touch when she reacted to her son as she did, and this caused Emily to develop more than a slight interest in Rochelle. Emily was becoming mildly obsessive in satiating that curiosity about this family whose life had commonality with that of her own family. She knew from experience that bits of background would enable the picture to develop more fully when other mothers talked about Rochelle and her lifestyle as they saw it. She couldn't wait to hear them, and she was going to start with Miriam, Rochelle's neighbor. Rochelle had one of those wannabe lives, a life other women could elaborate with gossipy gusto, so that it seemed much fuller and larger than it probably was.

Emily, Jojo and Lulie walked hand-in-hand to greet Miriam and Tenandra who were standing in the front door waiting for them.

"Miriam," said Emily after the children fled their mothers' conversation, "when we were talking about Rochelle Emory, why didn't you tell me she was your neighbor and the one who built that awful house."

"I don't tell anyone I know she lives there."

"Why not? We were talking about her. Why didn't you just mention it?"

"Well, you know what they say."

"No, tell me."

"There goes the neighborhood," she chortled.

CHAPTER 12

"You don't have one of those homeless meetings tonight, do you?" asked David while he was drinking his last cup of morning tranquility. Over his coffee cup, his full, round brown eyes followed Emily's movements around the kitchen. Reddish-brown hair framed her square face that smiled at her world. Broad shoulders and her five foot eight height enhanced the perception of stamina she had in resolving challenges life offered her.

He smiled at the memory of her running to greet him in the driveway shortly after Jojo was born to announce she wouldn't be returning to the college to teach. At the time, it seemed impossible to get by on only his sporadic sales of computer systems, but he veiled his uneasiness and said they'd make it okay. And they had. Life was better than okay. With a reason to work even harder, they had beat out a successful business together. Emily put her Master's degree in her back pocket, and they'd pack up Jojo and tote her between the house and office and work around the clock if they had to. He smiled again at the memory.

Emily stood at the kitchen counter packing lunches. Only seven more lunches left in the school year.

"What are you grinning about?" she asked.

"I was thinking about the day you announced your intention of letting your job at the college go."

"I had thought about it ever since Jojo was born. I was so scared you'd be angry because all that time I was pregnant, I swore I'd never let a baby get in the way of my career and a second income." Now, it was Emily's turn to grin. "You were so gracious about it."

"So do you have one?"

Called back from memory lane, she said, "Do I have one what?"

"A meeting."

"No," she said. "Not tonight. I don't have any meetings this week. Tomorrow is the open house at school, so we can see what the kids have done all year."

"I thought we already knew. They bring home enough work to give us each a part-time job. You'd think they were in high school, not grade school. When I was young, we didn't have that kind of homework in grade school. Why do they have so much homework?"

"It's designed to reinforce what they've learned that day in school. It's not so bad; we get to see them learn."

"Right. So why do we have to go to Open House?"

As he asked the question, Jojo and Lulie walked in and grabbed their lunches.

"Daddy," announced Jojo, "you have to see my story. We've been decorating our rooms, and Mr. Oberg has some new pets in the classroom. He brought in a snake, and we got to watch it eat a rat. Maybe the snake will do the same for you."

"There's your answer," countered Emily. "The teachers and the reptiles are waiting to see you."

"I suppose so," he said as he hustled the little girls out the door in a flurry of good-bye kisses and waving papers.

The night of the big Open House, as important to a grade-schooler as a debutante ball to a young woman, finally arrived.

"Hurry up," prodded Lulie. "We have to get there right on time. I have so many things to show you."

"Lulie, it's only 5:30. It doesn't start for another two hours," said Emily a third time.

"But we have to be on time."

They were on time.

As the Kristichs entered the lobby of their daughters' school, they spotted the Roses and moved across the room into their direction. The passage to their children's classrooms was strewn with the comfortable conversation of people who know each other well. The Roses and Kristichs parted company at Tenandra's class, and the Kristichs moved onto Jojo's classroom which had become a ripe fire hazard with all the colored paper, cardboard and art projects climbing the walls and padding the chairs and desks. Like ants ready to hoist their load to their catacombs, parents surrounded the teachers ready to hoist their children's achievements or failures into the teacher's presence. Because Emily volunteered in each of her daughter's classrooms and talked to their teachers then, she felt no need to join the throng engulfing those teachers. That enabled her to pour over the girls' works and laud them with gooey accolades.

It also gave her a chance to observe her latest curiosity. Rochelle showed up at the Open House not only with her two children, but also her, heretofore, unseen husband. Emily had been so engrossed in Jojo's work she hadn't noticed their arrival although Rochelle's outfit of tight fuchsia hiphugging pants and halter top set off by a cobalt blue long open jacket must surely have created a stir. Geoffrey Emory, already on the paler side of blond, seemed even paler next to his colorfully dressed wife.

"Hello, Mrs. Kristich." Samantha with adult grace and aplomb took over the introductions.

As she had already seen the snake, bulging with the rat lunch in which he had indulged, in Jojo's classroom, Emily wasn't keen on seeing the snake in Lulie's room, so she stayed at Jojo's desk while the rest of her family went to Lulie's classroom. Her position at the desk gave her a vantage point to watch the Emorys when they came to see Scott's work. People milling about the room screened her spying on the family that physically moved together but seemed to have no union binding them.

Rochelle tried to say something quietly to Geoffrey, but he moved away from her before she finished. She gave a small shrug as if to shake off the slight and moved further away from her husband. Scott took Samantha's hand and brought her over to his desk. Mother and Father followed mutely while Scott pointed at something Samantha was to observe. Father asked Scott a question, and Scott silently nodded his head while watching his father's shoes. Clumsily, Father put his hand on the young boy's shoulder and looked confused as he flinched. As if by telepathic direction, the family moved in one line out the door. There were no words exchanged among the family. Emily could follow their progress through the classroom window, so she saw them get into the family car, a dark Rolls Royce. She couldn't see the color of the car because the streetlamp wasn't bright enough, but she could see Geoffrey watch his family impatiently while they climbed into the sedan. Until her own family rejoined her, Emily sat quietly pondering the scene she had just seen. Family dynamics—probably one of the most open secrets in society. No one really understands them, but just about everybody is an authority in dealing with them.

Or so they think.

CHAPTER 13

It wasn't very much like the hospital in which Joan Chavez was used to working. In this clinic, the austere cleanliness and systematization didn't overtake one's senses like at the hospital. If anything, the clinic's physical attributes were almost opposite that of the hospital. Instead of the hospital's barren, yet hopeful, white, the clinic was a smoky beige. Instead of ordered cabinets and supply closets, items were stacked haphazardly on shelves and tables. Instead of muted efficiency, a block party atmosphere prevailed. Children laughed and played with toys in the waiting room while their parents gossiped and passed information to each other for finding shelter and food. As disorganized as the clinic was, Joan didn't mind not having structure on which to frame her life that she had at the hospital. She liked hearing the children's hubbub, and she liked the idea she was helping the community.

What she didn't like was knowing where the medicine for this clinic had come. That was the flaw in the whole set-up, and she was going to be caught in that flaw. She had crossed the line, and there was no way out. Sitting in the closet that had been designated the office of the director of the clinic, Joan rubbed her temples with both hands. This was one of those situations that only got more complex. To tell the truth and try to disentangle herself from the tendrils of illegality was only going to get harder to do. Even if she were to begin to extricate herself, she could lose her job, her license and the careful routine she had fabricated for herself. She would be without anything to give meaning to her life because her job was her anchor. Like a rat going through a maze, she wasn't going to find a way out, and Chad was going to make sure she was trapped in that maze. How could something that is doing so much good for people be so wrong?

Sitting there at the desk dwelling on misfortune wasn't going to help anybody. She was here to work to try to make lives better and healthier. Joan moved over to the medicine closet and went through the shelves stacking little boxes of medications that the clinic needed. She arranged them neatly, so the earliest expiration dates were at the front of the cabinet and would be used first. So that the meds wouldn't be given to patients incorrectly, she mixed the Spanish labels in with the English labels. That precaution would help any personnel who needed to provide directions to the patients of the clinic. They could read the directions in the language with which they were familiar.

The ringing phone zapped her senses and made her shriek.

"Hello. Hello, Ms. Chavez?" the voice on the phone questioned nervously. "Do I have Ms. Chavez on the line? Are you there?"

"Yes, I'm here," Joan answered impatiently.

"Um, yes, well, I was told to call you. Mr. Woodley. He's the one. He said I should call you. We are suppose to, um, meet and arrange, you know, the, uh, drop off."

"Who *are* you?"

"Oh. Yes, well, yes. I'm sorry. My name is Thomas. Thomas Oakhurst. I don't think you know me."

"Of course, I do, Thomas. You sit on the Board of Directors for Sustain and Shelter. So you are to be my courier? I don't know why Chad even thinks we need to have someone else in on this."

"Well, ma'am, I think he doesn't want to have to rely on only you to deliver the stuff. If you can't be there, then I can take it."

And with more people involved, more people get in trouble, Joan mused. "Right, and you're an insurance policy."

"Beg your pardon, Ms. Chavez? You said something about insurance?"

"No, skip it, Thomas. Do you know what you're getting into?

"Yes, ma'am. I know, but I would like to work with you. What you are doing is beneficial for all those people. I know we take the medications needed at the clinic back and forth."

"And did Chad tell you where we get them?

"Yes. He said you, through your connections at the hospital, were able to arrange a special discount for our clinic. He said you pick them up from the distributor, and that saves us shipping. What you are doing is so wonderful for all those people," Thomas said just before hanging up.

Yes, thought Joan. And illegal. That asshole, Chad, was going to make sure I will never be able free myself from this. Not only was he going to ensure that I continue stealing, he was going to involve another innocent person. That way, Chad would have two people to which he could attach blame and skirt any problems for himself. Chad, by maneuvering Thomas into this situation, had provided a witness to my stealing. Now, it was virtually impossible to report this crime and take the consequences because if I do, I ruin Thomas's life as well as my own.

Joan laid her head on the desk and started crying.

CHAPTER 14

For her next visit, Emily didn't bother to call ahead to the Sustain and Shelter office; she just showed up at 10:00 in the morning. By burying her head in some papers she was shuffling, Shannon avoided acknowledging her when she walked in the door. Emily proceeded to the file cabinet from where she had seen Shannon procure the data list last week and was stopped when Shannon jack-rabbited out of her chair and almost shouted, "I'll get it."

She rapidly continued, "I should have had it out for you ready for you to type when you came in. I'll do that next week. I wasn't sure you were going to come back, so I didn't think about getting it out. I'll be more careful next time."

"Why, thank you, Shannon. I don't want to put you out of your way," responded Emily warmly.

"That's what I'm here for," said Shannon, and those were the last words she said to Emily that morning.

It was different when Chad Woodley arrived about a quarter of an hour later. It was as though someone had hit Shannon's 'on' button because she switched from morose sullenness to delighted cheer.

"Hello, Mr. Woodley," she sang out sweetly.

"Hello, Shannon," he cheerfully greeted her, smiling eyes not quite looking into hers.

"I missed you yesterday," said a perky Shannon, her small even teeth making a cute little chipmunk smile.

"It's always nice to be greeted by you, Shannon, after I've worked so hard out in the kitchens. But, you know, Mr. Millup and I had to make sure things were running right. We do an important job, and we want to help as many people as we can," said Coach Chad.

"Oh, yes," tittered Shannon. "You are so wonderful to help all those poor people."

Playtime over and now down to serious doings, Shannon said, "There is a phone message for you. Kind of important."

Seeing Emily listening to their conversation as she typed the keyboard, she said almost imperceptibly, "It's you know who."

Chad squinted his eyes at her in misunderstanding, and when she repeated it a bit louder, he nodded his head and said, "Dial it for me. I'll take it in my office."

As he walked down the hall, he stopped at Emily's workspace as if he had not seen her there and said with hearty jocundity, "Well, well. Look who we have here. How are you, Mrs. Kristich? Are you finding everything all right? I'm sure Shannon is a wonderful help for you." He stopped short of slapping her on the back, went into his office and closed the door.

Shannon held the caller on the phone until Chad took the extension in his office. As Emily proceeded through the list of individuals, she recalled hearing no ringing of phones when she was at this office last week, and she hadn't heard any in the forty-five minutes she had been here today. Odd for an office not to have incoming calls.

"Shannon, why do you not have any calls to answer?" asked Emily speedily poking the keyboard.

There was no response from Shannon as she hid herself in the papers she had on her desk.

About to repeat the question, Emily stopped as the visitor of the week walked in the door. Ida McIvey didn't appear to notice Emily because she walked to Shannon's desk and said, "Please give me the key. I need to file these."

Shannon gave her a fierce look and slightly jerked her head in Emily's direction. Ida looked up with cheerless eyes, flushed slightly and said, "Oh. I was unaware of anyone else being here. Maybe you should file these, and I could see Chad."

"He's on the phone."

"I need to see him. I'll wait."

"Suit yourself," sulked Shannon. She picked up the papers and took her keys out of her purse which was stored in the bottom desk drawer. Trying not to obviously stare, Emily had a hard time seeing what key she selected. By keeping her head inclined toward her keyboard, Emily was able to look to her back and see Shannon open a cabinet set directly in the middle of the wall of files. She opened the drawer that was second from the bottom and put in the papers Ida had given her. From the sound of the drawer, it appeared to be fairly empty. It didn't have the heavy, slow slide that full drawers have; it pulled out quickly and had a hollow sound to it.

Emily looked up as Shannon completed the filing, and saw Ida watching her. Smiling at her, she asked, "Were you able to get any financial statements for me to study?"

"What?" she said caught off guard. "Uh, no. That is, I haven't had a chance to get them together. You know, end of quarter and all that. Lots of information to pull together. We'll get you some. Just need time and all that. You know how it is with figures."

"Isn't that what you just brought in? Weren't those financials?"

"What? What, you mean those papers? No, no. They were just worksheets, not financials. We'll work on them and try to have them for you. Soon, we'll get them to you soon." She fluttered about, hands twisting nervously.

"By next week's meeting? That would be helpful. There might be some way we could brainstorm some ideas for the budget."

"I don't know about that, but soon. We'll have them for you soon."

Emily got through the 'k' section that morning, but she never knew if Ida saw Chad because Ida was still waiting when she left.

CHAPTER 15

Two more school lunches, and then Emily would have her kids to herself the whole summer—zoos, museums, picnics, maybe even a trip south to Disneyland. She wouldn't have to share them with the world. Not that she didn't want her kids to participate in the world; it was nice, however, to think she could play with them and listen and talk to them. Jojo and Lulie would, in many ways, teach her more than she would teach them.

David walked in adjusting his sunshine yellow and red tie on the red pinstripe shirt and said, "What are your plans today?"

He had been a competitive swimmer in college and reveled in the California weather that never got cold enough for him to be unable to swim outdoors. The spring sun was beginning to tinge his face with a light bronze and bleach his blonde hair white around his face during his swims three days a week. The red and white shirt was a crisp backdrop for his healthy face.

"PTA luncheon, final meeting of the year," Emily said.

"Thank you," he said as he came up behind her and kissed her. "For what?"

"For being my wife."

She turned and beamed a lavish smile up at him. "No problem."

"How well do you know Rochelle?" asked Emily when she and Miriam were seated among the tropical greenery of the newest of the chic Pleasant Creek cafes. Plunked in the middle of a new high-rise office building, the restaurant formed an atrium that allowed the workers in the surrounding offices to observe the patrons enjoying their lunches. It was perfect for lunch with a bunch of ladies, and Miriam and Emily were enjoying a good gossip fest before said ladies arrived.

"Enough to wave hello as we pass through the guard gate in the neighborhood. Not enough to ask her where she bought her latest outfit. But that doesn't stop us from gossiping about her."

"What do you mean?"

"Ramona, the neighbor at the bottom of our property said Rochelle told her she was having plastic surgery."

"What kind?"

"I don't know. Probably a tummy tuck, so she can continue to look like dynamite in those strange outfits of hers. How she can look so good in such weird clothes is beyond me."

"Listen to you," bantered Emily. "You wear those caftans and sarongs and look fantastic."

"Okay, thank you, but she wears stuff no one else over twenty would wear and still manages to look good."

"Right. You wear stuff no one outside an fashion museum would wear and still manage to look good."

"Thank you again, but you're missing my point," Miriam laughingly said, and the braids swayed with her laugh.

"I'm making my point," Emily said returning the laugh.

After the wine was brought to the table, Emily said seriously, "Getting back to the Emorys. Have you ever heard they mistreat their kids? Does the neighborhood ever gossip about that?"

"When Scott was a toddler in the playgroup, he used to be an outgoing, smiling kid. As he got older, he got more and more quiet, more withdrawn. One time he was at the house, and the kids wanted to swim. He came out in a swim shorts that were too big, they looked like his father's, and a tee shirt and never took it off. They weighed him down so much in the water that he started sputtering around like he was going to drown. It scared him so much that we called his house for Rochelle to come get him. She never came. Ramona finally took him home and talked to Rochelle about how scared Scott had been. All Rochelle said was that he could take care of himself."

"Did you ever say anything to anyone?"

She hesitated before she answered. "The moms talked about it. I mentioned it to Harold. What are you going to do? Can't prove anything. We all decided we'd watch out for him and feed him because he never seems to get enough to eat. But after that, he never came back. When we asked Samantha one time, she said her father wouldn't allow it. It's pathetic how that kid is treated. We…well I'll be. Look who just showed up."

Both Miriam and Emily looked up just as Rochelle seated herself at Miriam's side.

"We were just talking about summer plans. What are yours?" Emily asked hurriedly in the hope that the gossip about Rochelle was erased, so she, hopefully, never heard a word of it.

"Ladies, everyone knows I have plastic surgery in the summer. I refuse to get old. I refuse to lose my good looks; I've got a lot of money invested in my body and face. Summer is the best time because I put the kids in camp, and I have the whole time to myself. No one to cart around or feed. Don't have to go to any of those stupid kids' outings. Just have to spend my time with my plastics guy. It's the best time of the year. No kids."

"So, Rochelle," Miriam began, "why'd you come today?"

"Geoffrey found out about this and told me to get my ass over here and make like a good mom."

Miriam choked on a piece of bread as Emily drew back and nodded, "Right. That's as good a reason as any."

CHAPTER 16

One more day and school would be out. Whose emotions are greater: the child because he has a summer of play ahead of him, or the mother because she has a summer of little routine ahead of her? Except, of course, for Rochelle. She had no routine ahead of her, just plastic surgery without her annoying kids. In the bustle of cleaning out desks, checking lost and found and presenting teachers with thank you gifts, Emily was dismayed to remember the monthly Sustain and Shelter meeting that evening. Maybe if she had bustled a bit more, she could have forgotten it completely. But then, Rochelle would have popped into her head as she had done the last few days, and Emily would still remember the good ol' S and S meeting.

Oddly, as she dressed for the assembly, she didn't feel annoyance as she had before the last meeting. Remembering Shannon's strange behavior, Ida's hedging on the financials, the locked file cabinet and Ralph Watkins' slow procedure through the donor lists gave Emily a curiosity about the Sustain and Shelter organization. What would it take to get into that drawer at the office? If Ida brought in papers, and if Ida is the treasurer, those papers have to be financial statements. If the drawer is locked, Ida must be hiding some kind of information. But from whom? Who else has the key besides Shannon? Maybe there's a key chest from which she could get the key. Might be wise to look into that and see about getting into that drawer.

Several cars were already parked when Emily pulled into the Sustain and Shelter lot at 7:15. As she headed her car toward one of the rear lots, she noticed Thomas sitting in his car apparently waiting. Even though she felt sure he saw her wave to him when she headed back to the building, he slouched into his seat and looked into the rearview mirror. Joan Chavez' car came into the parking lot just about the time Emily walked up to the back entrance, and the noise of the car door opening made her turn back to the parking area because there had not been enough time for Joan to park and exit her car. As Emily reached for the door, she observed Thomas getting out of his car to wait. Emily ducked into the hallway and watched Joan pull her car neatly into the parking space next to Thomas while Thomas opened the trunk. Curious, Emily stepped into the shadow of the almost closed door and watched through the window as Joan got out quickly, went to her trunk, extracted a box from her trunk and put it into the open trunk of Thomas' car. Neither one looked to see if anyone had watched them. Thomas, with his unyielding correct posture, hovered over Joan as he escorted her into the office.

Through the partially opened door, Emily heard Thomas say to Joan in a hesitating, unsure manner, "I, uh, well. I just wanted to say, you, um, you look nice. Tonight. You look nice."

Thomas was right, agreed Emily. In freeing her hair from the bonds of the severity of the bun she usually wore, Joan had softened the pronounced angles of her petite face. When she smiled shyly at the compliment, the blond curls, of which there had been no evidence when they were bound behind her head, added to her femininity and made her appear more approachable.

Emily hurried ahead to the conference room, so they wouldn't find her loitering and watching them. As she entered the room in great haste and found a seat next to Bo, Blythe Oberstein, dressed in a black and white short sleeve coatdress accented by black and white spectator pumps, smiled at her. Ida, with her hound dog eyes, guiltily looked away from her when she arrived, so Emily knew she didn't have to ask if the financial statements were ready for her. The older couple Emily had seen at the last meeting wasn't present. Rochelle gave her a small, bored salute. Wearing a tightly fitted white linen suit with a sweetheart neckline, she asked Emily, "Been to workout recently?"

"Yes, I went yesterday. Have you?"

"No, too much on my mind. My husband travels a lot, and when he's home I stick around."

"Guess you miss him when he's gone?"

Rochelle answered with a sarcastic expletive just as Rudyard Millup blustered his way through calling the meeting to order.

"The last meeting of the fiscal year of Sustain and Shelter Board is called to order at precisely 7:38 PM on Thursday, June–get the date right on that will you, Shannon."

Shannon nodded at the keyboard, and the meeting progressed.

There was no treasurer's report. "Suffice it to say," Mr. Millup assured the group, "the deficit has been taken care of by an anonymous donor. Mr. Woodley will still get his increase in pay."

Would the anonymous donor be on the list Emily was currently typing?Maybe she could pump the impassive Shannon to discover who the donor might be. Maybe. Probably not, but it was worth a try.

"…and Mr. Woodley wanted me to be sure to thank her," Mr. Millup filtered into Emily's thoughts, "for taking on the job of putting our donor and volunteer list into, what did you call it, Chad?"

"Database," said Chad with a forced smile.

"Database. Thank you from all of us at the office." With that statement, eyes turned to Emily expectantly. Not quite sure why, she smiled at them and tried not to look stupidly stunned at being caught not listening. It was enough because the meeting held the promise of being short, and no one particularly wanted to hear a speech.

"Then with that, meeting is…"

Mr. Millup was interrupted by Rochelle who said, "I will need to be excused for the next two meetings. I'm having some surgery."

"Okay, put that down in the minutes, Shannon," said Mr. Millup. No sympathy, no discreet questions. Apparently, the whole world knew Rochelle had surgery every summer.

Half listening to the wrap-up of the meeting, Emily was more intrigued with Chad's passing a note to Bo. Just like middle school, only this note wouldn't get snatched up by the teacher. Bo read the note, looked at Chad and nodded. Curious, Emily watched the two men, but her gaze was impeded when Rochelle got out of her chair after the meeting was adjourned. She certainly does look younger than me; wonder how old she really is. Maybe I should look into plastic surgery. Emily smiled to herself imagining her family's reaction to her taking time off from life for plastic surgery. As Rochelle turned to leave, Emily edged away from her seat, caught her eye and said to Rochelle, "I hope your surgery goes well. Are you going to be all right?"

"Of course. I already told you I do this every summer. I hate spending time with my kids. This is my excuse to dump them for the summer."

Emily stopped short of rolling her eyes as she said, "Good luck."

Their cars being parked in different locations, they parted at the door, but not before Emily saw Bo sidle up to Chad's office and wait quietly for him. Purses are such useful items. Always at the ready, they seem to be in one's hands—or not. Emily's purse suddenly dropped from her hands spilling its accoutrements of life on the floor and under the conference table. As she slowly bent to retrieve them, she also dropped some papers she had in her other hand. From under the table, she could see the two pairs of legs of Chad and Bo. They didn't bother to go into Chad's office, but the top of the table wasn't a good conductor of sound, so their conversation was heard only by themselves. Emily was able to pick up the last few sentences when Chad asked Bo as they were leaving, "So you'll do it?"

"As soon as I make the plans. May take a little time, but I'll let you know."

"Okay, but the situation needs to be addressed soon."

"Yeah, man, got it. Not to worry. I'll take care of it."

Papers and keys in hand, curiosity aroused, Emily approached her car, saw Blythe's car was parked next to hers and stalled getting in her own until she saw Blythe approach.

"I wanted to ask how things are going for you," said Emily.

"They're fine. In fact, I may have a line on a job. A real job working with children," she said enthusiastically.

"What kind of job?"

"I haven't got all the details. Next time I see you, I'll know more. You take care of those little girls. Teach them to take care of themselves, so they never end up in a mess like mine," Blythe warned.

"Thank you. Good night."

And that was the last time Emily ever saw the homeless Blythe Oberstien.

CHAPTER 17

David, Emily, Jojo and Lulie stepped off the school ground and opened the door to a summer of palpably hot days and refreshingly cool and balmy nights. They ran onto the playground of the Bay Area and sampled every tourist attraction they could find. They managed to include Byte on their outings when they went to the cool coast of California. Together the family made memories that would become integral parts of their lives. Even as they planned their days, there was a resignation to the days of summer falling into the blur of memory too quickly and with not enough time to savor the optimism of the season. They clenched the days as tightly as they could, but time wrenched them away, compacted them and stored them in the deepest prinkles in the brain to be triggered in the future by a taste, or picture or smell.

Emily's forays into Sustain and Shelter could not invade the secure comfort of her family's summer respite from their normal yearly routine. Shannon's brusqueness, which became more curt with each Friday Emily showed up at the office to do the input, did not deter

Emily from relishing the summer with her husband, children, mother and dog.

All of Contra Costa County attended the annual Fourth of July happenings.

Well, perhaps not all of Contra Costa, but it seemed the whole county was there. As Americana as it could be, Pleasant Creek Park was swaddled in enough plastic red, white and blue bunting to choke an environmentalist. A marching band engorged the gingerbread gazebo and performed Sousa marches and patriotic ditties so certainly and loudly that they danced in one's head for a continual week after the jubilee. Military bands harmonized the marching band in the gazebo and accompanied various units of military personnel in their fastidious, clean cut movements, the perfection of their dress enhancing the perfection of their bearing. The screaming whine of the might of the precision military planes greeted the onlookers from above with a show of American exactness and strength.

Contra Costans peacefully leisured through the day as bloated with pride in their red, white and blue as they were bloated with the questionably healthy delicacies and brews hocked by vendors at the festival. The Chamber of Commerce was out in force as local merchants presented their products and services. A myriad of non-profit groups set up booths for their ever-needed fund raising. It was at one of these booths where the Kristichs met Louisa and Bob after she had manned the booth of the agency for which she worked, Community Action Group.

"Enjoy yourself, Louisa?" asked David.

"It was okay. Genevieve, my co-worker, and I worked that shift together. She loves those things because she sees everyone in the county and can catch up on all the gossip. She tried to get her hair dyed into a red, white and blue stripe, but the strands of hair from one color kept falling across the other colors. It looked like she had electrical wiring for hair."

After the parade of war veterans passed, the family walked the park to view the ring of booths. At the farthest point from the gazebo almost behind the local Cadillac dealer's booth, sat the Sustain and Shelter kiosk. Had it not been for Lulie, they would have missed it completely.

"Look, Mom. Isn't that the place where you go on Fridays?" asked Lulie as she pointed to the cubicle.

"Where do you mean, honey?" Emily followed Lulie's pointing finger but didn't see the booth.

"There, in the corner behind the cars."

Emily ransacked the direction of Lulie's index finger until she finally had it in her line of vision. "You're right. That's it. They never said they were doing a booth. I wonder if it was a last minute decision."

"It couldn't have been," pointed out Louisa. "Those applications had to be in by May 15, so the organizers could get the equipment rented and graph out the space required in the park. They had to decide by then."

"We've had two meetings since then, and I haven't heard a word about it. Let's go see who's manning the booth. You'd think they would have asked for volunteers or something. No one likes to sit at those things on a hot day and certainly not for a long time. What a drag."

Rudyard Millup was just coming out from behind the booth as they approached.

"Rudyard," called Emily.

He didn't quite look like he was running away from them, but it did require a second call from Emily to gain his attention.

Dressed in his beige linen suit, complete with patriotically striped tie, he came over to them mopping perspiration off his face and neck.

"Well, hello, Mrs. Kristich. How are you?"

"We're fine, but it looks like you're hot. Is your wife here?"

"My wife? No. No wife here. She's much too delicate to come out in weather like this. I wouldn't allow it. It's too warm."

"Aren't you considerate, Mr. Millup?" Louisa said. Emily looked obliquely at her mother and surveyed the rest of her family to see if they picked up on her sarcasm.

"I'd like to introduce you to my family, Mr. Millup." Emily started with David and finished with Detective Bob Washburn.

Rudyard swallowed visibly. "*Detective* Washburn, you say? Is he related to you, Mrs. Kristich?"

Louisa smiled broadly as she said, "No, he's my good friend."

"I wasn't aware you needed volunteers for this booth. I didn't even know you were having a booth. Shannon or Chad never said a thing."

"Yes, well, you know how it is. We do hate to call on our volunteers for just everything. We don't want to chase them away now, do we?"

"But isn't that what they're for?" commented Louisa. "I work for Community Action Group, a semi-private social agency here in Pleasant Creek, and we use our volunteers for many jobs. The more volunteers you have, the more the work is spread around. They wouldn't be volunteering if they didn't wish to help."

"You could have called some people from that list I typed. There are so many names on it. Most of it's in the computer. I'm sure they would liked to have helped," offered Emily.

"I suppose so. I must be off. Have to get home to my wife," he threw over his shoulder as he rushed away.

"Interesting," was David's only remark in the whole exchange.

Bob Washburn, on the other hand, had many more remarks to make after the exchange. "Emily, tell me again who that fellow is."

Emily told him and added, "The president of the same board on which Ralph Watkins sat."

"Who's Ralph Watkins, Mommy?" asked Jojo. At that, David took her hand and reached to take Lulie's hand. As he guided his daughters along, he suggested they go find an ice cream stand.

Emily added when the children were gone, "The same Ralph Watkins that was found in the car at Del Oro Plaza. The same Ralph Watkins you told me not to talk about until he was identified and you gave me the word. Only, I found out about the i.d. at a board meeting. That Ralph Watkins.

"And let me tell you something else, Bob. There's a very strange financial situation going on over there."

"Like what?"

"Like I don't know. But I'm going to find out. I've sat on enough boards to know this doesn't feel like they're keeping their records correctly."

"So do you have anything concrete?"

"No, but I will."

"How?" asked an alarmed Louisa. "If you're going to do anything dangerous, I want you off that board now."

"Louisa," said Emily warningly. She repeated in the same tone, "Mom."

"Okay, okay, I know. I shouldn't have said that. But you need to be careful, and you need to tell Bob if you really do find anything strange. Many times, non-profits, especially if they're new, haven't been trained to keep records properly. I'm sure that's it. They just need some training. I'll get you the names of training organizations to pass on to them. I'm sure they just haven't been trained. Nothing to worry about."

"That's right, Mom, nothing to worry about.'

As the rest of the family, dripping ice cream cones held in their hands, approached, Bob advised, "However, if you do find something, you, please, let me know immediately. Fair?"

"Like you let me know about Ralph? Do you know anything more about what happened?"

"Okay, yes, I know a few things. I'll tell you some, but not with the little girls around. I'll tell you only if you promise to let me know any information you have. Got it?"

"Promise," agreed Emily.

The booth they approached was devoid of any decoration except a small, hand-lettered banner reading, 'Sustain and Shelter'. There was a plastic tube with dollar bills and coins in it sitting on the card table. In the lone chair was a man whom Emily had never seen. The tics with which he was affected prevented him from passing out the organization's pamphlets to passersby, so they sat on the table. Emily nodded 'hello', and the man smiled revealing three missing teeth.

"Do you work for Sustain and Shelter?" asked Louisa.

"No, ma'am. I eat there."

"It's nice meeting you, Mr...." probed Emily.

"George, just call me George."

"You certainly are nice to take time out to sit here, George."

"Yes, ma'am. Anyone who will feed me, I'll help 'em out. They're helping the homeless. And I'm a homeless." Perhaps the pride with which he pointed out his station in life could have been from the fact he had a group with which to identify.

"So they are," agreed Emily.

"Very interesting. You've got yourself involved in quite an agency," David said as they left the area. "What do you think about this group, Louisa?"

"I'm not really sure. How about for now just leaving it at there are agencies and there are agencies? I know they do some good things, but, honestly, if that's an indication of their organization abilities, I'm beginning to wonder."

Quiet prevailed as the family walked to their respective cars in the parking lot. The children were worn out from the day's activities; the adults were mulling over the scene with Sustain and Shelter.

Louisa interrupted the silences. "Bob has an idea."

Emily looked at the glint in her mother's eye and said, "Uh-oh. Who has the idea?"

Louisa tapped Emily's arm. "Stop that. You don't even know what I'm going to say."

"Experience leads me to believe it's going to be an experience."

"Oh, my, yes, a family experience. Bob has tickets to a carnival; he has enough for all of us. Wouldn't you like to go?"

"But, Mom, we don't even like carnivals," Emily protested. "I get sick on all the rides."

"This is not a carnival as you know it, this is the East of the Sun and West of the Moon. I don't even know if it could be lumped in the same category as a carnival. This doesn't even have rides," coaxed Louisa.

"Then those games are all rigged. It took David forty-six dollars to win a stuffed dog for Jojo at the last carnival we attended. By the time she brought it home, the sawdust that was used for stuffing left a trail from the car to her bedroom."

"This carnival doesn't have games, either," interjected Bob.

"Then how can it be a carnival if it doesn't have rides or games?"

"That's what we're trying to tell you. It's not like a typical carnival. It has people doing acrobatics. It has terrific reviews in the entertainment section of the paper."

"You mean stuff like rings and ribbon dances?" asked Jojo. "I love ribbon dancing."

"Kind of. It's fancier than that. Colors and acrobatics and gymnastics and good music."

"I'd like to take the whole family," Bob said. "It'll kind of make up for the slip-up about not telling you you know what. It's supposed to be a great show."

David acquiesced. "We'll go, won't we, girls?"

"Good. That's taken care of. One more thing–can we all go in your van? That way we can all go to San Francisco in one car."

"Right. Good idea, Mom. Give me details. And, Mom…"

Louisa interrupted her. "I know. I know. I won't be late. I promise."

"And we will all be on our best behavior, right, girls?" added David looking at this daughters.

Both girls couldn't have been more solemn in agreement if they were to meet Mr. Rogers himself.

CHAPTER 18

The July board meeting of Sustain and Shelter was not as muddled as the other monthly meetings Emily had attended. This was possibly because there were only five people present; however, Mr. Millup continued to foster the undercurrent of confusion that had become an integral part of his manner of conducting business. He began by giving a running comment of the people absent and the reasons for the absence. He got through the first few relatively easily.

Scanning the members, Mr. Millup pronounced, "As you are all aware, Blythe Oberserve has resigned."

"Oberstein," corrected Shannon.

"Whazzat? What's that you're saying?" he said, put out because he had been interrupted, or corrected, or both.

"Oberstein, her last name is Oberstein."

"Right. That's right. As you are all aware she resigned. She's off to take some job somewhere.

"I suppose we should all wish her well," he added as an afterthought.

"And Bo. Anybody know where he is?" Blank looks and shaking heads answered his query.

"Oh well, maybe he'll be back," Rudyard said.

"He'll be back," reassured Chad.

"What makes you so sure?" asked Rudyard.

"Don't worry. I know."

Rudyard looked at Chad as if he finally understood the meaning of Chad's statement and continued, "Then, there's Rochelle. She's off having some surgery. She'll be back next month."

"We won't have a meeting next month," interrupted Shannon again. She seemed to be enjoying putting him ill at ease.

"Huh, no meeting next month?" He looked quizzically at Chad Woodley who slightly shrugged his shoulders.

"Next month is August, and we don't have meetings in August. Remember, the office is closed the last three weeks of August for vacation." Shannon enunciated each word slowly for Mr. Millup's understanding.

"Right, oh, right. That's right. Let's see. Ralph Watkins, now, have you replaced him yet, Chad?"

Chad cleared his throat to explain. "I've got some names of community leaders and have been waiting until the summer is over to request they join us. There are some good possibilities. We'll have someone in by September, won't we, Shannon?"

Shannon's light turned on. Her evening was complete because Chad had talked directly to her. "Oh, yes, Mr. Woodley," she breathed.

"Now, who else is missing? Oh. Ida. Where's Ida?" Before Shannon could open her mouth, Mr. Millup looked directly at her and asked, "I assume you know the answer to that also?"

Shannon mutely shook her head and joined the rest of the surprised room looking around the table.

Joan said, "She's never late, and she never misses a meeting. She must have called someone. Did you check the answering machine?"

Shannon said, "We don't have an answering machine in the office."

Joan said, "Why ever not?"

Shannon said, "No one felt we needed one."

Joan gazed at her and said, "Of course, you do. Everyone has answering machines these days. Why they're like televisions. Everyone has TV's, sometimes two and three." Her mouth settled into a thin, grim line.

Wonder of wonders. Thomas cleared his throat and said the first words Emily had heard him utter in the meetings she had attended. He cleared his throat again and said, "She's right, you know."

Joan bestowed a smile of thanks in his direction which he mirrored when he realized it was for him. His smile achieved the same effect as Joan's softened hairstyle–it erased the severity of his demeanor and reinforced his pleasing looks.

A bit on the defensive, Chad said, "We always felt the office wouldn't receive the calls, the kitchens would. So we put the machine there instead of here."

"Well," said Joan not understanding the logic of their efficiency at all. "Do you think that makes sense, Thomas?"

The surprise at being addressed was evidenced in the slight jump of Thomas's shoulders. He cleared his throat importantly and said, "No. No, I don't think so."

Joan smiled at him, and he smiled back at her.

"So no one has any idea where Ida is?" asked Mr. Millup again bringing the group to the whereabouts of Ida.

To shaking of heads, he said, "We certainly can't conduct business with only us here. We'll have to adjourn and do all this in September."

Joan said, "Is there anything we need a decision on?"

"No, no, don't worry your pretty little..." he stopped as he caught Emily stiffening. With a nervous chuckle he continued, "Don't worry about it. I'm sure Chad and I can handle it in the office. If there's anything important, we'll call an emergency meeting."

"But wait." Emily tried to forestall the adjournment. "What about the fundrais…"

"The meeting is adjourned, Mrs. Kristich," declared Mr. Millup with unmistakable finality as he and Chad Woodley quickly exited the room.

A few minutes after being rebuffed, Emily walked over to Shannon and asked, "If the office is closed the last three weeks of August, does that mean I can't use the computer?"

"What?" She looked up from the laptop she was closing and gave Emily a blank look.

"Remember how Rudyard and you discussed having no meeting in August, and you said the office would be closed. Does that mean I can't come in?"

"Yes, no one can."

"So that means I better finish this by next week."

"Guess that's what that means."

"So what're you going to do in that three weeks?"

"What do you mean?"

"Well, do you work in the office?"

"Why would I do that? It's a vacation, why would I put in time at work?"

"Don't know. Some people use the time to catch up on jobs or projects. Do you need a board member to have the keys?"

"Why?"

"For emergencies?"

"No, Mr. Woodley and Mr. Millup can take care of that. Why should we give anyone the keys?"

"Public agency helping the public. Seems like it should be accessible to the public."

Shannon rolled her eyes at Emily and said, "Yeah, right."

CHAPTER 19

A tropical balminess bathed Sunday and set the spirits of the Kristich family into high gear for their outing. They picked up Louisa and Bob and set off through the Caldecott Tunnel, the Maginot Line of city and suburbs, and encountered the drippy dampness of a San Francisco summer. The rapid deceleration from warmth to cool is a fact of life in the Bay Area, and, as a result, sweaters and jackets have permanent residence in automobiles. The minivan approached the enormous blue and yellow tent set up incongruously among the sophisticated skyscrapers of the City—a blue blob among gray spires. David parked the car, and the family melded into the line of humanity waiting to have tickets checked. After entering the tent, the drapes on the doors dropped, darkness enveloped the crowd, and the show began.

Louisa and Bob were right. It was a carnival unlike any imagined, and the word carnival couldn't begin to capture its essence. Resplendent colors of sunshine, teal, magenta, orange, lime and blue blazed on the props and costumes used by the players of the carnival. Against the empty darkness of the tent, colors spewed forth in a dazzling luminosity that entreated the eyes to follow every move of the equilibrists as they contorted themselves into certifiably inhuman positions. Masques and disguises enhanced the suprahuman aura of the feats of the acrobats: noses the size of Cyrano's, hats the size of Mae West's, make up done in the magic of the rainbow. Pleasantly peculiar tunes tickled the ears and reverberated the tent with pitches and rhythms that seemed to encompass music of all ethnicities. Bodies were used as levers and held perpendicularly to two storied poles; the tightrope walker leapt in mid air between two wires; duets curved and bowed their bodies while wrapped as tightly as conjoined twins; a child walked horizontally up his vertically erect parents, and it was all done with daring charisma and charm.

"What did you guys think?" asked Bob Washburn as he put his hand through the crook of Louisa's arm after the family had left the tent.

"Thank you, Mr. Washburn. It was like wonderful," said Jojo.

"Oh, yes. It was beautiful," squealed Lulie. "Just beautiful. And those people had funny faces. Would you want a nose that long, Jojo?"

"I think people get them cut off if they're that long," said Jojo pedagogically.

"Yes, I would get my nose cut off if it got that long. Noses sure make people look different, don't they, Mom?"

"Right," agreed Emily, "and sometimes act differently."

CHAPTER 20

Emily had her chance to get into the file cabinet on the last day of her volunteering at the office of Sustain and Shelter. Deciding she would be bold and try to get into that locked cabinet was much easier in the comfort and safety of her own home than actually facing unknown consequences in a hostile office. Not only was the ever-gloomy Shannon present, but Chad strolled in at 10:00 that morning. Looking up from her desk, Emily saw him before he put on the facade of joviality, and the sulky darkness of his eyes gave them a swollen look.

When he saw her looking at him from the work desk, he wrapped his hearty greeting in a big smile, "Well, hello, Emily. You don't mind if I call you Emily, do you? And Shannon, sweet Shannon. Isn't the day just lovely? This summer has had such nice weather, not too hot, not too cool. What more could we ask for?"

He carried on his exultation of the glory of the weather down the hall and back to his office. Emily turned from watching his progress and glanced at Shannon who still wore the soft glowing aura reserved only for Chad. She called Shannon's name four times before Shannon's cloud evaporated enough to receive her attention. Eyes narrowed, Shannon looked at Emily and frowned. Since niceties hadn't worked on Shannon prior to this time, Emily decided to use the direct approach and gloss the wording a bit when she asked, "Do you and Chad date? I mean you and he seem so close; whenever I see you together you seem to be almost telepathic."

A little exaggeration was the grease for the wheel because Shannon beamed at the thought she and Chad might be on the same wavelength as she said, "We don't actually date. He and I talked together once and decided we had a better relationship than that. He told me he has never known anyone like me, and I was closer to him than any person in his life. I was his confidant. That's probably why you could see our closeness so quickly. You hardly know us, and you can still pick out our feelings for each other. You really think we're telepathic? And you could see that?"

She paused and said dreamily, "That's what we are, just like you said. Telepathic, almost spiritual."

It was cruel, but why waste the opportunity if the information were to pour forth?

"Have you two known each other long? A relationship like that must have taken quite a long time to develop, right?"

"Oh, no. We knew. Just like people falling in love." Her voice softened on the word 'love'. "We just knew. My cousin introduced us when I went to one of the kitchens to help feed the homeless. My cousin is homeless, more or less. Sometimes he lives with my aunt, but they don't like each other. So when they get tired of each other, he leaves. He and Chad are pretty good friends, and George, my cousin, knew I was looking for a job when I graduated from business school. So he introduced us, and Chad and I just knew."

This was better than Emily hoped for, so she pressed on. "Chad seems very dedicated to helping out people. Has he always done this type of work? I've been impressed by the good work he's done. Did he do this in the last city he worked."

"You mean in San Diego?" Emily's stab in the dark had worked. "I think so. He doesn't have any training or anything, just a good heart. When he was in El Paso, in Texas, he also did this. Also, somewhere in the valley. Modesto or Fresno. Some city out there. He just starts a little soup kitchen, and people see all that wonderful work he's doing, and they start helping him out. He works so hard for others. He's got the biggest heart. Then people see his good works, so they donate money. He takes that money and starts getting shelter and food for everybody. And then, then when he's really got it going, he turns it over to someone and goes to another city and starts one again. That's how he met Mr. Millup. Mr. Millup was so impressed with what Chad was doing, he started getting money for him to help his organization for the homeless somewhere in the valley—Modesto or Fresno or someplace like that. After a while, Mr. Millup persuaded the board of Sustain and Shelter to hire him. He's already got a medical clinic going."

Shannon sighed, "I'm so glad Mr. Millup hired him. Chad is so cool." She post scripted her accolade of Chad. "This is the first time he's started a clinic, though. I don't remember hearing him talk about any others, so it's been a rough go for a while. But he got Joan Chavez' help, so that made it a little easier. She's so bitchy though. It's good Chad is so nice, he can put up with her. Sustain and Shelter and the clinic have grown so much. It's wonderful what he can do to help to help all those poor, pathetic people."

Shannon's eyes were getting teary as she talked about the good-heartedness of her wonderful Chad. She pulled the bottom drawer of her desk out to retrieve her purse, rummaged around in its depths and pulled up a tissue to rub her eyes.

Chad called from his office, "Shannon."

"Oh," Shannon hopefully exhaled. "I have to go see what he wants." She vaulted out of her chair and all but ran down the hallway leaving her purse gaping on the desk, a key filled smile beckoning to Emily.

How easy it was to be daringly nosy and plan sneaky opportunities Emily had never thought would actually materialize. Here was the manifestation of her plans staring her in the face. Having no idea if Chad's discourse with Shannon was to be long (Here's hoping.) or brief (Perish the thought.), Emily planted her feet on the ground as if to stomp out her trepidation, got out of her chair and walked slowly past Shannon's desk. Quickly she shot her hand out to seize the keys and walked the five feet behind Shannon's desk to the locked file cabinet. However, just as she had done when she first saw Ralph Watkins lying dead in the car at the mall, Emily proceeded a few feet before the contents of Shannon's purse registered. Backtracking the few steps she had taken toward the filing cabinet, Emily looked down at the handbag and visually explored the miscellany of the purse. Confirming that she had, indeed, seen a gun, she reached out a finger and gently tapped the weapon. It didn't feel like plastic, and it didn't sound like plastic; in conclusion, it had to be a true weapon, concealed in a purse, concealed, in this case, under some fluffed-up tissues and make-up that had spilled out of a smaller bag. She tapped the gun again, looked at it without disturbing the contents of the purse, took a deep breath and proceeded toward the filing cabinets again. Knowing she had very limited time to get into that file, she fixed in her mind as best she could the display in Shannon's purse, so that she might retrieve the image later.

To the business at hand. As Emily proceeded by trying each one to locate the key among the seven on the ring, she raced through a scenario of what might happen should someone walk into the office while she had her hand buried in the locked cabinet. The gun in the purse crept into these situations, and the outcomes Emily painted for herself ended up with the gun going off. Once again, she reminded herself, get to the business at hand. Chad, contrary to the love Shannon knew he had for her, didn't want to keep the young woman around him more than a few minutes. This was one of those situations when time would flash by, and there would be no leisurely minutes allowed her to steal this file. There were stacks of blank copy paper stored on the file cabinets, so Emily grabbed a handful of them from one of the open reams, then ducked quickly onto her haunches to open the drawer of the cabinet with the key discovered to fit the lock of the requisite file drawer. It slid out sounding just as empty as she remembered.

In the file divider was a lone notebook with no label. She decided this had to be Ida's work as she riffled through the pages and scanned the numbers on them. Emily hoped she wasn't subjecting her body to an early heart attack with the physical stress this skulking around was causing because her heart was throbbing blood through her body at a bruising rate. She had expected a file with the few papers she remembered Ida bringing into the office; instead Emily found a notebook. A notebook is for many pages, and this was a low-budget, she assumed, operation. How many pages would it take to post the income and expenses of a low-budget operation? Maybe Ida was one of those bookkeeper types who used many journal entry notes and, therefore, had to use lots of paper. As she took out the notebook, she heard the door to Chad's office slam and assumed she would hear footsteps next. Hoping snapping open the notebook didn't send them running to see what she was doing, Emily took the papers out of the binder and quickly shoved the blank papers into the notebook, so anyone glancing at the file would see paper peeking at the edges of the file, slid the file into the drawer and closed it.

Even in the carpeted hallway, Shannon's footsteps became progressively louder until they beat a tympani drum punctuated with gunshots in Emily's ears. She had to move away from the files back to her workstation, so Shannon wouldn't begin to wonder what she might be doing standing in that location. Shannon had made it so clear that Emily was not to have anything to do with the files, she didn't want to pique the young woman's suspicions, especially now that they were on such familiarly friendly terms. There was also the gun factor; it probably isn't a good idea to rile a woman who carries a concealed weapon in her purse. Emily knew from her heart rate, higher than any she had experienced during exercise classes, she had just run the mile in record time as she took the ten feet briskly back to the computer. In her hand were not only the papers that once inhabited the locked file cabinet, but also Shannon's keys. Entering the passageway from the hallway was Shannon, not looking very ethereal either.

As Emily seated herself, the keys and papers shoved under her, she said, "Problems, Shannon?"

"I'm not to talk to you. You are here to work, and you must get that finished." She took her purse and slammed it into the desk drawer.

No, not the purse! Panicked thoughts whooshed through Emily's head. I've got your keys. Put the purse back on the desk, Shannon. Then another complication plunged into Emily's brain. Someone likes locks in this office so much, what if Shannon locks her purse in the drawer? With a key on the ring I'm sitting on? And if she can't find the key ring, what to do? Don't look for the key, Shannon.

And she didn't.

Adrenaline from the race with the papers was still pumping, and although Emily was rapidly jabbing the keyboard, nervous sweat seemed to flow out of every pore of her fingers giving the keyboard a slippery dampness. Watching Shannon and mentally pleading with her to please get that purse out or leave the room, so Emily could drop the keys in the drawer, made the morning as nerve wracking as if she were a squirrel hopping electrical lines in a lightening storm.

All Shannon did was file papers in the unlocked cabinet drawers. When she turned her back to Emily's area, Emily reached under her skirt, extricated the papers and placed them on the desk with the list of names she was typing. After Shannon had filed her first set of papers and turned to obtain more from her desk to file in a second drawer, Emily took the misappropriated papers, folded them and stuffed them in the drawer where her purse was lodged. The third time Shannon turned to file papers, Emily opened the drawer and put the papers lying there into her purse.

"Leaving already?" said Shannon hopefully.

Her voice was a howitzer in an open field, and it startled Emily into unnerved astonishment, so she jumped up from her chair and punched down on the key ring. A look of perplexity skipped across Shannon's face, so that, if she hadn't had an inkling of suspicion before, Emily was sure she did now. The literal pain in the butt Emily was experiencing had to be choked down because Shannon was still staring at her as though she had just witnessed a very alive Elvis walk through the door.

The still pumping adrenaline gave Emily extra speed with which to strike the keyboard, so she completed the list that day.

"Finished," she proclaimed.

Shannon said absentmindedly, "With what?"

"The list, Shannon, the list. I've finished with the list."

Instead of a verbal pat on the back one might have expected, Shannon said happily, "So that means you're gone? I don't have to see you anymore."

"Something like that. Do you want an extra copy of this stuff?"

"Yeah, Chad said something about that."

"I've got time; I'll copy it now. Is the copier warmed up?"

"It's broke. It's been broke awhile."

What an office! What efficiency! But a broken copier was probably better in dealing with the keys that were still embedded in Emily's backside because she wouldn't have to get up and have Shannon see her keys lying outside of her purse. Emily fleetingly wondered how big the bruise was going to be, and how she would explain it to David when he saw it. Somehow it didn't seem reasonable to suppose David would approve of her snooping in locked office drawers especially having stolen the keys out of someone's purse, more especially if she told him about the gun in the purse. Heavily dimmed lights in the bedroom can be very romantic. They're also good for hiding bruises.

"Do you want to make the copies?" Emily asked Shannon.

"Why would I want to do that?"

"I don't know, Shannon. It just seems if you work here, you would be in charge of making sure the paperwork is in order."

"That's not my job. You volunteered to do it."

Knowing there was a solution to the problem, which in this case was Shannon, Emily said, "If I take these to a copy service, can I be reimbursed for them?"

"I suppose so. Check with Ida, she'll take care of it."

"Okey, dokey. I'll do that. I wouldn't want you to have to risk doing it yourself."

"That's right. You leaving now?" There was that tinge of hope in Shannon's question.

"Soon." Just as soon as I can figure out what to do with your keys. Slowly gathering the papers containing the lists the printer was belching out, she dwelled on the matter of the keys. Shannon wasn't budging from the desk. The keys were still an aching reminder to Emily of their presence. What to do?

Emily reached into the desk drawer to procure her own purse, took her keys out of it and put the purse on the list she would copy for the agency. She then reached under her seat and put Shannon's keys in the same hand as her own keys. Gathering up the papers and purse in one hand and the two sets of keys in the other hand, she walked over to Shannon's desk to say good-bye. As she approached the desk, she shuffled her feet as though she had tripped over them and dropped both sets of keys. Shannon made no move to help Emily which was to be expected, and appreciated in this case, because Emily slid Shannon's set of keys to the foot of her desk where she would see them if she took some effort to look. Then she would think the keys had fallen out of her purse when she jammed the purse into the desk drawer. At least, that's what Emily fervently hoped she would think.

"Good bye, Shannon. I'll bring these next Wednesday before the office closes for the summer. What do you think, about four or five copies?"

No response.

"You're welcome, Shannon," Emily muttered as she walked out the door.

CHAPTER 21

The annual trip to San Francisco's Pier 39 occupied the Kristich's Saturday, so Emily didn't study Ida's reports that she had agonized so hard over getting. She did admire the blue-green tinted swelling on her left buttock, however, and gingerly perched herself into sitting positions when required for a day or so after the incident with the keys. The sight of the gun bothered her more than the pain of the bruise, and she became somewhat distracted from the day's doings when she thought about it. The family didn't seem to notice as they were caught up in the hubbub and took her silences for their talking space. A gun in the middle of the suburbs seemed so out of context, and a gun showing up in a charitable agency demeaned the charity of the organization.

On Sunday, the Kristichs drove to the mall where Jojo and Lulie were packed onto a bus with fifty other Jojos and Lulies and sent off to camp for a week. Being conscientious parents, David and Emily made sure their girls got away from home for a weekly camping trip every summer, so they would develop independent skills and socialize on their own. That's what good parents must do to make their children well rounded, or so childrearing experts proclaimed. Emily wasn't so sure about this almost universally acclaimed practice because she liked having her daughters under foot, but she bit her tongue and made like she was as excited that they could go as they were to be going. Standing on the asphalt made malleable enough for a slight footprint by the hot sun, the parents waved slowly and watched Lulie give her double time wave and shriek her excited good byes while Jojo smiled her tentative smile and waved a slow, doubtful good bye.

In the car, David put her hand in his, and kept it there the remainder of the drive home. "They'll be back soon. It's less than a week, and Saturday isn't so long away."

Byte, who whimpered as the kids boarded the bus, put her head on Emily's shoulder from the backseat and would have kept it there if it hadn't been for the car starting and lurching Byte out of her seat towards the floor of the backseat.

"I've got an important meeting with some people in Santa Rosa, Em, on Monday, but I'll get home as soon as I can, so you won't be lonely. I'm sorry. This could be a big sale. The guy wants hardware and software, and I don't want to miss any detail."

"No, David. You go ahead and get that sale. I'm fine, and they'll be back before we know it. I love you for thinking of me though," she said as she reached over and kissed him. "Maybe I'll call Mom and see if she wants to do something. There are closets and junk I can clean out. I've got end of the quarter reports to complete for your office. Don't worry." And, but she didn't say anything to David, some stolen papers to study.

David called it an early night because of his business trip in the morning, so before she went to bed, she brought out the papers still jammed in her purse. As she started studying them, she began to understand the diffidence of the agency in letting her have the financial statements. Looking like computer-generated sheets, the information was printed horizontally in a landscape fashion rather than vertically. If the sheets were computer generated, that indicated some computer somewhere was harboring this information, perhaps even the computer she was using at the office of Sustain and Shelter. Emily rather doubted that, but perhaps when the office reopened she could look at the files on the computer. That's if the indomitable Shannon could be thwarted. Assuming she had a quarterly report in her hand, although there were no dates to confirm that, and assuming she had the report for Sustain and Shelter, although there were no names to confirm that, Emily was dumbfounded to find over three million dollars taken as revenue. She arrived at that figure by adding several sheets of what she assumed were income accounts. Ida had many of the items coded numerically, so it was difficult for Emily to find the standard expenses of payroll, office supplies, insurance, rent for the kitchens, food and supplies. Ida had also devoted several pages to small amounts that might have been individual transactions, or they could have been back-up information for the coded line items. There were no long-term liabilities, and the only short-term liability was payroll taxes. Assets consisted of the office and furniture and a bank account of about $10,000.00.

Perhaps it was the late hour; perhaps it was the amount of papers in this file, but Emily couldn't make sense of the sheets. This paperwork included neither balance sheet nor profit and loss statement. Not having been trained as a bookkeeper, Emily was aware that she needed to walk through financial information at a slower pace than an educated accountant. However, working in David's office had taught her that deciphering numerical information was not an impossible task, so this shouldn't be a problem. But, if, in this cursory view, her estimation of the income and expenses were correct, Sustain and Shelter had equity of almost three million dollars in cash.

Some fundraising. No wonder Shannon carried a gun if she had to take those amounts of money to the bank.

"Hayley'll be sick tomorrow," announced David a couple of days after his trip to Santa Rosa.

Emily gave him a quizzical glance and said, "Is that in your crystal ball?"

"Kind of. She was sniffling and looked bad, so I predict she'll call in sick tomorrow. Every time she answered the phone, callers thought I was the one talking, her voice was so scratchy and deep. She was moving at half-pace too. Usually she gets enough office work done for two people; today she just did one person's work."

Both of them paused to see who would bring it up first, but Emily outsat him on this one.

"So do you want to go in, or shall I call a temp service and have them send over a receptionist type?" David asked.

She smiled. "Let me think about the day tomorrow." She started to verbally outline her schedule. "Clean out one closet, have lunch with Miriam and run that list I've finished for Sustain and Shelter. Yeah, I'll go in. It's better that way because I know most of the office procedures, and the temp would have to do on the job training. I'll be there."

"Thank you. I'll gladly pay you someway."

"That's right. You will take me out to dinner tomorrow night because I will miss my lunch with Miriam."

"I guessed that was coming. But for you, my helpmeet, I will gladly forsake our evening at home to take my one and only love out to dinner."

"I had no doubt you would."

Needing more space as his business grew these last ten years, David had moved into his second office. Of both offices, this was the only one David and Emily had the luxury of time and money to plan and decorate, and they had achieved a professional effect in its taupe, navy and persimmon decor. The wall of windows gave the waiting room occupants a panoramic view of Pleasant Creek from the second floor of the building and provided a pleasant work environment.

As much as Emily enjoyed coming into the office to work and having the success of David's business reaffirmed, she could still feel the twinge of nostalgia for the first of David's offices. The twinge wasn't so much for the cramped closet sized office they could afford with papers stacked inefficiently among pieces of computer equipment and software. The twinge wasn't so much for the late nights spent doing bookkeeping or the late days making contacts and hearing 'no' too often to keep one's spirits above sea level. And the twinge certainly wasn't for the worry which insinuated itself into every activity she and David participated, worry that a sale was missed, worry that a check wouldn't clear, worry that taxes couldn't be paid, worry that the business wouldn't have a market. But the worry that devoured so much of their lives was also the inducement which spurred them on to work the long hours and undergo the rejection and live frugally so payments would be met. And one day they had so much business they had to move into another office and hire more staff.

The twinge of nostalgia which Emily felt was for the closeness and bond which working together so tightly with David had given their relationship. It was for the time they had to spend together to make the business, time which was now fragmented into different parts of their lives and not given to one purpose only. It was even for the arguments of how to spend any extra money they had. It was for the effort and guts put into a goal they had together and finally seeing it materialize into an achievement far beyond their expectations which created the satisfaction of doing a job well. It was for the glue to their marriage which was lathered on with a mortar thickness many couples could not begin to have. Those early years of trial and error record keeping, product evaluation, job costing, and profit analysis had given them time together and business skills many MBA's would never have. Now they didn't have time together like they did in the past, so filling in for some of the staff was a way for Emily to keep in touch with David's office and his life outside their home, and working the office provided a change in routine.

Perhaps that's why the inefficiency of Sustain and Shelter bothered her so much; she knew what an honest, efficient business should look like. And perhaps that was why she stuck it out with the non-profit. She felt she could tweak Sustain and Shelter into an efficient agency with clean and honest records. To that end, Emily decided the first thing she would do at David's office that morning would be to make a second copy of the Sustain and Shelter donor list she had so diligently copied onto the computer. Instead of taking the list to a copy service, she could just as easily copy the list at David's business and charge Sustain and Shelter per page. Then, as a responsible board member, she could begin the task of cleaning up their mess.

CHAPTER 22

When David repaid Emily for her work at his office with dinner at their favorite restaurant, it was as pleasurable as when they had been dating and had just reached the exciting-to-be-with stage. The softly lit atmosphere prolonged the dinner through which they giggled and played footsies, so it wasn't until later that evening after they returned from dinner that Emily remembered the copies she had run off for Sustain and Shelter.

"David," she announced.

"Emily," he responded.

"I forgot to drop these by the agency, and I think they need them tomorrow because it's the last day the office is opened before vacation, and they'll want to get them filed. I'll run over there and put them in the mail slot."

"Emily, it's ten o'clock, can't it wait? You can get them in tomorrow morning."

"No. No. I can't. If Hayley calls in again and is sick tomorrow, I won't get them there in time because I'll have to go into your office. I promised them I'd have them there today. Shannon isn't known for her flexibility, and I get the idea it's not wise to displease Shannon."

"Emily," David protested, "This is volunteer work. It's not like your next paycheck hangs on getting a few papers to them. It can wait."

"But I'll worry about it all night. I'll be back in forty-five minutes."

"I should go with you."

"Don't be ridiculous. You stay here and relax. Byte will go with me, won't you, girl," she said looking at the dog lying beside their bed. Byte looked at her and lazily flopped her tail in agreement. "It's fine. Good bye," she said as she blew out the room after sliding a kiss across his cheek. "Come, Byte."

Her intent to keep the car idling in front of the building while she deposited the meticulously ordered papers into the mail slot and make a quick job of delivery was not what occurred. Instead, hearing voices and seeing the office of Sustain and Shelter backlit, she made a trip around to the rear parking lot to see what was happening. Byte, already sitting erect with attention, became agitated as she approached the back lot. Her headlights flashed onto the face of Chad Woodley unloading a carton out of a U-haul truck. There were no lights on in the building although a back door was standing open, but there was a car with its headlights shining into the back of the U-Haul enabling Chad to see where he was going. Although she didn't see their faces, she thought there were two other people with him, and the truck was packed with crates identical to the one Chad was unloading.

"Pónganlas en la oficina. Allí. Pongan las cajas allí. Necesito a hablar con la mujer," Chad directed the two men. Slowly they walked to the back of the truck, picked up one box and carried it tiredly to the back entrance of Sustain and Shelter.

"Mas rápidamente," Chad barked as he turned to Emily's van.

Chad, the container parked between his chin and elongated arms, clumsily duck-walked to Emily's car. As he approached the car, Byte rose up from her sitting position in the front seat to stand. The fur on the back of her neck stood up as if suddenly hit with a jolt of static. The low, deep growl emitted out of the back of her throat at Chad's approach beckoned Emily's right hand to rub her neck in attempted reassurance, but it didn't stop Byte's protective snarl.

Surprised, or annoyed, Emily couldn't decide which, Chad said, "Mrs. Kristich, what are you doing here?" He took a step backward from the car when he heard Byte's complaint.

"I dropped those papers you wanted copied. I figured you'd want them before vacation started. Shannon would probably want to file them; she likes things neat, you know."

"I'm sure it could have waited. You certainly didn't need to make a special trip for that."

"What are you unloading? These look like the boxes that were in the office a few weeks back." Emily asked.

"Unloading? Yes, we are unloading food and some clothing that was donated to the kitchens," he said as he staggered while trying to distribute the weight of the box. With each movement Chad made, Emily could feel the tension in Byte's body draw tighter and the growl get more intense.

"This late?"

"We didn't want to disrupt the office by doing this during the day."

"But shouldn't you be taking that to the kitchens? You'll be doing double work if you have to load it up again and take it to the kitchens."

"No problem. We do it all the time."

"Who's 'we'?"

Chad jerked his head in the direction of the headlights. "You know, some of the volunteers."

"You mean some from the list I was typing?"

"I'm sure their names are on there."

"Don't they know English? Why are you speaking to them in Spanish?"

In an attempt to lightheartedly chuckle, Chad choked as he said, "This allows me to practice my Spanish. You know how it is. Can't live in this state without knowing some Spanish. Soon I'll start practicing my Arabic. Great diversity we have here, you know."

"If you needed volunteers, why didn't you call some of the board? There are several of us who could have helped."

He abruptly interrupted her question by saying, "Well, good night, Mrs. Kristich. Thanks for the papers. I'll be sure to tell Shannon how well you followed her orders."

"Who are those people in the truck? Are there only two people? Would you like me to help you with the unloading? I don't mind, you know. I have the time now."

"No, Mrs. Kristich" he said testily. "I do not want your help unloading. This is heavy work…"

Byte interrupted him with a shrill bark. Chad jumped back and momentarily lost his balance, so the box he held slipped almost bringing him to the tarmac. Byte barked again—a deep, threatening bark.

Holding the box in front of him like a shield, Chad threatened, "Get that dog out of here. If he attacks me, I'll sue."

"Byte would only attack with provocation. Are you going to provoke her? Or me?"

"Get out."

Chad turned his back and tottered away from her car leaving her no option but to drive home. She drove out of the parking lot and had to swerve around the oncoming van that was too far in her lane. It was too dark to see exactly what type of van was usurping her lane, but she had a sense she had seen it before as it headed toward Sustain and Shelter. Van plus office. Van plus driver. Van plus Bo. She did a quick u-turn in the middle of the street, an advantage of driving late into the traffic-less night. Emily sped along the road, but too much time had elapsed for her to be able to catch up with the van. Cruising by the office, she didn't drive into the parking lot because she knew she wasn't invited to the party, and she didn't want Byte to be 'provoked'. She slowed slightly in a futile attempt to determine if the van went into the front parking lot of the building. Excuses, excuses, she thought on the way home. It wasn't that she was worried about Byte; it was that she was worried about what Chad might start. Byte sat as erectly as she could and didn't relax until a mile into the drive home.

"You and I must have the same taste in men, Byte."

Driving home she concentrated on the scene she had just seen and wondered why anyone would pack and unload boxes twice. Shannon was going to have a great time tomorrow snacking on the packing.

CHAPTER 23

Contra Costa County consists of a delta formed by two rivers, the San Joaquin and Sacramento. Just as the Nile and Mississippi yield their river deposits to form fertile farmlands, so do these rivers. In fact, before tracts of houses blanketed the land, fields of crops were in abundance relying not only on the rich silt of the rivers, but also on the irrigation provided by them. There are still some agricultural areas, but the rivers' delta area is now used more for water sport and boating than agricultural enterprises.

People take their boats in and out of the sloughs and the islands roosting among them. They fish on the banks and piers of the rivers. They camp and swim in the land and water set aside by the state of California for state parks. They walk the banks of the river in towns that once depended on the river for life, Port Costa, Port Chicago, Crockett, Pittsburg, Antioch, and Knightsen. These are little towns that were once the life of the county and are now, at best, picturesque unless they were fortunate enough to have a highway bisect them or a mall built in their midst. Then they have been granted a new means of existence.

It was near one of these towns along the banks of the river that a solitary walker first saw a body. The body was never meant to be seen as evidenced by the rope that was still tied around its feet. The other end of the rope must have been tied to some type of anchor to conceal in the folds of the murky river water the violation done to the body. Nature wasn't going to let this secret go untold; however, for the never-ending movement of the river had allowed the rope to be dragged repeatedly across a sharp object, so it was cut from its mooring to float to the top of the river.

There's a sixth sense which informs one he is about to approach a desecration. It produces a squeamish trepidation that sets adrenaline coursing through his being to prepare him for what he is about to see. In this case, there was also a vaguely familiar foul odor. There's also an ambivalent excitement surrounding the unbidden discovery because coming in touching proximity of death is a rare event in the lives of most of us. A few of us attend lukewarm funerals, or memorial services as they're now called, where the body oftentimes isn't present. We watch death on television, but there is a window to barricade us from the reality of the film we witness. Workers whisk death out of hospital beds sometimes before relatives are aware their kinsman has died. As a result, we are left with the conclusion of our long-livedness, and it is a jolt to our logic when we smell or touch death in its rawest form.

The section of the riverbank where this mutilated body was found is overgrown with reeds that wave sinuously even in the stillness of the day. This particular walker enjoyed this part of his constitutional because as he crested the reeds, their yellow green contrasted artistically with the sandy bank and the powder blue sky above. Many times pieces of river debris had floated onto the ridge of land by the river. Sometimes they were interesting shapes of logs refined into soft curves by the never-ending movement of the river. Sometimes they were pieces of trash thrown overboard by boaters. Sometimes they were spines of river plants devoid of form and color. And sometimes they were just good old unrecognizable flotsam and jetsam.

The body was unrecognizable, but he knew it wasn't flotsam or jetsam. His sense of smell alerted him to his encroachment of something gruesome, but his inquisitiveness quenched his caution, and he continued the advance. He picked up a stick, courtesy of the river, but whether as a weapon or a prod, he wasn't sure and slowly moved forward.

Nature is not only ordered, she is efficient. Nature not only governs the rules of creation and destruction, she provides the control for disposal. From the vultures in the sky to the maggots on the ground to the bacteria present everywhere, Nature is her own best waste management. Human beings look upon dead creatures with reverent discomfiture, but when the signs of death are erased as they are on bones bleached by sunlight, people look upon death with sophisticated interest. Nature has removed our kinship with the dead body by obliterating the recognizable features of our species and leaving the bones which we never see in ourselves as the final act in her clean-up process.

Unfortunately, Nature hadn't had the chance to complete the job of removing the identifying marks of humanness on this body. When the walker came as close to the body as his senses would allow, he gaped at the disfigurement set before him. There were no eyes, there was no nose, patches of hair remained on the scalp. Shards of skin still attached themselves to gray muscle mass. There was only a shimmering translucency to the soft body areas that remained because the river had washed out all color.

Not knowing how long he ogled the body allowing the shock to his senses recede, he turned and jogged back to town. He loped into the first store he saw open and gasped out his request to call the sheriff.

The discovery of the body on the delta of East County didn't quite rate the same news coverage that the discovery of the body of Ralph Watkins did which was probably because it was not found in the confines of Pleasant Creek. If it's not in one's backyard, then it must not be one's problem. However, because it was close to the opening of school, and because Ralph Watkins' murder had not been solved, there was a geometric progression, the validity of which was questionable, as to the magnitude of concern which parents felt about the safety of their children soon going off to school. Obliging their public, the news media played up the angle of children's safety, and parents worried appropriately, but after school started, parents worried about homework and teacher assignments and sports teams–matters closer to home.

As with the last unidentified murder, the news media reworked the story using the few known data with as much creativity as it could muster. The reporters made a valiant effort, but it is hard to squeeze facts out of silence. The only definite item reported was that the body was that of a woman as marked by the cleft in the chin, the proportions of the pelvis, and other forensic evidence. If dental records had yielded an identity, it was a well-kept secret. The woman's body might have stayed a secret of the river had it not been for the rope working loose from its heavy anchor. Beyond that knowledge, there was no other information, and very few people were interested enough to search out more news.

Emily wanted to know. Two unidentified bodies showing up in the same county within a couple months of each other mightily piqued her curiosity. Then, on the day Emily reported the body of Ralph Watkins there was that statement Detective Yoshiwara let slip about a body found in a similar state. She combed newspapers from several different Bay Area cities to look for bits of information to piece together a composite of the woman found in the river. She searched the newspaper archives at the library for information regarding the body she had heard discussed in the detectives' car. She called her local paper; she even called the county sheriff's office, but they couldn't release information on a police matter. No reports of missing women could be tied to the body in the river. The body remained unidentified, and from the paucity of facts Emily could garner, it appeared very few were interested enough to try to claim the woman.

She even asked her mother and Bob to dinner.

"So, Bob, what do you think about this woman found in the Delta?"

"What woman?" asked Louisa.

"You know, that one that fellow found a week or so ago," responded Bob. "I don't know, Emily, what do you think about it?"

"Well, you know, what's happened?"

"Don't know; out of my jurisdiction."

"But you could find out, right?"

"Not really. I don't have any reason to. Do you have any reason for me to find out?"

"Yeah, Em, why all the questions? Do you know the woman?" asked David.

"Now, how would I know her? From what I can gather, no one knows her. Or, do they, Bob?"

Bob shrugged. "Got me. Apparently, there's no identification yet." Emily sat back and with a spoon swirled some of the cream sauce left on her dessert plate. "Right, that's what the sheriff's office said. And the sheriff/coroner's office wouldn't tell me anything."

"Emily," David said warningly, "what's going on?"

"You called those offices. Why didn't you just ask me?" interjected Bob.

"I am. You're stalling."

"No, I'm not. I don't know anymore than you know. How can I be stalling?"

"Well, then, tell me this. That body you mentioned in the car the day you took me home. What do you know about that one? Has it been identified?"

"What body?" asked Louisa for the second time that night.

Bob sighed before he explained. "There was a body found in San Joaquin County a few weeks before the one at Del Oro Plaza. My partner let it slip when we took Emily home because it had some similarities to the one she found. The day had become very long, and traffic was awful. Emily was so quiet, and he was just thinking out loud. No one out there has been able to come close to identifying the body. But they will. We were a little more fortunate in the timing of finding Ralph Watkins. Whoever shot him didn't hide the body as well as the person who shot the other fellow. The decomposition of the San Joaquin body was greater than Ralph Watkins, so there's less to go on."

"Was it shot in the back of the head?"

Bob hesitated and looked at the three adults sitting at the table. "I'm not at liberty to say."

"Bob," said Emily testily.

"Okay, then, was the body in the river shot in the head?"

"Maybe."

"What do you mean 'maybe'?" asked David.

"Just that. Maybe. Take it for what it's worth. Now, why are you so interested, Emily?"

Emily sat back and looked at the occupants of the dinner table. "Just curious." She reached for empty plates and got up to take a stack to the kitchen. As she took her stack of dishes to the kitchen, she remarked, "And, you, Bob, are not helping satiate my curiosity."

CHAPTER 24

There are two days of the school year that are universally greeted with pleasure and anticipation—the first and the last. The first day of the school year, as promising in its sunny warmth as its sunny expectations, had arrived. Now it was time to look forward to the last day of the school year.

Lunches made, Emily and the minivan with its young cargo charged forward into the new school year. Amid the brightly colored lunch boxes and backpacks and new school clothes, some with room to grow and some with store tags still hanging on them, Emily, Jojo and Lulie renewed last year's friendships and met the new teachers. Having made sure her daughters were firmly ensconced at their desks, Emily walked out the school. As she did, she saw Rochelle walk in the schoolyard with Samantha and holding Scott by the hand.

Samantha stopped when she saw Emily and said brightly, "Hello, Mrs. Kristich."

At Samantha's cue, Scott smilingly mimicked his sister with a more subdued, "Hello, Mrs. Kristich."

"Hi, kids. Rochelle. How was your summer? You look great, Rochelle. Must have had a successful surgery."

"Good summer. Good surgery. I keep forgetting things, but the doctors tell me that sometimes happens with anesthetic. I hope it will go away soon. Other than that, I felt good so quickly that I drove out to camp and brought the kids home early. We had a wonderful summer, didn't we, darlings?"

Both children smiled as though they had just eaten a three-scoop ice cream cone.

"Rochelle," said Emily, "would you like to join our carpool this year? I didn't mind taking your kids home those few days last year, and if it would make it easier, I'd be glad to do it this year. I don't live that far from you."

"I'm one step ahead of you. Miriam Rose and I have decided to do that. If you'd like to join us, it'd make the driving that much less for all of us. Give me a call."

"Yes, I just might do that. Sounds good."

As a parting afterthought, Rochelle, her red horizontally striped pants and coordinating red vertically striped tunic matching the brightness of her smile, called out, "I'll be seeing you at the PTA meeting next week."

"Oh. Right. I'll be seeing you," Emily's voice faded off uncertainly.

Emily whisked into her car, and as Byte jumped into the front seat to greet her, she said, "Sit down. We don't have time for that now."

She sped the car through the gates of Bluebird Hill as quickly as they would open, jumped out of the car and ran onto Miriam's front porch. The alarm was on, so it took some time for Miriam to get the door open.

"Hello, what blew you in in such a fury?" Miriam said as she opened the door, and Emily jumped in.

"Miriam, I just saw Rochelle at school."

"Doesn't she look great? We'll have to get the name of her surgeon in case we ever want to use him. I've seen lots of plastics, but I've never seen one done as well as hers. She was telling me about the hospital stay. She invited me to coffee, and we had the best time. She didn't talk much about the actual surgery, though."

"Yes, but that's not why I came. I came because…"

"I'm still not sure what she had done." Miriam was still on the surgery tangent. "Do you know?"

"How would I know? I just saw her. The reason I came…"

"She probably had a nose job. Everybody gets nose jobs. And maybe pads in her cheeks. I thought I had heard she was having a tummy tuck, but I would think it'd be hard to do all that at once. Besides she has that figure to die for already."

"Miriam." The peevishness in Emily's voice stopped Miriam. "Wait. That's not what I came to talk about."

"But you asked if I had seen Rochelle."

"I know that. I was asking because I saw Rochelle at school with her children."

"So?"

"You told me she never takes her kids anywhere. You said she has other people get them, or they walk or something. I do not recall ever seeing her at school except for the Open House. Don't you think that's odd?"

Miriam cocked her head and thought and finally said, "You're right. Maybe Rochelle's husband wants her to bond with their children like he likes her to bond with the community. But he's not been home that much that I know of. Maybe they're more relaxed with him gone. Maybe I'll have her to coffee, and we can talk about that."

"Maybe that anesthetic affected her relationship with her kids and made it better."

"What anesthetic? What are you talking about, Emily?"

"When I saw her, she said she had been affected somewhat by the anesthetic, and it made her forget things."

"You may be right."

"Maybe she's trying to prove something. You do know she called me to do a carpool with her kids? Would you like to join us?"

"I knew that–about the carpool. Rochelle already asked me."

Miriam closed the speculation. "Oh, Emily, who cares? The kids are back in school, so let's go to lunch. We haven't gone but a few times. It's time to start up again."

And they did. They took Byte back to Emily's house, picked out their restaurant and topped off their lovely, meager meal with a hearty raspberry-almond torte.

CHAPTER 25

"Mom, we have a field trip in three weeks," Jojo announced when she and Lulie plopped themselves and their school accoutrements into the seats of the car. "Here's the permission slip, and the teacher wants to know if you can come."

"Does the teacher want to know, or do you?" smiled Emily.

"I guess both of us want to know. Can you?"

"Sure, honey."

"Oh, good."

"Where is it?"

"Sacramento."

"Sacramento? That's quite a ways away.

What's there for you to see?" "Indians."

"I didn't think there was a reservation there."

"Don't know about that. It's a museum, and it shows about California Indians and what happened to them. All the fourth grades are going, so we have to take a bus, but the moms have to drive. So you might have to drive."

"No problem. School is getting going early this year, isn't it? You've got Back to School night next week and then a field trip in October. We're going to be busy."

"I know, but it's fun. I like school."

"Good." Emily changed the subject. "The Emorys might join our carpool."

"You mean Samantha?"

Emily nodded her head.

"Wow. Everyone likes to be with Samantha. She's the nicest big kid in the whole school. I'd like that."

"Lulie, that okay with you?"

"Okay, Mommy," Lulie said agreeably.

Back to school night already.

Echoing Emily's own thoughts, David neutrally inquired. "Didn't we just do this? It seems like we were just at the school not very long ago. Doesn't it seem like it to you?"

"The summer went by too fast. It was almost four months ago when we went to Open House."

"Was it really? I guess if they change the name it's not the same thing, right?"

"I guess so," she grinned.

It started out as déjà vu of four months ago. The Kristichs met the Roses, accompanied by the Emorys, at almost the same location as last spring in the hall of the children's school. This time, instead of Samantha cordially calling out the greeting, Rochelle did.

"Emily. Come and meet my husband, Geoffrey."

Smiling politely, Geoffrey Emory protruded his right hand in David's direction and said, "I'm Geoffrey Emory."

David returned the handshake and said, "I know. We met at this same shindig last year. It's nice seeing you again."

Geoffrey captured Emily's interest this evening. She stood slightly behind David while he tried to draw Geoffrey out of his taciturnity. It didn't work, so David talked mostly with Rochelle, Harold and Miriam about the school and the kids. Geoffrey stood away from the family group, and although he wasn't quite bored, he wasn't quite paying attention. He looked absorbed in thoughts of his own. It wasn't hard for Emily to imagine him absorbed only in his own world. He must have been aware of her staring at him because he caught her eye and lifted his lips slightly at her tentative smile. The gesture accepted her notice, but it did not admit her into acquaintance of him. She just couldn't pigeonhole him. He didn't play the part of a typical husband or father, yet he was here, so there must be some type of curiosity as to what his children were doing in school.

Emily watched while David small-talked with Rochelle for about ten minutes until the children tugged their parents off to view the pieces of artwork created by their unsophisticated hands that would soon become integral components of their homes—until they were accidentally broken. While Jojo demonstrated to her father and sister an experiment recently done in science class, Emily had another chance to watch the Emorys. Rochelle bent down to look at Scott's desk, and he pulled out a reader. Having asked him to read to her, she listened to his halting words and followed along the line of text with her finger to guide him. When finished, she put her arm around him and gave him a hug. With bewilderment Emily saw Scott look up and return the quiet smile of his father. Gone were the awkward, robotic movements Emily had witnessed last spring in their family cluster, but the demonstrative warmth that

Rochelle extended to Scott was not apparent in his father's reaction. He continued his quiet smile at his son but still stood to the side of the family. Samantha still put a protective arm around Scott as they left the room. The family still walked in single file as they had before. However, this scene was different from the one in the Spring. There was something missing. The irony was that whatever was missing was positive.

David came to the desk where she was sitting and said, "Lulie wants us to go to her room. Are you ready?" Looking at her he asked, "What are you studying so hard? You look as if you're solving the problems of the world."

"Umm, maybe. Did you notice how quiet Rochelle's husband was? He didn't say anything after he introduced himself. He didn't seem a part of the family, do you think?"

"Quiet, yes. But part of the family, I don't know. The little boy seemed more alert, though. I did detect that. Is that what's bothering you?"

"I thought you only had eyes for me."

"I do, but there's no harm in looking. It's the pursuing that's wrong.

"I'm not sure."

"Why are you so interested in that family? Just because that gal dresses like she has stock in Victoria's Secret? Lucky she has such a knockout figure. On anyone else that skin tight sheath would have looked like someone had overpacked a gunny sack."

"I thought you only had eyes for me."

"I do, but there's no harm in looking. It's the pursuing that's wrong. Besides I haven't seen anything better looking than you."

Laughing, she said, "That's acceptable."

He put his arm around her as they proceeded to Lulie's class.

CHAPTER 26

"We missed you this summer, Bo," Emily greeted the young man with the tanned face and sun whitened hair.

"Hey, cool. Went hiking with some of my best buds. Took the summer off before the big dissertation. Figured the relaxing memories would get me through the writing."

"Were you gone the whole summer?"

"The whole summer. Just me and the dudes."

"You weren't home at all this summer?"

Bo slowly shook his head. "Why?"

"Where did you go?"

"Down to Mexico. Practiced my Spanish and saw some of the best of the best."

"Did you take your van with you when you went hiking?"

"Sure, man, it's got my gear in it."

"But, wait, are you sure?"

"You giving me the third degree?"

Emily smiled and started to ask him another question when Joan Chavez walked up with a brown haired man shorter than she and dressed in a brown suit. His brown suit was accented by a brown and beige tie that matched his beige shirt and brown shoes. Instead of drabness as one would expect with so much mud color, his brown eyes and full faced smile brightened his under-coordinated clothes.

"Emily, I'd like to introduce you to William Nguyen. He's our newest board member."

Neither woman mentioned Ralph Watkins, but Mr. Nguyen said, "I'll be taking Ralph's place."

"Did you know him?

"Not really. I just knew who he was. He was assistant administrator at the hospital where I work. I'm in accounting there."

"The way you said his name, it sounded like you might know him," Emily replied. "Are you a computer expert like he was?"

"Better."

"We could have used you last summer," Emily said.

"So I heard."

"So, William, if you work at the hospital, you must know Harold Rose, right? He and his wife are good friends of mine."

William looked confused as he tried to place Harold, "No, I don't recall the name. Are you sure he's at County?"

"County? Oh, no. I'm sorry. He's at Mercy. Sorry for the confusion. So you're at County? Is that how you know Joan?"

"Yes, she's the reason I'm on this board," he said smiling at Joan. Emily turned to Joan, "But, Joan, if Ralph Watkins was at County, does that mean you knew him there?"

Joan, her face ashen, looked away before she responded, "Excuse me?"

Emily rephrased her question, but then Rudyard called the meeting to order. Joan rushed over to sit by Thomas as they all took their seats. Thomas smiled gently when he saw Joan sit next to him.

Rudyard, not one strand of his distinguished hair out of place, opened the meeting at precisely 7:38, or as he proclaimed, "Right on time."

Emily and Thomas looked discreetly at their watches, but everyone else seemed to accept Mr. Millup's concept of time as fact.

"Welcome, everyone. Hope you had a nice vacation. We had a profitable one as you will see from the financial statements we will be passing out shortly," Rudyard said.

As he continued his diatribe, Emily forgot about asking about the relationship between Joan and Ralph as her brain did a back flip. To finally be getting the financials meant there should be an explanation of the budget she had already seen. Maybe, just maybe, this organization is finally getting established enough to arrange itself in a more orderly manner.

"...and welcome, Rochelle. You are looking more beautiful than ever," Rudyard declared as a few people looked obliquely in Rochelle's direction and smirked.

Emily took a mental leave of absence from the next portion of the agenda to try to review the purloined financial statements she had hidden among the tablecloths in the dining room linen cabinet. Even if she had completed her muddled journey through them, there had not been a plausible excuse for Emily to reinstate the financials to their resident drawer at the office. She didn't have any reason to go to the office as she had finished the input before the August vacation. Even if she were able to think of some excuse to enter the office for any period of time, the disagreeable Shannon acted as the office Charon at the river Styx. It was not a pleasant to cross her path, and there was no silver coin for Emily to bribe entry into her domain. After stealing the papers, Emily had rationalized that no one would want the documents during August as that's when the agency was on vacation. Or so they claimed. But if they claimed a vacation, was it possible that they didn't really go on vacation? Bo said he was gone the whole summer, yet his van was driving around late at night. What kind of vacation was that? And if they didn't go on vacation, what were they doing?And if they used that time for something other than vacation, what was it?And, most importantly, who were they? And why was she even thinking on the tangent of 'they' doing 'something'? The answer could be August's coming and going, and she had begun worrying about who would want those statements in September.

Jerked back to the proceedings by Bo's nudging her with a stack of neatly mimeographed balance sheets and income statements, she absently took a few of the pages and passed the stack to Thomas who carefully took the copies, lined up all the corners and placed them scrupulously on the table next to his binder. He then took his pen and angled it across the upper right hand of the papers in readiness to take notes. Emily's earlier thought track was too intriguing to let loose of it, so she didn't look at the papers until Chad got up to present the papers to the group.

"In your hands you have the information some of you," Chad stared in Emily's direction, "have requested. We held off getting the information to you until we had our fundraiser this summer. We knew we would have good news to report to you after the huge success of our summer work. You will be just delighted, believe me. Of course, some of the credit goes to Shannon." He smiled at Shannon, sitting at the word processor in a brown and pink sundress, her cleavage bisecting the mound at the top of the dress's too-small bodice. She basked in happiness at being condescended to by Chad.

"Rudyard and I almost single handedly developed a fundraiser for the Pleasant Creek Fourth of July festival." He held up his hand as though he had heard applause. "Now this was a lot of work, but we got it organized and off the ground and took in a substantial bit of revenue."

Joan asked the obvious. "Why didn't you tell us at the May or June meeting? We could have helped and lined up some volunteers. We've got the list Emily worked on, don't we? We could have used that."

At that remark, Shannon stepped out of the circle of glory to shoot a glowering scowl at Joan for daring to question Chad's procedure.

"Well, yes, we could have. We decided we could handle it because that is, after all, our job. Rudyard and I have so much experience at this kind of thing that we are true experts. What we do for this organization, the time and effort we put into it, is what makes Sustain and Shelter the fine group it is. If all community non-profits did as well as we did, Pleasant Creek wouldn't have nearly the problem with homelessness that it does. Our group, thanks to Rudyard and me, and the volunteers, of course, oh, and you board members, stands head and tail above the rest."

Most of the board members looked away from Chad. If he tooted his horn anymore, there was going to be a tremendous traffic jam right there in the boardroom.

Satisfied he had rebutted Joan's point, he said, "Please turn to the papers in front of you."

After a five minute pause, he said, "Now, since there are no questions, we'll proceed to committee reports."

No questions? Emily's brain screamed. You bet there were questions. Emily, having scanned the income statement in the five-minute time allotment, wanted a tidy answer to explain the questions stumbling over each other in her mind. She had gone over the pilfered statements enough, so she thought she knew some of the figures. Even in her confusion surrounding the stolen papers, Emily knew these figures were far different from those on the papers at home. Mentally comparing the two statements, she knew she couldn't ask the questions that were looming like billboards in her cortex. She knew she couldn't ask someone to explain the difference because this second profit and loss statement clearly stated there would never be an opportunity to explain she had the other statement and why. There is a vast difference between revenues of three million dollars as shown on the stolen statements and revenues of seventy five thousand as shown on these statements.

"Wait, Chad, I have a question," said William Nguyen. "I know I'm new to the board, but can you explain to me on this statement just exactly how much your fundraiser took in and what exactly the fundraiser was?"

Rudyard's eyes narrowed only slightly at the speaker as Chad said, "We were given an opportunity to set up a fundraising booth on Fourth of July at the local carnival. We actually took in quite a bit of money which was very pleasing."

"Yes, but how much?" Joan asked.

"Quite a lot. Enough to wipe out any debt we had. Plus we received some donations."

"Again, how much?"

Turning to Rudyard, Chad asked, "Do you remember the exact figure?"

Rudyard didn't answer for a short time and then cleared his throat. "Yes. Yes, I do, as a matter of fact. We took in about $5000.00."

That's all? If so, for what organization did Emily hold the different profit and loss and income statements? Emily, mightily confused, could only begin to conjecture the meaning of the other statement. If you can't hit 'em in a frontal attack, try the rear. Barring that, try a flank attack.

"Did Ida prepare this report?" Emily asked in her best ingénue voice.

There was only the slightest hesitation before Chad said, "Ida?" He glanced at Rudyard and repeated, "Ida?"

Rudyard nodded slightly.

"Yes, Ida prepared the report. She is, after all, a certified public accountant," Chad said.

"Then we could ask Ida about this, couldn't we? She would have the exact figure. It should probably be its own line item, don't you think? I'm surprised Ida didn't put that in. Shannon, if you'll give me Ida's phone number, I'll ask her about this."

Shannon looked at Chad who looked above Emily's head.

"Shannon? Can you give Emily the phone number?" asked Bo.

"Well, I could. But, right now, I don't have it with me. I don't keep that information on me, you know. Wouldn't want the privacy of any of the board members messed with?"

"Then, I'll stop by the office tomorrow and get it from you, okay?" asked Emily.

Shannon pursed her lips in thought. "No. No, I'll get it to you. I just have to locate it. Within the next couple days. I'll get it."

Thomas cleared his throat and carefully asked in his softly timid voice, "Why isn't she here? Does anyone know where she is? She wasn't at the last meeting, either."

Rudyard and Chad looked at each other and then at Shannon who shrugged. "Why would I know where she is?"

"Didn't she call in? Usually board members call when they're going to be absent," stated Thomas.

"Didn't call me," said Shannon.

"Didn't call me," said Chad.

"Didn't call me," said Rudyard.

"Maybe we should call her," pointed out William Nguyen. "If she hasn't been here for two meetings, and no one's heard from her, perhaps there's some issue that needs to be addressed."

"But we might be invading her privacy. Some people could get angry about being discovered doing something they think people might not like. We really have no right to go nosing around her business. We'd better leave it at that."

Chad's summation of the situation surprised the board members into silence that allowed the agenda to be finished quickly.

As the meeting drew to a close, Rudyard arose and said, "We don't want to have this information fall into the wrong hands as it is confidential. Therefore, please pass the financial statements to Shannon who will destroy all but the master copy."

People readied the papers to hand to Shannon, and Emily protested, "Rudyard, we should, as board members, have copies of these available for reference. This is a tremendous aid in decision making."

"Turn it in, Mrs. Kristich. It's in our bylaws." Rudyard's frosty tone brought another protest from Emily.

"But we don't have any copies of the bylaws either. We need…"

Rudyard had abruptly turned and presented his back to her.

Taken aback, Emily reached into her folder to retrieve the financial statements, and was about to put it on the table when she realized she had inadvertently picked up two copies. She slid one across the table to Shannon, who was checking off board members' names on a list as she received their copies. She slid the other under her notebook and hoped that in the flurry of shuffling papers no one noticed.

CHAPTER 27

Angrily Emily strode out the room and into the parking lot. Rochelle's Rolls was parked next to her van looking like Beauty and the Beast of the vehicular world. Although Rochelle had left the conference room to arrive at her car before Emily, she had not opened her car door yet and appeared to be waiting. At the same time Emily registered Rochelle's apparent waiting, her attention was caught by the staccato stepping of high heels on the pavement. Emily glanced up and saw Joan walk to the passenger side of her car and open the door. As she did that, Thomas, whose gold car was next to Joan's blue one, opened his door slightly. If it hadn't been for the courtesy light going on when the door opened, Emily doubted she would have noted his door opening. Emily stopped at her car door and pretended to fumble with the keys while trying to unlock her door, so she could watch Thomas and Joan. Although Joan leaned down into her car as though she were looking for something, Emily was positive she saw Joan's hand shoot out in Thomas's direction and hand something to him. Emily's anger and her observation of Thomas and Joan's action had impeded her awareness of Rochelle waiting by the Rolls until the other woman hovered closely enough to her to almost touch Emily.

Startled, Emily said, "Rochelle. I didn't realize you were standing there. That was quite a do in there, wasn't it?" Emily attempted to laugh off the lingering anger over Rudyard's rudeness, but the laugh stuck in her throat and came out a gag.

Without a preamble, Rochelle, the spikes of her hair tipped gold to coordinate with her gold lame short skirt, long blazer and white lace hose, said, "Emily, be careful. Don't ask those people too many questions."

Emily's surprise at the drama of the statement dissipated long enough for her to catch the fright in Rochelle's eyes before the woman turned and slid into her car to speed off. Rochelle's warning gave her pause before she started her car to return home, so she sat in the driver's seat of the van staring until everything in her visual range became a gray glaze. Shaking her head to clear the glaze and will herself back into awareness, Emily turned the ignition on her car and slowly pulled out of the driveway of the parking lot and realized she was following Joan's car. Without planning to do so, Emily followed the car until it turned into the parking lot of the strip mall that housed the Safeway.

"Now's as good a time as any to pick up a few groceries," she muttered to herself as she whipped a left turn into the last entrance of the parking lot.

"And a little exercise is just what I need," she continued to mutter as she parked her car away from Joan's and far away from Safeway's entrance.

She stayed in the car and waited a few minutes to see if anything transpired in the direction of Joan's parked car. Sure enough, she saw Thomas's car pull in next to Joan's. The glow of the overhead parking lot lights not only enhanced the slowness of Thomas's movements as he exited the car and looked furtively behind him, it also cast a dying sun gloom to them. Emily slid down in the seat of her car, her head aligned with the steering wheel allowing her to see him through the rungs of the wheel. He looked in the direction of the car but gave no recognizing start, so Emily assumed he didn't see her or realize it was her minivan.

He reached for the door of Joan's car and quickly slid into the passenger side of the car.

Emily continued to watch, but that was all she could do. No action was perpetrated in the car she was observing, but even if there had been, she wasn't sure what to expect. Relief that she wouldn't be called upon to act tempered her disappointment at events leading to another piece to put into the puzzle that had developed around Sustain and Shelter. Surmising they must be doing some planning, although for what she couldn't begin to guess, she started to get out of her car. Then she changed her mind because she couldn't see a lighted, safe path to the store without the occupants of Joan's car seeing her. She closed the partially opened door and was getting ready to start her car when Joan drove out of the lot with Thomas.

"Oh," groaned Emily. "There's no way I can follow them. I can't get to their side of the lot fast enough."

She shoved the car door open, marched into Safeway and bought her groceries.

Frustrated by the evening's occurrences, she threw the door between the garage and the kitchen open and burst into her quiet home. Before she went to the dining room to obtain the megabuck financial statement, she hopped up the stairs to capture some of the peace of her sleeping daughters. They were sleeping quietly, but their peace didn't allay her agitation. Maybe David would have some words that would calm her.

"David, are you asleep?" asked Emily quietly as she entered their bedroom. Although he had left a light on in the room, his light snoring told her he wouldn't be using it to read the book propped across his chest. It was probably just as well. During the drive home, she was undecided as to whether she should tell him her thoughts about Sustain and Shelter and the strange events of the evening. By not waking him, she made her decision to keep quiet about her musings. Maybe later when she had more concrete, not abstract, thoughts.

Byte, however, having roused herself when she heard Emily's car enter the garage, was waiting for her. She blinked at Emily, raised up her hind legs and luxuriated in a prolonged stretch. Sitting at readiness in anticipation of Emily's action, she waited. As Emily left the bedroom to compare the two financial statements in detail, Byte loped downstairs behind her mistress. Emily sat at the kitchen table with Dr. Pepper for a caffeine crutch, and Byte heaved herself onto the area rug in the family room and through partially closed eyes watched Emily's head move between the two statements.

Emily's comparison was fruitless. Unlike the first set of papers, these just received were printed vertically on three sheets. These included a profit and loss statement and a balance sheet. She found nothing to validate her suspicions. The few expenses she could match to both sets of financials were the standard expenses of rent, utilities and phone. The salary figures didn't match, and they weren't quite lined out as in the other set of financials. By adding extra zeroes to the page passed out this evening, she couldn't make the figures match the larger ones on the older statements. If she hadn't physically lifted the macro financial worksheet out of the locked cabinet at Sustain and Shelter, she would throw her assumption about the significance of that document overboard. It would be nice to find Ida to answer some questions. All the examination of the statements did was trigger questions popping into her head at a rapid rate.

The lateness of the hour was beginning to divert her thoughts. No, they were actually turning in on themselves and eroding any logic they might have had, so that a state of anomie was developing in her head. She had to contact Ida who should have the key to the two statements. First thing in the morning, she decided. She'd go to the office and trap that little twit, Shannon, and make her produce Ida's phone numbers. As Emily readied herself for bed, she contented herself that would be proactive. Then she could make some headway. Turning off the light, she lay in her bed and was just ready to nod off when her mind replayed the scene in the parking lot between Thomas and Joan.

Joan. Joan knew Ralph. Joan had never said anything about knowing him either. What was it Shannon had said about Joan and the clinic Chad had set up? Ralph was at the hospital, so was Joan. The clinic was a mini-hospital. What were the financials saying? Why was Chad so defensive? Where was Ida tonight? Why is Rochelle afraid? Why don't you go to sleep? Why are you thinking about all this? Where is Ida? Why is Rochelle afraid? The thought pattern sing-songed in her head as the grandfather clock struck two o'clock accompanied Byte's snoring in the dog bed in their bedroom. David's percussive breathing added to the orchestra in their bedroom, but the music wasn't the kind that would let her drift into sleep.

CHAPTER 28

This is going to be easy decided Emily as she walked into the empty office of Sustain and Shelter. No Shannon; no Chad—that she could spot. Emily reached across Shannon's desk and pulled a small directory of telephone numbers toward her. She quickly riffled through the roll and copied the information for Ida McIvey. As an afterthought, she flipped to the 'O's' and copied Blythe Oberstein's particulars. Even homeless people could use a cell phone. Sure enough, on Blythe's card was not only a cell number, but also a post office box.

As Emily turned to leave, she heard giggling coming from the hallway. Deciding the noise could only be coming from Chad's office she walked back there. Polite people would knock before they entered a closed door, and Emily reached up her hand to do so. However, hearing the low murmur of a man's voice weave in and out of the giggling, Emily decided this was not a situation calling for manners. Emily edged the door opened, and Shannon, sitting on Chad's lap, saw her first.

Shannon jumped up. "What are you doing here?"

Emily held up the paper on which she had written information for the two ladies and said, "I came to get Ida's phone number."

"You mean you just walked in and took it?"

"That's what I mean."

"You can't do that," Shannon said.

"Perhaps. But now, I have the information, so I can call Ida and find out what she's up to."

"I heard from her this morning," interjected Chad.

"Did you now?" Looking at her watch, Emily said, "It's 8:17 AM. Even if you've been playing handsies-feelsies for only fifteen minutes, that means you talked to Ida before 8:00, right?"

Chad nodded. Shannon, watching Chad's movements, mirrored his nod.

"You talked to her that early? You were able to get a hold of her?" Again Chad nodded. "She said she had been on a very long vacation earlier this summer and forgot about the meeting last night. Said she didn't even have the minutes from the last one to remind her that we were having a meeting last night."

"Okay," agreed Emily. Turning to Shannon, she said, "Chad and I have some things to discuss. Why don't you go sit at your desk while we do that? Then you can resume what you were doing here."

Shannon looked at Chad and indignantly marched out of the room when he nodded his agreement to Emily's suggestion.

"We're going to do this with the door shut, Chad," directed Emily. As she turned from closing the door, she asked, "You setting up a little May to December here?"

"What are you doing here? You're not scheduled to come here anymore."

"True. I wanted to get Ida's number to find out those answers we were looking for last evening. Shannon and you made it very easy for me to do so."

"We don't give out information like that. It involves privacy issues."

"These privacy issues you keep bringing up—would those be because you don't want people to know where you live? You don't want them to have your phone number?"

"What do you mean? I don't care if people know where I live. I rent an apartment—near the kitchens, so I can be available whenever I'm needed. I do much more for this organization than most executive directors do, you know. I'm worth every penny paid to me."

"And how much are we paying you?"

"You should know. You saw it on the statements I passed out at the meeting last night."

"Right. I was able to memorize all those numbers when you gave us so much time to study them. If I recall correctly, the salary figures weren't lined out; they were lumped into one figure, one nebulous, could-mean-anything figure. That's a problem. That's why I need to call Ida. I need to find out what's happening within this organization."

"Shannon's been told not to give out private information. How would you like it if we all had your phone number and address?"

"Actually, that would be fine. As working members of this board, we should all have each other's information. It makes situations like this much easier to address."

Chad began to wheedle. "Of course, Mrs. Kristich, you're absolutely correct. We'll talk about that at our next meeting. I'll put it on the agenda. Now, thank you for your time." He reached out to open the closed door.

"Okay, Chad, I'll get hold of Ida to find out what's happening." Chad's eyes narrowed slightly; this time his demeanor was one of efficient business. "I couldn't agree with you more, Mrs. Kristich. I noticed those numbers after the meeting. When I talked with Ida this morning, I pointed them out to her. She told me she'll have them worked out by the time of our next meeting."

"What did she say?"

"Just that she had to do the financials in a hurry, so there may be some mistakes on them. She felt very badly about the errors when I told her about them. I told her to fix them, and she said she would."

"Then, I'll have the information from her before the next meeting, won't I?" Emily smiled. "Maybe Ida and I can locate an independent auditor to study the financial records."

Chad about-faced from business pretense to a threat. "Don't do that, Mrs. Kristich."

"Excuse me?"

Chad's tone became even more threatening. "Don't do that. Don't call Ida. It won't help you; it won't help the board. Don't go into matters that are no concern of yours."

Emily cocked her head and looked at Chad. "You know, for someone who has supposedly worked on non-profit boards, you don't know much. The public is the group to which you must answer. The board of directors for any non-profit has a fiduciary responsibility to make sure the agency is responsible and performing its services efficiently. If that isn't happening, then the board must deal with the consequences. If you're in anyway inhibiting the responsibility of this organization, then we have to know about it, so we can get back to the job we're supposed to be doing."

"Then, it's time for you to resign the board. You obviously don't understand how well we're functioning and taking care of those poor, down and out people. Resign, Mrs. Kristich."

"Or what?"

"Just remember, you've been warned. I'll accept your letter now, if you wish."

"Don't wish to do that. We need to figure out what's happening. I'll start with Ida."

Chad's eyes narrowed as his face tensed. "Get out," he said.

Emily returned his stare. "Yes, I have other errands to run." She turned and slowly walked out the door.

The only errand Emily was going to address could wait until after she called Ida. At home with the two copies of financials in front of her, she dialed the number she had purloined from Shannon's file.

It did not surprise Emily that there was no answer. It didn't even surprise her that the answering machine wasn't up to taking a message; indeed, it couldn't give a coherent greeting. Ida's voice answered, but her sentence looped back into itself, so the information was garbled. Too many messages on the machine? Ida hadn't been around to pick them all up? How long had Ida been gone from her house? After a quick perusal of the financials, Emily dialed her mother at Community Action Group to ascertain she could meet her for lunch. This would be her other important errand of the day.

"And see if Genevieve would like to join us, would you?"

"Why ever for? All she'll do is gossip."

"That, Mom, is what I'm counting on."

The last call she made was the one to Blythe's cell phone. Blythe didn't answer, but Emily was able to leave a message that she wanted to hear about the new job and find out if Blythe had truly resigned the board of Sustain and Shelter.

CHAPTER 29

Fried onion ring in hand, Genevieve threw up her arm and waved at Emily as she entered the restaurant. Louisa, chin in her hand, looked at the wall as Genevieve continued her endorsement of the onion rings.

"These onion rings are *so* good, Louisa. You must have one. But only one because I just love them, and I'm so hungry. Emily is coming up right behind you. She has on such a cute outfit. Oh, if I were twenty years younger, I could wear those cute clothes. Do you like this shade of rose?" Genevieve pointed to her hair. "My hairdresser says it's called 'Rouge'. It goes well with this outfit, don't you think?"

Louisa nodded as Emily slipped into the chair next to her mother.

"What goes well with the outfit, Genevieve?" asked Emily after she had given her mother a quick kiss on the cheek.

"My hair. Do you think this color is good with it? I just love it when my hair matches my outfit."

"It complements it beautifully, Genevieve. And to think you started the fashion thirty years before any high schooler thought of dying his hair rainbow colors to match the outfit. You are a trend-setter."

Genevieve giggled as she finished the onion ring. Louisa glanced at her daughter and quickly looked away smiling.

"Thanks for joining me on such short notice. Genevieve, it was especially nice of you to take your time. I've got some things I'd like to know about, and it's in the social action field, so I knew you'd know the answers."

"Well, I'm sure your mother would know since she's a wee bit older than I am and has been around the block of community groups. But I do keep up on the information especially now that I'm executive director of Community Action Group, so you're probably right to ask me instead of Louisa."

Louisa breathed deeply and smiled serenely as she looked at her co-worker.

Emily cleared her throat, gave her order to the waitress who had appeared just at that moment and patted her mother's thigh under the table. Neither daughter nor mother looked at the other. All the better to control the guffaw that would surely erupt at Genevieve's perception of the office doings.

"Yes, Genevieve. Now, tell me about Sustain and Shelter, you wise woman, you."

"Well," launched Genevieve, "you don't remember this, but I know you do, Louisa…

"…because of my great age, you know," interrupted Louisa.

"Yes, well, no. I mean, I remember it also. But there was a time Pleasant Creek was convinced it didn't have any homeless people. But we know that's all wrong. We knew it at CAG and tried to warn the city council and the board of supervisors that we had an impending problem. Do you think they wanted to hear about it? No way. So we dealt with it best we could. Remember those people, Louisa, that couple, the Gridleys?

She sat on our board and then resigned because she felt we weren't doing enough to address the problem. Then they founded that organization? Well, that was Sustain and Shelter. They were old then, they must be dead by now. That was ten, twelve years ago."

"No, they're alive and kicking. Maybe they're not kicking, but they are alive," interjected Emily.

"Are they really? My, they were getting up there then. I think he's still there. I've met some of the other new people. Let's see. There's a homeless lady, Blythe or something. She's a nice person, but who's going to listen to her? I mean, they should listen to her, but they won't. The Gridleys thought she would be a wonderful spokesperson for the homeless.

"Oh, and Joan Chavez. You know her, Louisa, she sits on our board. Her father actually helped the Gridleys start Sustain and Shelter, but then he died—cancer, I think. She took over for him. Hmm, who else do I know? They're getting new blood. Heaven knows they need it. I mean, their fundraisers are so old hat. It's amazing they keep going. They need some major grant money from somewhere. Although, they have a clinic, I heard. For the people who can't get MediCal or Healthy Families. That clinic provides everything free. Now, that's a service for those people living out here who can't get medical help, even state programs. So they must be getting money from somewhere.

"Must be that new guy, the new executive director. Can't believe those old board members let him in. I heard he really started to shake things up, wanted to wipe out a bunch of the old board members to bring in new blood. You know, some of those board members think once they're on the board, they've joined Britain's royal family and everything they say should be the proclamation of the kingdom. It's like they're glued to that conference room with Liquid Nails. Nothing's going to move their butts off those chairs. Even when times change and needs change."

"So what about this new guy?" asked Louisa. "Do you know him?"

"No, met him once. Has kind of an attitude. But if that's what's going to jumpstart that board into making Sustain and Shelter a good organization, maybe they need a cock of the walk. Do you know him, Emily?"

"You could say that."

"You like him?"

"Cock of the walk fits him pretty well. Cock of the walk bordering on asshole. Seems he's good friends with Rudyard Millup."

"Rudyard Millup. Oh, what a handsome man. He could make my blood boil. Made his money in real estate, developed many of the tract areas around here in the seventies and eighties. Sometimes, I think he was on the board just to make sure the homeless didn't interfere with sales of his homes, but I certainly couldn't prove that. He is such a good looking man."

Seeing Emily curl her upper lip at her remark, Genevieve asked, "You don't think so?"

"It must be the generations, Gen. Maybe he's just not my type."

"That must be it. You just don't have good taste in men; your generation really doesn't like those strong, good looking he-men. I just get breathless thinking about him."

When the food arrived, Genevieve took a hiatus to admire the plate of food she had ordered. Emily took a breath and asked, "Do you know Ida?"

With a mouth half-full of her first bite of ostrich burger, Genevieve exclaimed, "Ida. Oh my, yes. I'd totally forgotten poor Ida. She's a bookkeeper by trade, maybe an accountant, no, I think bookkeeper, but, by now, she might have her CPA. Well, anyway, it doesn't matter. It was a good profession for her because she was so timid, and, that way, she could stay with her books and numbers. She was a kind lady, just not sure of people and easily intimidated. She would probably welcome being part of the wallpaper. Poor Ida. Tall, gangly, could have been attractive, I think, but just had no self-confidence. Is she still around? My, I hadn't thought of her in years." As she swallowed the bite, she waved her hand at Louisa, "You remember her, Louisa, from the rummage sale days.

Remember the rummage sale we used to have? Ida would tag the clothes and junk and just panic if someone asked her to help out a customer. She worked longer shifts than anyone else."

Louisa nodded. "I do remember her. Quiet, nervous and hard working. Tell her hello for us, will you, Em? Ask her for her number and maybe we can go out for lunch. Want to do that, Gen?"

Genevieve nodded as she chewed her burger as Emily and Louisa began eating their meals.

After she carpooled the kids home later that afternoon, she tried to call Ida again. Of course, there was no answer.

That machine is as garbled as those financials decided Emily. That thought prompted her to retrieve the financials again, but a homework question from Lulie interrupted her study of them. When the girls had finished the homework for the evening, Emily cornered both of them. "So what do you think about Halloween?"

"It's fun. I like it. Especially the party at school," responded Lulie.

"She's asking you what to make for your costume for Trick or Treat," Jojo interpreted for her sister.

"Oh. Oh. This will be the best costume. I want to be one of those people with the noses."

Emily gave her a perplexed look.

"You remember, Mom. Like at that carnival we went to. With Gramma and her friend. Remember? They had those long noses, and their outfits were bright, bright colors. Remember, Mom? Please make one of those for me. Please, Mom."

Could a Mom be forced to retire from motherhood if she couldn't replicate a costume for her young child's Halloween? That might be a crime in league with telling a toddler there is no Santa Claus. The bright color wasn't the problem. It was going to be the nose. How does one make a six-inch long nose that would stay on a pug nosed little girl?

As if Jojo knew her thoughts, she said, "Maybe with papier mâche, Mom."

"What? What did you say, Jojo?"

"Maybe you could make the nose with papier mâche. You know, that stuff you do art projects with? We did one in class last year. You make the wheat paste and water and put wet newspaper around a form. Have you ever done it?"

"Right, I have. That's a good idea, honey. How do I get it to stay on?"

"Make little holes and put string through, so Lulie can tie it on her head. That might work."

"Maybe you should be the Mom, Jojo, and I'll be your kid. You have some good ideas."

"Then I might turn psycho like you. No, I want you for my Mom. Do you want to know what I want to be?"

"Is it going to be hard? Do you think I can do it? And, by the way, the word is psychic, not psycho."

"Oh, yes. This will be easy."

Thank heaven. Aloud Emily said, "Do you promise?"

"I promise. I want to be a skeleton."

Good. A skeleton is available in every drug and variety store. "That sounds great."

"With all the bones labeled."

Emily's smile faltered as she said dismally, "All of them?"

"All of them. And the bones that the store doesn't put on their costumes? Well, we'll put those on. Okay? But don't worry. I'll help you. There is an anatomy book that you or Daddy had in college in our library."

Emily looked at her daughter thoughtfully. Jojo was nine years old, still had baby fat cheeks with freckles that looked as though fairies had left their dancing footprints across her face, and baby fine strawberry blond hair. Sometimes her little girl face belied the intelligence sitting behind it, but most of the time she wore an earnestness equal to that of any adult. Louisa always said the next generation was smarter than the last. If this child and her sister reflected the rest of the upcoming generation, the world would probably be the better for it.

Labels on a skeleton suit shouldn't be difficult with aid from *Gray's Anatomy*; it was still the nose construction that presented the largest obstacle in this costume creation. Was this how a plastic surgeon felt each time he reconstructed someone's nose?

CHRPTER 30

On a day so gray and cloudy, going outside was like being wrapped in a blanket of ghostly hush, Emily and Byte took a lengthy walk down the bike trail to the pond in the park. Pricks of cold air peppered Emily's nose mounting a perception of autumn's smells—the smoke of wood stoves, dankness of the ground that the sun was too weak to dry out, moldering leaves so weighted by damp they would never again cavort with gusts of wind. The undesirable chill precluded the usual population of the trail by bikers, joggers, and other dog walkers.

For just that reason, Emily and Byte embraced that chill because there were few creatures by the pond, and it meant Emily could take Byte off her leash. The canine cruised past the lagoon congested with reeds, water grasses and lilies. Almost as loudly as a horse, her rhythmic legs pummeled the ground propelling her massive chest around the water where Byte decided to exercise her prowess over the ducks and geese milling about. She snapped at the ducks and growled, pulled up short and did a u-turn to strafe them again. The birds, in turn, exhibited their dominion over her in the air. They fluttered their wings clumsily, bleated their squawks and scattered themselves in disorientation until they launched themselves into the air in agile suppleness and rode the air currents with speed and grace.

"Come on, leave them alone, Byte. They fly higher and faster than you do. You're matched wit for wit."

As Emily watched the ducks glide to safer harbor, an arrow of geese thrust across the sky, their strident cacophony announcing the coming of winter. It was only the first of October, so Emily discounted their harbinger of the change of seasons. The rainy season had been starting much later these last few years, so that Emily was positive the geese were wrong.

Emily should have believed nature's announcement.

This year the geese were right, she was wrong.

The rain began on the day of the Sacramento field trip for Jojo's class. Thankfully it was only a manageable drizzle until after the children boarded the return bus for home. Two other cars of chaperones left with the bus, but the three moms riding in Rochelle's car stayed to forage among the picnic tables and museum for lost articles and trash young eyes and hands might have missed. The bus and the other two carloads had left early enough to miss the rain, but Rochelle's car was deluged in what began as a series of splotches overburdened with water on the windshield. By the time Rochelle's Rolls was close to the 680 interchange, the rain and highway oil non-mixture had created such a peril that it took the collective concentration and support of the mothers to help Rochelle drive.

"Would you like me to try it, Rochelle?" asked Miriam.

"No, I'm all right, I think. Just watch that back side for anyone coming up on my sides. I'm trying to see what's ahead of me, and the wipers can't push this wall of water away fast enough. What worries me is getting back in time to take the kids home from school," mumbled Rochelle. "They might get frightened if we're not there when we said we would be."

Emily inconspicuously glanced at Miriam in the back seat and shrugged her left eyebrow in question at the apprehension Rochelle expressed in regard to the children. Miriam was shifting her focus between the second lane of the eight-lane highway and the shoulder and gave only a barely perceptible return rising of the eyebrows.

"They'll be okay. There are phone numbers on my kids' emergency cards, so if David can't get them, my mother can. Once we get off the highway, it'll be less crowded."

"Right, until we get to the Benicia Bridge. Then there'll be a bottle-neck," confirmed Miriam.

"At least it's in our own back yard, though," said Rochelle as much to calm herself as the other occupants of the car.

By the time they reached the interchange, there were no discernable drops of rain. The drops had synthesized, so the car was traveling into a blockade of water to which there seemed no end. Rochelle found by hunching over the steering wheel to the beginning point of the windshield wiper arc, she could see enough of the road to maintain a straight trajectory in the lane. It appeared they would make it to the bridge in relatively good time because the rain forced the traffic to move at the same pace, and there had been no fender benders in the area—yet. The women were still concentrating intently on the road and not yielding to the inflexible paralysis in which their muscles were locked. Rochelle was still bent over the steering wheel, the muscles of her back no longer hurting, just anesthetized to the ache she would surely feel tomorrow.

The diligence they were bestowing on Rochelle's driving was probably the reason the crack of the bullets didn't intrude into their consciousness. Rochelle's hunched position was probably the reason the bullet didn't bloody her. And the unexpected anticipation that anything as foreign as a bullet entering their vehicle probably kept their astonishment to a minimum. It was only with the second bullet that flew in front of Emily's face and into the passenger's side window that her attention was diverted from the road. Emily, startled, snapped her head to her left and realized what had happened. So it was with the third bullet that shattered into the back quadrant of the driver's side window and furrowed Miriam's cheek that the women were astonished and became alarmed. The speed with which the bullets propelled themselves into the car was too fast for the minds of the women to perceive and comprehend. The moments were too fleeting to react as one should, so they were unable to see the car from where the salvo was discharged. Even if they could read a license plate in the opaque rain, it was too late as the car had passed them at a speed dangerous in dry weather and absolutely treacherous in wet weather.

As Rochelle pulled the car to the side of the road, Emily, in the growing density of the autumn afternoon, subconsciously registered piteous terror on her face. Emily was just as horrified as Rochelle to realize Miriam had been struck in a drive-by shooting. This was a phenomenon that occurred in gang wars and on Southern California freeways. This did not happen to middle class, suburban ladies, mothers, yet, and on their way from their children's field trip. Miriam's lower left face was a sheet of darkened red in the gray light.

"Miriam," screamed Rochelle looking at her sitting in the back seat. "You're bleeding."

"I am?" she questioned dazedly as she swiped her hand across her forehead.

"Miriam, on your left cheek," said Emily as she pulled tissue after tissue from her purse. "You were facing us, and the bullet got your cheek."

"What bullet?" Miriam asked in surprised unawareness.

"The one that just flew into the car. Don't you see them? Look, there's water pouring down Rochelle's window."

The three of them, too agitated by what Emily had just said to feel the wrenching of constricted neck and shoulder muscles being yanked into different positions, stared at water coursing down the inside of the driver's window out of three small holes. As if on cue, their heads turned immediately to the right, to Emily's window where they saw water gushing out of one hole there.

"Three holes," said Miriam. "Three bullets."

"We've got to get to an emergency room. Now," yelled Rochelle in a panic. "Now! Get us there, now."

Rochelle's high pitched scream and rapid breathing compelled Emily out of the car to run to the driver's side in the silvery, shining glut of water. She yanked open the driver's side door and pushed Rochelle into the passenger's seat. Being thrust across the side of the car calmed Rochelle, so she wasn't hyperventilating, but she was in hysterical tears wrung out of her body with wracking heaves.

"Relax, Emily. It's only a facial wound, and it's not deep. Harold says facial wounds tend to bleed worse than they actually are. Let's get home to the kids. Then you can take me to the emergency room."

"Are you crazy, Miriam? You're in shock. Don't you feel that on your cheek? We have to get you to a hospital. We have to report this. Don't you understand what's happened? You've been shot," Emily bellowed.

"I know that." Miriam returned a quiet roar. "Get me home. I want my kids and Harold. Then we can call the Highway Patrol or the police or someone. Do it my way."

"Not this time, Miriam. We go to the emergency room now. You can have Harold then; he might even be on duty. Whatever, we're going to the hospital. Be quiet and sit still."

"But I don't want to go to the hospital. I want Harold," she whined.

"You're going to the hospital."

Emily turned up the heat to keep Miriam warm and out of shock. Miriam laid her head back on the seat holding the blood-drenched tissues to ineffectively staunch the bleeding of her cheek. Rochelle was heaped in a sobbing curl on the passenger's side of the seat. Emily thought once she was off the highway and onto the city streets, driving would be easier. But the rain-blackened streets coupled with the sheeting of the rain absorbed any light that might have guided her to the hospital. The wetness that had drenched her clothes as she rushed out of the car into the rain on the highway seeped into her awareness with itchy discomfort. Rochelle's car plodded along the shiny, black, tarry looking streets until the women saw the lights of the emergency room at Mercy hospital. Emily pulled up behind an ambulance already occupying the canopied entrance to the emergency room.

Yelling, "Stay there", she ran into the rain which had become frigid as the day subsided into night. Emily dashed into the entrance presented by the automatic glass door and shouted to no one in particular, "My friend's been shot!" Heads started at the sight of the woman wearing drenched clothes, sodden hair and screaming.

"Where?" asked the receptionist with practiced calm.

"On the freeway. Before the bridge."

"Is she there now? Where should we send the ambulance?"

"No, she's in the car." Emily seemed astounded the receptionist didn't understand where Miriam was. By then, two nurses had swept through the double doors of the emergency room pushing a gurney. Emily rushed in toward them and said, "This is Dr. Rose's wife. Is he here?"

Almost as quickly as the receptionist left her desk and went to the emergency room, Harold appeared, the tails of his open white coat flurrying behind him.

"Emily, what is Treva telling me? She said Miriam's here."

"She's been shot, Harold. On the freeway. Out there, she's in the car–the Rolls out there."

"Okay, look, you stay here. Give Treva the information. We'll need to report it." To the nurses, he said, "Let's go."

As he added the unneeded, "Now!", the gurney was whisked out the doors to the car.

Harold yanked the door of the car open and peered into the dimness. He heard Rochelle's whimpers in the front seat, gave her a cursory, expert scan to gauge her condition and then moved his attention to the back seat. The outdoor lights cut the darkness enough to see Miriam's nonchalant smile as she quietly said, "Hi, babe. I've been hurt."

"You've got a mess there."

"My face burns a little."

"You're in shock."

"I don't think so. It's a face wound. You always say they look much worse than they are."

"That's not quite the way I said it. Be quiet, or I'll drug you asleep."

As Miriam, strapped onto the gurney and wired to an I.V. drip, was wheeled in, Harold walked over to Emily standing at the receptionist's desk.

"Is she going to be all right?"

"I hope so. What angle did that bullet come in? Could you tell?"

"She was sitting in the back seat, near the middle, so she could talk to both of us. Rochelle didn't get hit because she was slumped over the steering wheel trying to see the road before the rain blinded the windshield. The bullet whizzed by me. But I don't know how many bullets there were. We counted three holes in the front side windows of Rochelle's car, but there might have been more shots that we didn't hear or didn't get into the car. I think the one that hit Miriam came in at an angle on the driver's side window because that's how the cut in her cheek looks. If it had come straight at her in the back seat, she might have a big hole in her cheek. I can't even tell you when we realized there were bullets in the car. Miriam's face just started to bleed. Is she going to be all right?"

"That bullet may still be in her face, and it looks like some glass is embedded in her cheek. The trick now is to prevent infection. If I'm picturing what you described, the thing grazed her face and may have lodged near the ear. If it has, it could have damaged the ear. We'll have it x-rayed at the hospital.

"You'll have to stay until you give information to the Highway Patrol."

Harold nodded assent when she asked if Treva had already called them.

Then he asked, "Can you get Rochelle home? And then could you go to the house and take our kids with you to your house? I'll call them and let them know you're coming. Let me tell them what's happened, and I'll pick them up when I can."

"Yes to all of the above. Leave the kids with me, and I'll get them to school tomorrow."

"Thanks, but I want them with me. I'll leave here as soon as I get Miriam settled in and check with the docs who will look after her. I don't want my kids without a parent when something like this has happened. Try not to tell them what happened; that's my job. They'll be afraid for their mother, and I can help them through some of that."

"True. Come anytime, no matter how late. David or I can even bring them to you. Just call us."

The Highway Patrol showed up quickly, so reports could be taken allowing Emily and Rochelle to be dismissed.

Emily, extremely cold from the rain sodden clothes she was wearing, turned to Rochelle as they climbed into the back seat of the highway patrol car. This time it was Rochelle's car that had become part of a crime scene. "You okay, Rochelle? Harold's with Miriam now. They'll take care of her."

Rochelle, body jarring, uneven sighs interspersed among her low moaning, shook her head, "I can't go home. I can't deal with this. It's going to be so bad about the car and the holes in the window. What will I say to the kids about the car? And to Geoffrey. Oh my gosh, what will I say to Geoffrey?"

She became as hysterical as when the shooting first occurred.

"But, Rochelle. You have to go home. What about your kids?"

She started to cry more.

"Do you want to leave them home with Geoffrey? Is he even home? Is he traveling? Samantha and Scott need you."

Emily's last statement was the wet blanket to quench Rochelle's enflamed hysterics, as if anything wet were needed on a day like today. Using the palms of her hands to wipe her distended, glassy eyes, she straightened herself. Just as she encased her body in a rigidly straight posture, she straightened her emotions into placidity.

"Let's go now," she directed the patrolman as he entered his own car. "Actually, you should stay with Miriam's children. I can drive myself home now, so I'll take you to Miriam's and then take all of you home."

"Are you sure? Do you want a drink or something? A tissue?" Emily asked in disbelief at the quick change in Rochelle.

"No, I must get back to the children. I'm just fine," she smiled at Emily. I've been so upset. I just wasn't thinking. Shall I take you home?"

"Rochelle, your car isn't going anywhere except to a police lot. Look, we're in a police car. You can't drive; the officer will take us home. You sure you're okay?"

"Sure, I suppose so. I need to get to the kids." Confused, Emily watched Rochelle carefully until she was dropped off at her house. Rochelle exited the car without a thank you or acknowledgment of help received from anyone.

CHAPTER 31

When David returned home from work that evening, he remarked, "Tonight's a school night. What're the Rose kids doing here? I thought we had a family rule the kids couldn't have guests after dinner on a school night."

"Special circumstances," responded Emily. "So tell me. I can only imagine."

Emily hedged a bit. "Well, Harold asked that I pick them up because he didn't want to leave until he made sure Miriam was okay."

"Leave where?"

"The hospital."

"What hospital?"

"Mercy."

"You mean Mercy Hospital where he works? Why didn't Miriam just leave with him?"

"Um, it's like this. She couldn't."

"You mean she hurt herself."

"Not exactly."

"Why couldn't she leave, then?"

Sighing deeply, Emily explained, "She was shot."

David's voice was suffused with incredulity when he asked, "With a gun? What do you mean Miriam was shot?"

"Just what I said, David. She was shot in the car," explained Emily.

"Whose car?"

"Rochelle Emory's. On the freeway."

"How do you know?"

"Because I was in the car with them. The bullet passed me, but one got Miriam. In the cheek."

"You were in the car? You almost got shot?" Anger was surmounting his agitation. "Wait, did you say Rochelle?"

At Emily's nod, David asked, "Isn't she part of that Sustain and Shelter? That Rochelle?"

Again Emily nodded.

Angrily David cornered Emily and said, "What in the hell is going on? Do you think this has anything to do with Sustain and Shelter? That screwy Sustain and Shelter was okay with me until something like this happens. What is going on over there? Why were you women shot at? Why was Rochelle's car shot at? You will resign that board now."

"David, don't you dare tell me what to do? You are my husband, not my keeper. Now, calm down, and I'll tell you what I know, and then we will decide together what to do. You know better than to tell me what to do." David's anger added to the frustration of the day, and Emily's voice reflected it.

Chastised, but still angry, he mumbled, "I'm sorry. I don't like you being threatened that way, though."

"I know. I'm not sure what's happening." She interrupted her thoughts to ask him, "Besides, what makes you think Sustain and Shelter has anything to do with this? We were on a school field trip. That was a random happening. Just a, not just a, but, I mean, it was a drive-by shooting. No one was even thinking Sustain and Shelter. What made you tie that together?"

"I'm not sure," he said slowly. "It just seems the people who are connected with that group that I've met are on strange side. In this case, strange equals bizarre. Maybe not bizarre, but, at least, out of the ordinary. And what happened on the freeway is bizarre. I can't pinpoint why I think they're connected. It's just that, with all the volunteer work you and your mother have done, I've never heard of an organization this out of whack. I keep remembering that scenario at Fourth of July."

"Maybe. You may be right, but it could just be only a coincidental occurrence. It probably doesn't have anything to do with the group. However, it couldn't hurt to talk with Bob Washburn about all this. I would think the drive-by shooting was chance, though. It doesn't make sense someone would know who was in that car. I think I want to talk with Bob. I told the highway patrolman what happened, but I know Bob and think he could help me sort through some of this. Would you like to go with me?"

"Give him a call. Try your mother first. He's probably with her."

He wasn't at her mother's. In fact, Louisa reported, he wasn't even in town.

"Why do you want him?" Louisa tried to not seem too curious.

In an attempt to play down the seriousness of the afternoon, Emily said lightly, "Miriam was shot in a drive-by shooting, and I want to see if he knew the officer who took the report."

Echoing David's reaction almost verbatim, Louisa shouted, "Shot? What do you mean Miriam was shot? With a gun?"

"Just what I said, Mom. She was shot in the car."

"Whose car?"

"Rochelle Emory's. On the freeway." In still trying to alleviate the significance of the situation she said, "Rochelle drives a Rolls Royce. Don't you find it ironic a Rolls should be shot at? Doesn't seem in keeping with its image, do you think?"

Mom didn't bite and didn't seem in a mood to want to play with irony, so she asked acrimoniously, "Who's Rochelle Emory?"

"She's a neighbor of Miriam. Miriam never liked her until she got to know her. Anyway, we all went on a field trip together for Jojo's class."

"You mean the children saw it?" Sarcasm became disbelief.

"No, Mom, they were on the bus."

"But you saw it? You were in the car. My heavens, you could have been killed."

"But I wasn't. I'm okay. Miriam got shot in the cheek. Harold is with her now. But he'll have to file a report, too, and I want to talk with Bob about it."

"What makes me so mad about this is I can't even tell you to be careful. It's not like you were somewhere you shouldn't have been. I mean, you were helping out the public schools, for Pete's sake. What could be more wholesome than that? And Miriam gets shot for doing that? Something's totally out of balance here."

Emily waited quietly while her mother blew.

Finally Louisa said, "Bob will probably call tonight because he said he might be able to get back tomorrow or the next day. I'll tell him and find out exactly when he'll be home. I'll let you know, okay?"

"Thanks, Mom."

"Okay, Emily. And, Em?"

She knew what was coming next, so she braced herself for motherly concern. "Yes, Mom."

"Be careful. Please. Something's going on, isn't it? Do you know what it is?"

"It was one of those things, Mom. It just happened. Don't worry."

"Right," Louisa sarcastically said as she disconnected.

Although the phone call was over, Emily still felt her mother's concern and her husband's frustration. She looked at the raindrops on the window which obscured any recognition of the yard outside and replayed the afternoon's events in her head. The damp air and the cold moistness gave an eerie feeling to those events. If it weren't so dark and wet, she'd leash Byte and take a long walk. Maybe tomorrow.

CHAPTER 32

October began an encyclopedia of precipitation—soft rain, cold rain, gray rain, drizzle, pelting rain, sleet, warm rain, sporadic rain, freezing rain, hail, gentle rain, even rain mixed with weak sunshine. There were few sunny lulls in the wet to dry things out. When everything started feeling spongy, the grumbles about the bad weather started. Tempers became short and despondency became prolonged, so smiles and cheerfulness were in short supply.

Emily didn't mind. She looked at the gray rain and saw the promise of a lush and green spring to be followed by an even lusher and more colorful summer. The days that rained softly allowed Byte and her to work in the yard preparing the moist soil to receive bulbs and seeds for spring's new growth. During the hard rains, they'd wait for the lull between storms and take long, reflective walks in the relaxing drizzle that allowed Emily's mind to amble in and out of the events of the days just as Byte ambled in and out of the bushes and undergrowth. In light of the next few weeks' occurrences, it was a respite for Emily to have that time to herself. During the next few days, she used the time spent indoors to create Halloween costumes for her daughters. Each day she'd put another layer of newsprint on Lulie's nose, so that it soon became as long as Pinocchio's. Her admiration of her handiwork was interrupted by a call from Bob Washburn.

"Emily, I got back to work this morning. What's this your mother tells me about a drive-by shooting?"

Emily retold the story and asked, "I was curious to see what the follow-up would be, and I thought you could help me there."

"It won't be in my jurisdiction. Probably California Highway Patrol. I didn't see anything posted or hear anything around the station, but I just got here. Who was involved?"

"I can't tell you anything about the car because we couldn't see it well in the rain. There were three of us, and Miriam Rose was shot in the face. We took her to Mercy's emergency room, and I told the highway patrolman what I just told you, but I thought I'd run it by you because I know you, and you can tell me what to expect."

"I'm sorry, Emily. Guess I can't help you much. I'll listen around here and see what I can find out. Sorry I'm not much help."

As he made noises to close the conversation, Emily stopped him. "Wait, yes, you can. You can help me, I think. I've been trying to decide if I should ask you this. But I just can't believe no one did anything about it. And if I'm upset they didn't want to help and kept their mouths shut about it, then I shouldn't do the same thing. Maybe, I'm off the wall here, but my curiosity is killing me."

Patient man, that Bob Washburn. He never indicated annoyance with Emily's lengthy preamble. He never indicated he was behind in his own work because of the four-day conference he had just attended. He sat at the other end, straightened up some papers on his desk and listened to her stumble around with her question.

Finally she got around to it. "Do you remember that body that was found floating in the river before school started?"

"Sure. You know who it is?"

"No, but there're a couple ladies missing from that board I sit on. It's that non-profit organization. Remember this summer when you met Rudyard Millup? David thinks the group is screwy, and he's probably correct. One lady told me she was going to get a new job, but I didn't get the idea she had to resign because of it. That might be logical, but the other one lady who is missing is their treasurer. I've tried calling her several times over the last few days. No one seems concerned about her not being at the meeting last week. I had to steal her phone number from the office. Ralph Watkins, the body they found at the mall, that day I saw you there. You recall all that?"

She heard his assent. "Remember how I told you he was on that same board. Maybe that's why my mind wants to put them together. Plus David being so mad about the shooting. Chad was kind of threatening, too, when I talked about her, the treasurer, that is."

"And Chad would be? Who is he?"

"The executive director. He's not the problem though. I'm not concerned about him. It's the treasurer I'm concerned about."

"What's the lady's name, Emily?" Detective Washburn said quietly.

"Ida. Ida McIvey. Kind of skittish all the time. She came into the office one time when I was there. Mom and Genevieve, Mom's co-worker for years, even remember her."

"Yeah, I know Genevieve; her mouth is as brash as her hair," interrupted Bob.

"You got that right. But listen. Even they described her the same way. Nervous, but good-hearted."

Emily started to relate the story of the two financial statements, but stopped because she couldn't draw the conclusion she wanted to without knowing to whom the body in the river belonged.

"I'll check on it. Do you have any other information about her?"

"She wasn't at a meeting one month; that's not unusual because people will have other obligations, but then she wasn't there a second month in a row. Usually someone would have some kind of contact with a board member. The director would need information of some kind especially from the treasurer. In the last board meeting it came out no one on the board had questioned her being gone. Wouldn't you think someone would be curious as to where she was? The reason that was given for not contacting her was that it wasn't good to invade people's privacy. Chad and Rudyard said it's a disruption of privacy, and we don't need each other's phone numbers and addresses. I've sat on several non-profit boards for a long time, and we always get that information."

"How about a description?"

"Oh. Thin, on the tall side for a woman, brown hair with lots of gray in it, wore glasses, about sixty or sixty five."

"Who's the other woman?"

"What other woman?"

"The one you mentioned earlier. You said there were a couple women missing from the board."

"Oh, you mean Blythe? Blythe Oberstein. She's a younger woman, homeless, but you'd never know it by looking at her.

"Those bozos, Chad and Rudyard, said she resigned the board to take another job. I don't know why she'd have to resign to take a job; people can work and volunteer with a little time management. I've tried calling her also and can't get an answer."

"Anything else, Emily?"

A pause and then, "No."

"Are you *sure*?"

"Right now I'm sure," she asserted positively.

"But I'll be the first you tell when you're ready if you have something, won't I?"

"Yes. That is, if…"

"If, what?"

"If you'll tell me who the body is. I won't tell anyone. I just want to know if it's Ida or Blythe. It'd be nice to find out before anyone else does. This time."

"You got it. It's a deal. But don't forget your part of it."

"I won't. And, Bob?"

"More deal?"

"Kind of. Don't tell my mother, okay? She's a little worried about this now; I don't to worry her anymore."

"Oh really." Bob chuckled. "I've never known her to worry about her children. Not telling her anything about this might be the easiest part of this whole deal. But don't you forget your part of it. I'll let you know what we find out."

Leaving too early to carpool kids home from school that afternoon allowed Emily to visit Miriam at the hospital. As she entered her room, private, no less, Emily asked, "So, how's it going?"

Tiredly, Miriam replied, "Okay, except I can't talk too well. I hurt, too. More than when it first happened."

"And you didn't want to go to the emergency room. I'm sorry you hurt, Miriam."

"It's not your fault."

Miriam's speech was much better sounding than Emily had thought it would be. She was understandable. The part about it not being Emily's fault bothered her. What if David were right? Then it would be Emily's fault. What if the shooting weren't chance? What if Sustain and Shelter were involved? But then how would anyone know Emily was in the car? If it weren't coincidental, then she was going to feel devastated to know she had caused a friend's pain.

"Has Rochelle been to see you?"

"No, I would have thought she would want to see the damage. She carried on about it enough in the car. You would think she was the one who was hit."

"That's true."

With nurses rumbling through patients' rooms and visitors plodding the hallway outside, hospitals aren't places that are most conducive for conversation, so Emily cast about for some light topic to discuss, but she couldn't come up with anything suitably comfortable.

"Harold told me the glass set up an infection, and you were lucky the bullet didn't shatter your jaw. I'm glad it wasn't any worse."

Miriam nodded at her and didn't offer anything except, "Me, too." She didn't want to discuss the shooting.

Miriam's vivacity and nonchalance had been burst almost as surely as if the bullet had penetrated her personality instead of her cheek. Her reluctance to talk about the incident coupled with Emily's unwillingness to cause any more discomfort stilted their conversation. There was an undercurrent of sadness because of Miriam's depression over the infringement to her person, and Emily didn't know how long it would take for her to recover.

After another pause filled with discomfort, Emily asked, "Miriam, have you seen the kids?"

Miriam just shook her head.

"They're too young." She was downcast.

"Couldn't Harold sneak them in?"

"He thought about it, but he said it wouldn't look good as head of the department to do that. I'm going home in a couple days."

"Tell me what your kids are going to be for Halloween," Miriam changed the subject.

Emily told her and closed the visit saying, "I'll be glad to help with the costumes for Eli and Tenandra."

A half-hearted wave and a tight clench of teeth from Miriam sent Emily on her way.

CHAPTER 33

Emily ran to the phone and grabbed the receiver with wheat-pasted hands, the result of another layer of papier mâché on Lulie's nose for her costume. Actually, the nose was coming along quite well; it was going to be a true work of art. The first couple layers had been discouraging as they limply hung onto the form of chicken wire, but now that the shape was assumed, it was looking realistic–as realistic as a six inch long bent nose could look. Emily was beginning to have some of the satisfaction of an artist in a creation well done.

"Hello."

"Emily, it's Detective Washburn."

If it's Detective Washburn and not Bob, it must be official. "Go ahead."

"How well did you know this Ida McIvey?"

"Not well, at all. I met her maybe three times. I bet I didn't say ten words to her. Mom knows her better than I. Maybe you should ask her what she knows about Ida. Why?"

"That body in the river, the one you were so concerned about, is Ida McIvey according to dental records. Can you think of anything, anything at all, that you've forgotten to tell me?" Emily was surprised to hear his tone of voice. He wasn't calling for small talk; he was calling to interrogate.

"I really can't. I can't think of anything right now."

"Remember our deal. Even the most insignificant detail is important. Think. You might not realize it's important, but anything you may have seen or talked about to someone could be vital. Anything." He said the last word with emphasis.

She knew the financials were something, but what? If she said something now, and it turned out they were nothing, what then? It was so much easier dealing with honest record keeping, the simple kind, like David's business, that she understood. It was much harder trying to match Ida's records, so they agreed. Her hesitancy to respond prompted him to ask again in an even more forceful tone of voice. The forcefulness of his voice made her back off from offering the financial statements to him. If she were wrong, it wouldn't do to bugger up the works.

"Come on, Emily. Tell me anything. Do you think you know something? If so, tell me. Now. Tell me now."

"No, nothing. I don't think I can remember any conversation or–I just can't think of anything." She said weakly, "Sorry."

"Right. Okay, here's the situation. I'm telling you this because I don't want the Ralph Watkins situation replayed between us. I don't want you to find out about this identity somewhere else. Understand? You're the one who pointed us in the direction, so you need to have some closure. Are you sure you don't know anything else?"

"You keep asking that, Bob. What are you looking for? I know very little about the woman–just what Mom and Genevieve told me—and, now, what you've told me. Help me out here. What do you want? It's like you want me to pop out with some solution to the lady's death. How would I know? Was she shot in the back of the head like Ralph? Or like that other person you and Detective Yoshiwara were discussing? That one in some other jurisdiction, like maybe down in the valley. Is that it?"

"Yeah, as a matter of fact, she was."

"And you think that's a connection? That doesn't make sense. It almost sounds like you've got a serial killer on hand."

"No, not a serial killer. These are too, for want of a better word, clean. Like the people were shot to get rid of them. They must've had information. If Ralph and Ida were privy to information, then they may have used that information against some people. We don't know what the info was, however."

"Was that other guy an accountant or bookkeeper? For any organizations? Like non-profits?"

"What makes you ask that? What do you know? You have something that could help us, don't you?"

"No, I don't. I don't have any concrete information, just supposition. You know better than I do that most killings, if they aren't based on some kind of emotional passion, are based on greed. Money equals greed. At least, I think, in my layperson's perception of things that is how crime goes. Passion or greed. Only takes one; sometimes, maybe, it takes two."

"Add power in there. Passion, greed or power. In some ways, you're right. Crime all boils down to one or more of three motivations–passion, greed or power, the great fallibilities of human nature," Bob said sadly.

"Poor old Ida. She didn't strike me as passionate, greedy or power-hungry. She was just an older lady who tried to do some good throughout her adult life. Mom and Genevieve said she was pretty much afraid of her own shadow. Kind of like the old spinster stereotype."

"Yeah, well, she wasn't a spinster."

"You sure? She could've fooled me. Then, how come when I called all those times, the answering machine answered, and her husband didn't? Seems like if she were married, her spouse would be home sometime. And how come the husband didn't report her missing? Even if he didn't like her, he would still report her gone."

"I'll tell you why. You remember Rudyard Millup, your friend you introduced us to on Independence Day?"

"Not my friend. Genevieve thinks he's a wowzer. I think he's a pain in the butt, a supercilious and condescending jerk."

"Right. Well, he condescended just long enough to become Ida's husband."

Emily's mouth dropped. She would have dropped the phone except the wheat paste for the papier mâché had glued her hand to the receiver.

"Emily, are you there? Emily?"

Emily gulped. "I think so."

"You think so?"

"Bob, are you sure? That doesn't make sense, Rudyard and Ida. It just doesn't mesh right."

"Why not?"

"I saw them together. Even together in the room, they weren't together. There was even some story about his wife being a homebody who never went out because she was so delicate. He even said that; she was too fragile. If you saw Ida and Rudyard together, you'd never, I mean, never, think they had any connection. He was so, so, almost mean to her. If she were loaded down with stuff and needed the door opened, he'd be the last person to offer to help her. In fact, he'd probably trip her just to make sure that the stuff fell out of her hands. This makes no sense. Are you sure?"

"Positive."

"Then, why didn't someone tell me? I've been on that board almost six months. Why didn't that come out?"

"Oh, he didn't live with her. He has his own residence. I know you know something. I know you're aware of something." Bob cajoled a bit. "Maybe it's something you don't realize. Maybe you heard something or saw something. You have to let me know."

"Let me call you back in a bit. I've got a cake in the oven that's getting overdone," she lied. "Talk to you soon."

Emily would have thrown the phone into the cradle except it was still glued to her hand, but she did hang up quickly, so she didn't hear him say, "Don't forget."

Staring at the phone and not really seeing it, Emily replayed the tableaus of Rudyard and Ida's being together in her mind. As hard as she tried, she came up with no whisper of their being at all related. It was the most tenuous of professional relationships she had seen, and, as a spousal relationship, there was nothing. Nervous, fluttering, insecure, gangling Ida and boisterous, pushy, egotistical, handsome Rudyard. Maybe that was the reason their relationship was a void, and they displayed no substantiation of it. They didn't match. Nothing about either of their personalities was analogous to the other.

And what about the interchange concerning reporting her whereabouts? There was no concern on Rudyard's part, and there was no desire to deal with reporting her missing. If anything, he pushed it away as insignificant. He never said anything in the conversation to disagree with Chad in reporting her absence. Ida's husband was silent on the issue. Emily tried to picture the scene and remember how Rudyard acted. She scrutinized her brain hoping to read Rudyard's facial expressions when discussing Ida. All Emily could remember from that meeting were the financials; she had been so surprised to finally have some hardcopy of the business of Sustain and Shelter. In her mind's picture, it was as though Rudyard weren't present.

Then, that begged the question. Why would a man like Rudyard marry a woman like Ida? Passion or greed? Just like crimes. Marriage could be passion or greed or power or all three, theoretically. Some marriages were a crime. Genevieve had talked about Rudyard's motive for helping the homeless. Keep them out of his tract developments, so that buyers wouldn't be put off. Passionless Ida and greedy Rudyard. What would passionless Ida know that greedy Rudyard would want kept secret? Ida was a money manager. Did she manage Rudyard's money? If he were doing criminal activities with his money, would Ida know about it?

As the receiver of the phone was still glued to her hand, she dialed her mother's office number with the other hand.

"Mom," she preempted any openings her mother offered. "Did you know Ida McIvey was married to Rudyard Millup?"

"Who? Ida?"

"You know, the lady Gen and you were talking about at lunch the other day. Ida and Rudyard."

"Rudyard, that bozo that Genevieve thinks is so good looking?"

"Ida and Rudyard—they're married. Or they were. Ida's dead now."

Louisa's surprised silence punctuated the conversation. "Dead? Ida's dead? Are you sure?"

"Bob, your Bob, just told me not only that she and Rudyard were married, but also that she's now dead. Remember at dinner a few weeks ago I asked about the body in the river? And remember the body was a woman? Well, Ida hadn't shown up at the Sustain and Shelter board meetings for a while, and Chad was so annoying about giving out her phone number. I took the number from the office the next day, called the Ida's house and never got an answer. So on a hunch, I asked Bob if that body could be Ida's. Poor old Ida, this is sad. Bob said they identified her, and it's Ida. He also said she and Rudyard were married."

"So Ida was married," mused Louisa. "Guess Ida had some passion in her after all. Wonder how she managed to use that passion to trap Rudyard."

"Maybe Rudyard used passion to trap Ida."

"Perhaps. I would think it's the other way around. She would want him more than he would want her. She must've made some super power play to snag him. Yeesh, bet that marriage was a crime."

"Don't know how it could have been. They lived apart," said Emily.

"Yeah, like I said, the marriage was a crime. I'll see if I can pump Genevieve for any more information." Louisa chuckled, "This'll probably be the first time in our friendship that I can one-up her in the people and places gossip. Poor old Ida. What a sad life."

Emily looked at the phone for a few minutes as she mentally pieced together the latest puzzle pieces. Mechanically, she used her left hand to unpry her right hand from the phone, washed her hands at the kitchen sink, and went to the dining room to get all the financial statements she now possessed. As she laid them out on the table, she puzzled over Ida and Rudyard. Bob, in his usual way, gave only a bit of information. There was more to be had. Emily looked at the papers, but the figures swam in wavy black ink. Quickly, she gathered them up, stuffed them into a file and jammed them into their hiding place. She grabbed her keys and stormed out to the car. Bob might not give her the answers she was seeking, but she knew someone who might.

CHAPTER 34

Dexter's California Deli provided the bribe that would unlock the answers. Emily picked out a turkey pastrami and provolone cheese sandwich for herself and a crisply fried Monte Carlo for the bribee. A huge chunk of praline cheesecake should obliterate any objections the bribee had to answering Emily's questions. It was far better than packing pellets and would give the poor woman some nourishment.

As she hoped, Emily found Shannon in the office loitering through a *For Style* magazine. Emily placed the bags from Dexter's—warm, spicy odors subtly emanating from them—on Shannon's desk before the young woman was aware of Emily's presence.

Shannon looked at the bags and then at Emily. "Oh, no. Not you.

What're you doing here? I thought Chad told you to stay out of here."

"Is he here?" asked Emily.

"Not quite."

"Not quite? What's that mean?"

"Um, well, I expect him soon. Real soon."

"You sure?"

Shannon looked at Emily and then at the bags from Dexter's still sending out inviting whiffs of good food.

"Well, maybe not for a while. Sometime this afternoon. Why're you here?"

"Just thought I'd see if there are anymore people to be put on your donor and volunteer list. I thought there might be some new names to add, and I had a little time before I pick up my children, so I thought I'd stop by. Since it was almost lunchtime, I thought you might like to have lunch with me."

Shannon reached for the bags. "What'd you bring? There are only a few names, but you don't have to do them. Chad doesn't want you in the office. He says you're too nosy and could cause trouble."

"I figured you might like one of those Monte Carlo sandwiches, so I ordered that for you."

"From Dexter's?" Shannon squealed delightedly. "Oh, that's one of my favorites. Oh, thank you. I just love them."

"Then praline cheesecake for dessert."

Shannon, mouth full of sandwich, nodded with excitement.

Emily ate slowly and small-talked with Shannon who, with each bite she took, answered Emily's questions more readily.

"Any word from Ida?" Emily asked cautiously.

Shannon raised her shoulders defensively, but Emily pushed some fresh strawberry jelly toward her. Shannon started to smear it on her sandwich.

"No, we haven't heard a word from her. She has some accounting to do, and Chad is pissed it hasn't been done."

"Doesn't anyone know where she is? Chad hasn't heard? Seems like she would have told the executive director if she were going out of town, don't you think?"

"Seems like it."

"Maybe she told one of her friends or her family, and they forgot to call here to tell you."

"Don't know about friends. But she doesn't have any family." "No husband? Surely, she has a husband."

"Not all of us have husbands. Even you told me that when you first came. Young women have so many opportunities, you said. Here you are, assuming Ida has a husband. Husbands aren't so important. I, we, can get along without them."

Emily nodded agreeably as Shannon spoke. "That's true. So many things for women to do nowadays. Wonderful options. My mother knows Ida from way back when and said Ida was always doing good things for organizations. She made the most of the options for her generation. My mother, who's a social worker, also said Rudyard has always been prominent in helping the homeless in Pleasant Creek. Said he's a wonderful support." Mom, forgive me for lying, Emily thought. "Probably Ida and Rudyard know each other quite well, don't you think?"

"Maybe." Shannon had reached for the cheesecake, so Emily pushed it closer to her and handed her a fork. "Rudyard hates her. Calls her a dried-up old prune. Says she's a blithering idiot. He never talks to her. When I've seen them together, he never talks to her."

"Is that how he talks about his wife?"

"Don't know. He doesn't ever talk about her, at least, not here in the office. He doesn't talk to me. I haven't ever met his wife. It's like he keeps her locked in a closet." Shannon chewed as she thought. "I don't think I'd like to live that way. In the background like that. I think I heard he's had a couple wives; one died. Don't know about the other. I think that's what I heard."

Emily nodded and started to clean up the lunch trappings. As she reached for wadded up napkins, Bo tramped into the office.

"Where's Chad?" he demanded. As Shannon shrugged her shoulders in ignorance, Bo paced agitatedly.

"When's he coming back?"

Shannon scowled. "Why do you care?"

"I need to talk to him. That idiot, Chewy, beat it off to Mexico. We need another day cook. How am I gonna keep that kitchen running?" He trudged off to the back of the hallway.

"And your habit fed?" mumbled Shannon.

"What do you mean?" asked Emily.

"Chewy is Bo's supplier," Shannon snapped. "Didn't you know that? Chewy is the biggest non-secret in this whole organization. Bo doesn't care if Chewy is gone and can't cook. He can always find a cook. Bo wants the coke Chewy brings up from Mexico. It's supposed to be some of the best quality."

Emily's mouth dropped somewhat. "Well, Shannon, you are a veritable well of information. Lots of miscellaneous information. I bet you know things that go on here that even the head honchos don't know."

Shannon smiled in smug agreement. "If you only knew. I could hang some of these people around here." That said, Shannon went back to the hallway to find Bo.

"Been nice talking to you, Shannon. You call me when you're ready for me to do the input. Anytime," Emily called to her retreating back.

Shannon waved Emily off with her hand.

"You're welcome, Shannon," Emily muttered as she left the office.

Emily saw the blue sedan when she checked for the all clear as she exited the parking lot of Sustain and Shelter. There was plenty of time to leave the driveway of the building and drive onto the street to go home– she thought. However, as she pulled onto the street, the blue sedan screeched into a swerve in front of her car barely giving her enough time to stomp her brakes before hitting the car. Chad Woodley pushed open the driver's side door and bounded out of the car.

"What're you doing?" he yelled at Emily. Surprised by the greeting, Emily stared at Chad.

"What're you doing?" Chad repeated.

"Well, I, well I stopped by to ask Shannon if there were more data to put into the computer. That's what I volunteered for."

"You're not supposed to be here. You're not welcome here. I've told you that."

"Chad," Emily said coldly. "Do you know what a volunteer is? A volunteer is a person who gives; that means they don't expect payment, and they give that time and talent because they want to help people. Non-profits are not set up to make money. That's why they're called non-profits. If a non-profit makes no money, there is nothing to pay workers a salary, and you have to have manpower from somewhere. That's what volunteers are for. Do you realize you have to have them to make a non-profit work? That's a basic tenet. I'm a volunteer. You can't keep me from volunteering just because you don't like me. I'm on the board. You need my help. By definition of a non-profit organization, you need my help."

Chad slammed his open palm on the hood of her minivan. "I don't want you here. I don't need you here. Get out."

"Don't you touch my car. You do that again, and I'm calling the police. Now, get your car out of my way. I'm going to call the board members and report this behavior; you, obviously, don't understand how charity organizations work. I do not need to be fired as a volunteer; you need to be fired as an executive director."

"You can't do that to me," shouted Chad. "I run this organization. You can't touch me. Don't threaten me with empty words, or you'll be sorry."

"Threat? I'm not threatening; I'm promising. That threat you just made, Chad. That won't cut it. Get your car out of my way."

Chad raised his hand.

"Don't even think it," said Emily.

Lowering his hand, he glared at Emily before he moved his car out of her way.

CHAPTER 35

Emily's heart raced just a little faster than the speed at which she was racing to get home. Deep breaths and gripping the steering wheel didn't do much to douse her anger with Chad. Non-profit meant enough money for operating social welfare programs–programs to make the world better. The only profit that would be made in any non-profit should be used to go back into the program and make the services available to that many more people. People became greedy when profit was involved. Shannon had told her Chad set up other organizations that provided shelter for the homeless. Maybe he was tired of seeing the profit go back into the programs. Perhaps, greed was taking over. Perhaps, Ida found something that indicated Chad had succumbed to greed. Perhaps, that was why the poor woman was dropped into the river. Greed or passion Emily had told Bob. Bob added the power aspect. It only took one, but, in Chad's case, did it take two? If so, what would be the passion part? Greed was easy to discern, power could play a role. Emily had seen Chad's power play over Shannon, had seen it in the meetings and had just witnessed it, again, in threats to her. But passion? Emily hadn't seen that–yet. Power and greed. It takes two in Chad's case.

Just short of ramming her minivan into the garage, Emily stormed out of the car into the house. She didn't even say hello to Byte. Instead she charged into the dining room, found the financial statements and began to pour over them slowly. Only then, with the need to delve into minutiae, did her heart slow down. Once again, she scrutinized the papers detail by detail. This time she compared the line items by title instead of amounts. The numbers had taken on a life of their own, but the words hadn't. The last few weeks, when she did bother to take the extra time, to look at the statements, it had been to compare numbers. There were so many lines on the papers, and the numbers were so haphazardly arranged, that she hadn't thought to look carefully at the several pages of account names. Ida had created accounts within accounts, and had used sub-accounts on each of the pages to group various combinations of numbers. Talk about standard accounting practices. Emily doubted Ida had used them. Ida must have been very adept at working the numbers the way she did because only she would understand the key to the organization.

And there it was. Instead of looking at the individual trees, Emily finally saw the forest.

The difference she discovered was a provision for capital reserves on the statement passed out at the last meeting, while on the million-dollar statement, there was none. And there was no category that would appear able to absorb that overage in net income. If there were no line item to which that overage could be posted, that meant there was an exorbitant amount of cash lying about. It, obviously, hadn't gone into the statement off of which the organization worked. If it had, there would be plenty of money on which the organization could operate. The public expects the money it donates to be used to help people. In this case, Sustain and Shelter was supposed to be finding shelter for homeless people and sustaining them. Three mil could provide a lot of shelter and sustain a lot of people.

It would be difficult to justify to the public why an association like Sustain and Shelter had that much money, so it probably wouldn't be in a bank. If it weren't in a bank, where could it be? The sum was too large to be left lying about, so it had to be in a bank. But if it were in a bank, it would be questioned. Legally, it had to be questioned because any daily transaction of $10,000.00 or more in cash had to be reported to the Internal Revenue Service. If it were in a bank in the United States, it had to be legally questioned. In a bank in the United States. A foreign bank doesn't report to IRS, so maybe a foreign bank wouldn't ask as many questions. Say, a bank in Mexico or the Caribbean. Chewy was on his way to Mexico. Shannon said Chewy was a drug supplier. Would Chewy also be a courier?

Images of the late summer night when she dropped the copied list of donors at Sustain and Shelter edged into her mind. Boxes of food, Chad had said. Boxes unloaded at night. Boxes with no labels. Boxes unloaded out of a generic trailer. Were the boxes coming or going? Chad had said they'd go to the kitchens, but why had they unloaded them at the office? Byte growling at Chad before the dog had even met the man. Three million dollars. Big boxes could hold a lot of dollars—maybe even three million and especially if there were many big boxes. Or many deliveries. When had Shannon eaten the packing from other big boxes? June? July?

Emily sat back in the chair, hands supporting her head as vignettes of activities of Sustain and Shelter taunted her logic. Too bad she couldn't do another lunch for Shannon. Then she could ask her from where those boxes were coming or to where they were going. Such a stretch.

She dialed the number of the Pleasant Creek City Offices. Upon prompts from the insipid voice directing her to press almost as many numbers on her phone as there were pages of financial statements from Sustain and Shelter, she was finally connected to Bob Washburn.

"That's quite a phone message system you've got there. This is Emily."

"We've had just a few comments about it, believe me. Seems they still have to work out the bugs."

"It's money laundering, Bob. Maybe not money laundering in the classic sense, but a type of money laundering."

"The phone system?" He snickered. "That's one thing you could call it, I suppose. It's been called lots of other things, some of them not as nice as that."

"No, Sustain and Shelter. It's money laundering."

He quit chuckling at his joke. As quickly as one could whisk on a mask, Emily could hear the change from doubtful comedian to serious cop. "Tell me about it."

She proceeded with how she had stolen the first set of financial statements after Ida had brought them in, then went to the night of watching Chad load boxes, talked about the drug and Mexico angle and finished with receiving the second set of statements at the last meeting.

"When you told me Ida and Rudyard were married, I had to think. The first time I compared the statements, I couldn't find any similarities. I couldn't find any relation among the numbers. Ida has complicated the statement I stole so much, I couldn't make it match. I kept trying and trying, maybe trying too hard. After we hung up, I got them out and compared the line items. There's no capital reserve on the first statement, the one I stole. Do you know what capital reserve means?"

"Kind of. It's for extra money you don't have budgeted for something."

"Right. In a non-profit, you can't make any profit. That's the tax status you have. But you never know how much money you'll take in through future donations, so you keep some, at least, you hope you can keep some in reserve, to make up for the lean times. Then you use it for start up for the next year's budget. You reserve it. The megabuck statements didn't seem to care for reserving that money. So where does it go?"

"In a bank?"

"No, not that much. A bank would want to know where all the cash transactions originated, especially currency. They have to answer to IRS. How many two bit non-profits would have a few million dollars raised during fundraisers like that joke they had at Fourth of July?"

"So why do you think all that's important?"

"Because at the last meeting, when the financials were passed around, Rudyard and Chad claimed they had made all this money at that booth, and that's why they were able to pay their bills. They claimed they made $5000.00, but that's wishful thinking for the amount of effort put into the booth. They couldn't have made much money with a set-up like they had."

"But that doesn't say how they got all the money on the financials."

"Bob, don't you see? They can get all kinds of money from drugs or pimping or gambling or whatever. A lot of it could come from big cities. Who's on those big city streets?"

"Lots of people. Pedestrians, streetwalkers, panhandlers, street salesmen, and…"

"That's right," she broke into his list. "Homeless people. Only they might not be homeless people. They could be people who look homeless, and maybe they aren't. Maybe they're just collecting money for something illegal. Then they pass the money to another so called homeless person, so money changes many hands before it even gets to the money launderer. A non-profit could be an almost flawless way to hide money. If anyone ever questions how they have that money, they could say they got a bunch of cash donations, and they don't know from where they came. They could take in all kinds of money. Shannon, the secretary, said Chad started these homeless organizations in other parts of the country–El Paso and San Diego. Those are cities near the border, and over the border are banks. I've heard some of the foreign banks don't ask many questions about how the money was made. They don't even care if it's hard cash."

She was getting excited because the idea was explaining itself. It was gathering momentum because each new idea that popped into her head seemed so plausible.

"I've read about mules. You know what they are"

"Sure, people who carry drugs across the borders of the U.S."

"And money. They carry money. What if those boxes Chad was unloading had more than food and clothes in them? What if they had money also? They could carry it across the border, say it was for charities or something there and give the clothes or food or whatever away but put the money in a bank."

She talked faster because he hadn't agreed with her, so she wasn't even sure he was listening.

"And here. Here people are always giving stuff like food and clothes away, so if they got caught with the money in the boxes, they could say it was anonymously donated and put in there by one of the workers who didn't know he was suppose to send it to another location to help, or even left in a pocket by the donor who didn't remember it being there. Or they could say they didn't know how it got there, and they'd almost be telling the truth."

She continued excitedly. "It's a cheap front, too. All they had to do was take a small percentage of the money they got illegally, set up a few soup kitchens, and people would even donate a bunch of the supplies needed to run the organization. They'd donate money, so the money laundering gang didn't even have to use their illegal money for operating costs. America donates over twenty four billion dollars to charities per year, and these people took advantage of that by setting up a pull-the-heart-stings agency as their front operation."

Emily took a deep breath, "What do you think?"

"Okay, I'll think about what you said. It makes sense. But, Emily, who killed Ida?"

"And Ralph?"

"Ralph? What do you mean Ralph?"

"Ralph Watkins. The guy in the parking lot."

"I know who he is."

"Might as well throw that guy in I'm not supposed to know about. Bet he was tied up somehow with all this. Bet if you checked Chad's work history, he headed some organization in the South Bay or maybe even in the Valley. Bet there were shady goings-on there also. There's just as much need for homeless organizations down there as there is in our part of the Bay Area. If whatever he's doing here is working, you know he tried it somewhere else."

"Think so?"

"I do. I think they, Ida and Ralph, knew what was happening. I never knew Ralph, but I met Ida. She was too nervous. Bet old Rudyard married her to control her. Or maybe she caught him and thought she had such a stud that she'd do anything for him. She probably had a hard time doing anything too risky. Maybe she wanted out. Maybe, oh, no—I hope not." Emily took a breath deep enough to be heard by Bob on the other end of the phone.

"What, Emily? What are you thinking?"

"What if Ida were killed because they realized I had the financial statements she had put in the drawer? What if Shannon figured out what I had done? Bob, that would mean I'm responsible for Ida's death. I hadn't even thought about that. What if I caused her death?"

"Emily, if that were the case, that someone killed Ida because of allowing you to get those statements, then they would have killed Shannon also. Do you think those people with Sustain and Shelter killed Ida?"

"I don't know."

Bob's silence made Emily realize she had hit upon something.

"Emily, did I lose you? You there?"

"Yes, I'm here. I just can't believe Ida and Rudyard. I can't believe Ida is dead."

"I understand."

After a pause, Bob said, "I'd like to see those financial papers, if it's okay with you. Could I come over?"

"No problem. See you soon."

No problem except to get Lulie's nose finished. In the time she had, Emily slapped another layer of paper and wheat paste on the nose and got the mess cleaned up.

Emily seated Bob at the mahogany dining table in the red walled dining room and produced both sets of financial statements.

"I think this is the key right here," she said while pointing to the Capital Reserve category on the working statement. She pulled out some worksheets where she had manipulated the numbers in the margins on the purloined papers, so they matched, more or less, the numbers on the 'legal sheets'. She also pointed out the lack of that category on the hidden statement.

"What it appears Ida did is take the categories on the private statements, the one for Chad to see, and lump some of those numbers together to give us the for-show statements. From what I can determine, and I'm no accountant, these income numbers on the private statements are whittled down by reversing some of them and taking some of the zeroes off. She also has these in code; I have no idea what the actual revenue categories are. But on the for-show statements, she manufactures some revenue sources, like donations, grants, fundraisers—the kinds of sources you'd expect a non-profit to receive.

"Okay, Emily, answer me again. Why do you think it's money laundering?"

"Because of the hidden report."

"But that could be anything. That could be something legitimate that one of the employees is involved in. Or, perhaps, there's another organization that requires a separate operating system. Maybe there's a reason to have two sets of financials."

"Yes, but from the time I've been asked to join that board, I've asked for financial information, and they've dilly-dallied around getting it to us. When they finally gave us the reports, they said the last fundraiser made this money for them. I was at the last fundraiser; you were at that fundraiser, and it was a pretty poor excuse for any type of fundraising."

She told him, again, of the night she encountered Chad unloading boxes. "If they were legitimately unloading boxes of food, why would they do it at the office? Why not at the kitchens where they serve the food? And why late at night? They keep legitimate working hours during the day. Why not then?"

"Who's the 'they' you keep talking about?"

"That's part of what I'm not sure about. I saw Chad; Byte growled at Chad before she even met him, so that makes me really suspicious of him."

"Don't think that argument's going to get you far. It's a bit abstract."

"I realize that, but you know when a dog distrusts someone, you tend to do the same."

"Somehow I don't think dog distrust is a legal precedent for evidence."

"Yeah, yeah, I know."

Bob nodded and asked, "Who else was there?"

"That's what I'm trying to tell you. I'm not sure. Rudyard may've been there. I saw Bo's truck/van thing. Later at a meeting he said he was on a hiking trip with his dudes, so I'm not sure if that was Bo there. Chad sure wanted me gone, though."

"Dudes?"

"That's what he called them. He told me he was gone the whole summer. You know where Bo said he went hiking?"

"Mexico?"

Emily nodded thoughtfully. "Of course, it could be a coincidence."

Bob agreed. "It could be.

"So do you have any ideas who might have murdered the two people?"

"I can think of lots of them. This is the quirkiest bunch of people in one spot that I've ever seen. I don't know if that would make them murderers though. But that's not really fair to judge them on that basis, is it?"

"No. It's not legal either," said Bob.

Conversation waned as each analyzed what had been said.

"There's something else to all this." Emily picked up the conversation. "It's kind of discouraging, too. Most of the people at Sustain and Shelter feel they're really doing something to help homeless people. The sad thing is they are, and if Sustain and Shelter is a front for something illegal, then it's as if their work has been useless."

"Emily," returned Bob, "deeds done with good intentions are very seldom useless. Will you let me take these papers?"

She nodded. "I'll also give you this. When no one was forthcoming with board members' addresses and phone numbers, I made this up by looking on the internet. Not all the information is there because it's only what I could come up with on my own, but it might help you." She pulled out a copy of the address list of the board members from another stack of papers.

Bob stepped out of her house into the rain, and she and Byte stepped out of her house into the garage to go pick up the kids at school.

"Is my costume done, Mom?" inquired Jojo. Her solemn face belied the excitement in her voice.

"Is my costume ready, Mommy?" echoed Lulie without Jojo's gravity. Lulie pranced her excitement into the car.

"We have to wear them to school in two weeks." Lulie emphasized the two weeks. "We have to have a costume."

"I just have to paint your nose, Lulie, and, Jojo, *Gray's Anatomy* lists more parts than are available on any of the store costumes. What do you want to do about that?"

"It's very important we get the whole name on the skeleton. I don't want like pecs for *pectoralis major*. It has to be *pectoralis major* just like that. Okay?"

"But, honey, that's a muscle; the costumes just have bones on them."

"Then we must color in the muscles with paint or something."

"How much homework do you have tonight?" sighed Emily.

"None because I finished it in school."

"Then we'll get the paint, and all of us will work on your costume. Tomorrow night I have a meeting, but we can finish the next night. Got it?"

"Great."

Great. Whatever happened to those body parts with names like funny bone, elbow, anvil and Adam's apple? Emily hoped David was up on his anatomy tonight.

CHAPTER 36

Although she arrived ten minutes before the meeting was to start, Emily was perturbed to see no other cars in the parking lot. No lights on in the building of Sustain and Shelter confirmed no one had arrived early to set up the conference room for the monthly meeting. Emily recalled the first meeting she had attended and feared this October meeting was to be another fiasco on that order. She went to the back door and tried it to no avail. She marched around to the front door and tried it with the same results. Deciding to wait until the 7:30 start time, she stood on the porch of the converted house.

After two or three minutes, Joan Chavez strode to the porch. She looked at Emily, did an about face and started to retrace her steps to the parking lot. Emily called out to her, but Joan started walking at a faster clip. Hoping to intercept Joan, Emily broke into a trot and reached for the tiny woman's arm. When she had clutched her raincoat, Joan stopped, and Emily whirled her around to face her.

"Joan, where are you going?"

Joan said nervously, "It doesn't look like there's going to be a meeting. Did you get a call there wasn't going to be a meeting? I didn't either. I must have been out. They would have called, don't you think? I'm sure they would have called. I have to go now."

But Emily hadn't let go of her raincoat, and Joan was impeded from moving forward.

"Joan, why didn't you tell me you knew Ralph?"

"I really have to go, Emily. Let go of me."

"Joan, I asked you something. Why didn't you tell me when you described him that day we were told he had died?"

"I didn't tell you because…Emily, I can't even tell you now. Please don't ask me. Please don't ask anymore. It will keep you safe." She was near tears as she implored Emily to let her go.

Just then Thomas drove up in his car and parked. He rushed out the car and hustled over to the women.

"What's going on here? Do you need help? Is she bothering you?" He addressed Joan kindly.

Emily released Joan who looked at Thomas, and the tears started flowing, "She asked about Ralph. I don't want her to know what we've been doing. It's too dangerous for her. There've been too many warnings."

He reached his arms around Joan in comfort, and she fell into him. He smiled softly as he said, "You don't have to continue this. We can work this out together."

Among blubbering heaves, she said, "But what about you? That's the reason Chad got you involved. He knew if someone else were involved, I would be less likely to back out of stealing drugs. That's why he put you in it. I'm so sorry. It seemed so commendable to help those poor people at the clinic; I didn't think about people getting hurt. I'm so sorry."

Totally bemused, but totally curious, Emily stood in the middle of her own private soap opera watching the couple bond in their turmoil. Knowing good manners dictated she should leave, common nosiness took the upper hand, and she stayed.

"Back out of what? What are you doing? Look, Chad is a schmuck. I've already told the police suspicions I have about him. I think he's doing drugs. Are you doing drugs?"

Joan's tear-stained face shot an alarmed look at Emily. "No. No drugs. At least, not that way. No, it's different. I'm not a drug pusher. I'm not."

She began crying hysterically. Thomas took his handkerchief and dabbed her face gently before he encased her in his arms again.

For a few minutes, he held her, eyes closed. When he opened his eyes, Thomas looked over Joan's head and explained to Emily, "Chad told Joan they could open a clinic if there were medicine. He said there was no way with their limited funding they could purchase medicine. Chad preyed on Joan's willingness to help by pointing out she worked in a hospital and had access to drugs. Then he let her draw the conclusion to steal them from the hospital. That way, he stays clean because he can say he didn't tell her to steal the drugs. He manipulated her and appealed to her wanting to help these people."

"Why a clinic? That's just more exposure for Chad. If he's using Sustain and Shelter as a cover, why add more components to it?"

In between a few sobs, Joan said, "Because I pushed for it. So many people need help, and the county can't serve them all. I thought it would be such a good idea. I could direct it, and then more people could get medical help. It's my fault."

With a hopeful smile, he said, "Joan, the good thing about this whole thing is my being able to work with you and get to know you."

She looked up and smiled.

Feeling as welcome as police at a beer bust, Emily started to leave.

"Wait, Mrs. Kristich," Thomas yelled after here and came rushing to her. "Wait. Please don't say anything to anyone about this. Please let us work this out for ourselves. We'll go to the police."

There it was again. Don't say anything about this. Bob had told her not to say anything about Ralph or Ida. Now, she can't say anything about

Thomas and Joan. What would happen if she were to say something to someone about some of this? Who would be hurt? Who would be helped? Don't say anything. Don't these people understand how dangerous this could be?

"Thomas, what about Ralph? He was murdered. Joan could have been the one to murder him."

"No, she wouldn't do that."

"But you don't know for sure, do you?"

"No, perhaps not, but she's such a special person. Look how much she risked to help people out. There are many people who can't afford medical care. Just give us a few days. Please. Please wait a week, and then you can go to the police. I promise."

She looked at him smilingly pleading; then she looked at Joan visually begging and reluctantly agreed.

"Look," Emily said. "I'll wait a week to tell what I know. You're better off if you go to the police yourself and tell them what you know. I'm going to give you the name of a detective to talk to. If you're smart, you'll get an attorney and go see the police. Give your attorney the name of this detective. I know this man, and if, next week, I ask him about your talking to him, and he hasn't heard from you, I'm going to tell him what I know. Understand?"

"We understand," said Thomas.

Joan nodded in agreement. "We'll do it, Emily."

Thomas took Emily's hands and smiled a broad thank you.

CHAPTER 37

Within the next few days the costumes came together surprisingly well. Jojo was pleased with the muscle structure they had painted onto the bones of the skeleton. As David had pointed out, it looked like a first year biology student had forgotten to read his anatomy lesson before he dissected a cadaver, but that didn't bother Jojo. There were neatly lettered labels on each of the anatomical parts, and, fortunately, David convinced her she didn't really need all the bones and muscles on the skeleton. She just needed enough to give the idea of what she was trying to accomplish. Lulie's costume looked like it could be almost any surreal creature until she put on the carefully constructed nose. Then the costume came to life and looked like a creature of the spectacular East of the Sun Carnival ready to ignite anyone's fantasy.

Emily had to admit it was interesting to review the anatomy of the human body. Her child had picked an interesting activity and involved the family in creating it. The Kristichs should probably get 'Family of the Year' for being so together and focused as a family in doing a holiday project. Their joint costume making had turned out just like family magazines promised it would; it brought togetherness and laughter into their hearts. And learning. They had all learned something that would have value in their lives. She had decided Miriam needed to see the costumes and hear the tale of her family's enterprise.

During the drive to Miriam's Emily continued congratulating herself and her family for adhering so nicely to the ideal family image. Miriam needed some cheering up, and Emily thought she would pop in and see if she wished to go get a milkshake or malt for lunch. Obviously with her cheek…no, make that her buccinator…now that the Kristichs, utopian family that it had become, had studied its anatomy, correct terms should be used. Anyway, with her infected buccinator still healing, she couldn't very well do a real lunch. But they could find a good hamburger joint, so Miriam could have some robust liquid diet.

As Emily jaunted along in her minivan with the costumes in the backseat for Miriam's perusal and Byte in the front seat for Emily's company, she continued the cerebral pats on her family's back. Close to the gate of Miriam's hill but still on the main road before the turnoff to her street, Emily was so engrossed in her self-satisfaction that she didn't see the car coming toward her van. She was in the process of outlining the speech on how to be an outstanding mother when she accepted 'Mother of the Year' award, so she didn't even see the car cross the solid yellow line of the two-lane road. Later when she thought about the day, she would try to convince herself she didn't see the oncoming car because the drizzle created a sequined gauze and interfered with a clear view of the road. When she was honest with herself, she would admit she was daydreaming and wasn't paying attention to the road. As the avenue on which she was traversing had relatively few houses lining it and even fewer mature trees, her attention wasn't pricked until she felt the grayness of the day darken quickly as the car sped toward her.

She sensed, rather than saw, Byte's stiffening. The dog's body posture was enough to jostle Emily out of her dreamy daze to look attentively at the road. However, it was too late because she could not swerve to avoid the oncoming blue car. It had built up such a speed that when it hit her front quarter panel, the van slid onto the shoulder of the road and up onto the sidewalk. There it slammed a white fence and mowed down the straggly brown skeletal remains of flowers behind the pickets. Although her seatbelt was secure, Emily's head flew forward and was stopped in its backward arc by the headrest of her seat.

Byte compacted into the foot space of the passenger's seat with a howl. Emily shook her head to clear the gray mist that blended with the gray day and tried to turn her head to the right to stop the yowling by comforting the dog. Subconsciously she reached out her right hand to pet Byte, but the dog wasn't in the seat. Desperation at the thought the dog might be hurt overcame bewilderment at what had happened. Emily gave her head some help to turn by taking both her hands and placing them on the sides of her cheeks to force her head to move to the right. Byte lay compressed into the footspace of the car that was too small for her body. There was no more crying, and her eyes were closed.

"Byte," Emily cried. "Byte, wake up. Come on, Byte. Wake up. You can't be dead."

She leaned over the passenger seat to the dog as if by scrutinizing her closely, she could will movement back into the dog's body. A bullet spider webbing the passenger side of the window broke her intense concentration on the dog. She reared up and screamed, "Shiiiit! Not again!" Swiveling herself back into the driver's seat, she reached to unhook the seatbelt to get out of the car to go to Byte's side and release her. Her eyes, out of habit, glanced into the rear view mirror.

"No, it can't be!" she heaved just as the navy car came up quickly and wheeled over the sidewalk ready to ram her left rear end. She relaxed her back against the seat and squeezed her head against the headrest hoping to prevent it from flying forward. Byte was already pinched into a tight position, so she wouldn't be moving with the impact—if the dog were even able to move—if she weren't dead. Knowing she was unable to do anything to prevent it, she watched the oncoming crash in the rear view mirror with wide eyes not only at the anticipation of a horrible invasion onto her car, but also because she recognized the blue car and the person driving it. Only that blond head would be able to reflect any color in the meager light. The impact on her rear end deterred any other thoughts. In light of the circumstances this was a positive occurrence because Emily was enveloped in mixed feelings of panic concerning Byte's demise and consternation at what conclusion her brain was racking up concerning the identity of the killer.

As hard as the minivan had been hit both times, the car that had hit her was a robust, older American model, so it was heavier and able to drive off at a fast clip without any apparent damage. If Emily had paid more attention to car models when David talked about them, she might have been able to identify the year. She couldn't get the license plate, nor could she see the face of the driver, but she knew that pale blond hair, and she was dismayed that she thought she knew the driver. Even knowing the driver, she was still too dazed to figure out how it came together.

Her first priority was to check out Byte whose eyes were still closed. She couldn't get out the driver's side door because it had been jammed shut by the collision. It was easier to ease between the two front seats and go out the side door. Clearly the best way to get to Byte was using this technique to get to the sliding side door and open it to get to the passenger side door to extricate the canine. Emily stepped out of the car just as the drizzle became a hard rain. Standing in the shower, she opened Byte's door and knelt down to pet her.

"Byte, come on, Byte. Open your eyes. Please. I'll help you. Come on. Please be okay," she pled with the dog. Water sheeted off her raincoat as Emily continued petting and cajoling the dog to good health. Raindrops spattered the dog and the vinyl seat of the car, and it was those raindrops that brought Byte out of her oblivion. As she blinked the rain off her eyelids, they popped open and gave Emily a baffled look. Byte blinked as the rain hit her eyes and tried to get up. Even though her paws were lying under her curved body, she seemed to be bent in the middle and was unable to find footing to lift herself off the floor. Trying to give the dog more room in which to maneuver, Emily moved the front seat to its most rearward position. Emily reached under Byte and tried to turn her head and body toward the open door. If Byte had been a cup dog, there would be no problem; however, her ninety pounds made for no light task. Then, Emily brought Byte's front paws into her hands and let Byte use her hands as a push-off to heave her body out of the foot space of the car. It worked. Byte was able to push against Emily's hands and loosen her body out of the cramped position and onto the ground. Still looking perplexed, Byte shook to bring herself to complete consciousness and to shake rain off her coat.

"How are you feeling, pup?" smiled Emily hopefully.

A tentative wagging of the tail signified she was functioning, albeit slowly. She walked in a small circle a few times, came back and gave Emily a swipe of her tongue which set Emily to sputtering away the dog lips. Emily returned the affection with a hug around the ruff of Byte's neck.

"It may be time to invest in a dog seatbelt. You're lucky you went down instead of out the window."

Emily opened the back hatch of the vehicle and urged Byte to enter into it. Emily put the dog's front paws onto the ledge and lifted while the dog simultaneously jumped. After closing the hatch Emily crawled back to the driver's side through the side gate and rummaged around in her purse for the cell phone. Just as she dialed 911, the phone beeped and discharged its last spurt of energy.

"Moral of the story," muttered Emily, "plug in at night. Now we've got to get this baby started, or it's a wet walk to Miriam's."

Emily was able to get the car off the sidewalk. No one had come out of the house to complain about the fence, so it was mandatory to get to Miriam's to contact the police. She knew Miriam was home, and she could use the phone there. She calculated she could probably get to Miriam's house which was only a left turn and gate opening away. The front of the car was deformed enough that steering was a feat in itself. Holding the steering wheel in opposition to the tires on the bent frame of the car to get the car to move in a straight line, she tried turning left onto Miriam's street. That was near to impossible, so she stopped the car at the bottom of the hill, got out at the gate, pressed the code for the Rose residence and let the rain finish off her already wilted hair. While the gate slid open at its interminably slow pace, she got Byte out of the car, put her leash on her, snatched the bag holding the costumes and her purse to proceed through the now-open gate in a trek up to Miriam's house. If Miriam, dressed in a purple and red caftan, were not still recuperating from their highway shooting, Emily would have fallen into her arms with relief as she opened the front door.

Miriam said, "Well, well, look what the proverbial cat dragged in. Only in your case, it looks like your literal dog is dragging you in. Or maybe you're dragging the dog—it's hard to tell, you both look so bedraggled. What happened?"

Holding the bag out to Miriam like an offering, Emily said, "I wanted to bring the kids' costumes to show them to you because I was so proud of what we had all created, and someone banged my van from the front and rear—deliberately. Then they shot at my car–just like Rochelle's car on the freeway. Whoever hit me ran my car up into someone's yard at the bottom of your hill, and I need a telephone to call the police. My phone is lying in disgrace at the bottom of my purse because it ran out of energy. My car is lying in a huddle at the entrance to your gate. Your homeowners' association is going to have it towed away as unbecoming to the neighborhood aura."

"I doubt it. Harold's president of it, and they call us with their complaints. Look, right now you're upset. Why don't you take a warm shower, and I'll get you some tea to drink? Then you can call the police. Towels in the guest bath are clean. Go on up. I'll get a towel for Byte and dry her off. We'll get to the costumes. Take some time to calm down, okay?"

"Can she stay in your garage? She was hurt during the collision, and I didn't want to keep her in the car. I want to watch her for a while. I think she's okay, but, after I talk with the police, I probably need to get her to the vet. And being wet like she is, I don't want to put her outside because she needs to dry off. Is that okay?"

"No, she can't stay in the garage."

"Oh." Emily was taken aback.

"But she can stay here with us. Poor thing has been traumatized." Miriam bent down to rub the dog's ears. "So have you. Go on up, Em. If you need to, lie down on the guest bed. Then we'll look at the costumes."

I came over to comfort Miriam, and she's the one comforting me. Emily appreciated the irony as she trudged up the stairs to take a warm and comforting shower.

CHAPTER 38

"So I'd like to talk to Detective Washburn as soon as he arrives. Tell him it's about Sustain and Shelter and give him my name, Emily Kristich, please. It's extremely urgent. Then you'll send someone over to look at the car, will you?" Emily restated the request she had made to the police operator. "Thank you. Yes, that's the address."

"Are you all right?" Miriam asked anxiously. The shower had washed some color back into Emily's face. She didn't look as ashen as when she first showed up at Miriam's door.

As Emily nodded affirmatively, Miriam said, "It's now my turn to take you to the emergency room."

"No, truly, I'm fine. I'll have a headache tomorrow, but, right now, I'm fine. Byte seems to be doing okay."

"You got that right. She wolfed down the roast beef sandwich I gave her. I think she thought she was supposed to get my fingers for dessert.

"So tell me about the accident," Miriam said as she brought tea to Emily. "Give me all the details."

"Okay, but look at these costumes while I tell you. Jojo and Lulie gave me the design. They thought of them all by themselves. Jojo's is really creative. Some people won't know what Lulie's is if they haven't been to East of the Sun and West of the Moon carnival, but the nose is what makes it. I suppose they'll think she's a court jester with that extra long nose. Look at this nose, isn't it just..." Emily's adjective trailed off as she looked at the nose and then looked out the French doors of the breakfast nook to the Emorys' house on the hill, then back at the nose. For a few minutes, time stopped as she stared unseeingly at the apex of the hill while the rain percolated at the windows.

"Em, are you okay? I really think I need to take you to the hospital. You look like you're getting ready to pass out. Like a concussion or something. We need to go to the..."

Emily jumped up. "Miriam, I'm sorry. When the police come, tell them about the car and where it is. Please. Please let Byte stay here. I'll be back." She grabbed her raincoat and ran out the back door, but then peeked her head around. "If Bob Washburn calls, tell him where I am. Tell him to come as soon as he can. The officer I spoke to said he should be calling in soon, and she'd give him the message."

"But where are you?" shouted Miriam. She didn't get the answer from Emily. Instead, she got it as she followed Emily's progress up the hill to the house at its top until Emily was shielded by the line of firs planted to protect the Emorys' house from its neighbors' interest.

Emily began the odyssey to the Emory house with determination, but as she slogged through the rivulets of water and the slimy mud on the road, her boldness flagged. Even with her aerobics training, her heart pumped hard enough for her to hear its beats correspond to the cadence of her footsteps. Neck muscles started tightening, but whether it was from the accident or wariness in approaching the Emory house, she wasn't sure. As she tramped through the turbid water washing down the road, she smiled slightly to herself thinking the conclusion she had drawn seemed preposterous. The effects of the accident must now be wearing off, so she felt she was more clearheaded than she had been at Miriam's house. It was thought of in such a flash when she looked at that nose. It's almost ridiculous. Almost a joke. But, then, why wasn't she laughing at the humor of her conclusion? It was just a costume, a Halloween costume, at that. It wasn't a disguise. Lulie, her six year old daughter, held the key all the time, and no one realized it, least of all Lulie. Someday Emily might tell Lulie how the nose on her costume made her mother draw such an outlandish conclusion. But, again, if it's so outlandish, why keep going?

As she was almost at the Emory house, she decided she'd stop in and ask a few questions. She arrived on the front porch, waited a minute for her heart to slow the output of blood, rang the doorbell and heard a rendition of the Westminster chime. No response. She rang again. No response. As she turned to leave, the door opened slightly. Platinum hair warily edged around the door. Slowly a face emerged, saw Emily, smiled tentatively and invited her in.

Emily guided her body in through the opening keeping her back to the other closed half of the double doors. Looking around the room, she was appalled. If the outside had been an architectural gaffe, the inside was a decorating nightmare. The interior of the house was as disjointed as the structure of the family living in it. There were three levels including the ground floor. The oak balconies on each floor provided the hallways for each tier and circled the entire level giving the house the look of Shakespeare's Globe Theater. Two stairways sited at each half of the surrounding balcony provided egress to the next level.

Various area rugs of bold colored geometric designs, Chinese flowered pastels and deep hued Persian patterns were scattered across the black marble floor that covered the entire downstairs area. In one area a blue leather sofa and chairs were arranged around a big-screened television for an entertainment area. There was an ebony dining table with seating for twenty around which were twenty wrought iron chairs for the dining room. A French Provincial grouping covered in sea-blue moiré satin designated a parlor. The kitchen, placed on a wall near the dining room setting, was a red and black glass tile galley affair. If Emily had not been standing in a house, she thought the place could easily have been a furniture store because of the variety of groupings set about the downstairs. Before the woman of the house said anything. Emily had ample time to survey the interior of the house.

Not surprised to see her, Mrs. Emory greeted Mrs. Kristich but didn't look her in the eye. Her body carriage drooped so much that even the spikes of her hair seemed limp. Emily cocked her head in scrutiny of her. The longer she looked, the less sure she was in her conclusion.

Emily's clear voice was searching as she said, "I came to talk about the car."

"Your car? What do you mean your car? I don't know anything about your car."

"I didn't come to talk to you about my car."

"What do you mean?" Anxiety filled both the voice and the face.

"Come on, you know exactly what I mean. I came to talk to the person who hit my car."

"Well, then talk to me," laughed the woman nervously.

"No, you aren't the one I came to talk to." Emily paused.

"When you said you had a job, I didn't think it meant you had to go away. It was as though you fell off the face of the earth. I didn't understand where you went. I never saw you again, Blythe."

"That's right. You will never see her again. There is no Blythe. That pathetic, homeless woman is gone."

"No, she's standing right in front of me. She's not homeless, and she's not pathetic, but she's still on the face of the earth."

"No," the woman screamed. "No, you can't do this to me." She clamped her hands on her head and turned. With hands still on her head, she turned to her other side. "You can't know about this. Don't you see? You're going to ruin this. You can't ruin it. I told you to stay away. I warned you. You can't do this to me."

The platinum haired woman raised her fists against Emily who grabbed them and held the woman's hands in the air.

"You can't do this. You're going to ruin it for all of us. The children. They need me. Me. They need me. Don't you see? I'm the one who protects them. She neglected Scott, and Samantha couldn't be there all the time to make up for his mother. You can't ruin this for them. You can't ruin it for me. Those children need me. There is no Blythe. She's gone. Leave us alone."

She wrenched her hands from Emily's grip in a downward jerk and ran out the door into the rain sobbing the same phrases repeatedly. Emily, her back still to the wall, surveyed the garish house from the third floor balcony to the bottom floor. Seeing nothing but costly and outlandish furnishings, she turned to the partially opened double doors to go back toward Miriam's and, she hoped, to find Blythe to calm her down.

"Stay right there, bitch," warned a husky voice. "Turn slowly and come to the center of the room. I've got a gun, and you must know by now, I can kill in one shot."

Emily hesitated.

The voice was more demanding. "Do it now, or you'll never get the chance to move again."

As Emily turned slowly toward the voice coming from the second floor balcony, she wondered why the change wasn't apparent last summer. The voices should have alerted Emily to the fact Rochelle wasn't Rochelle. If that hadn't, there was the change in Scott. In less than a summer, he had started reading. Why, Emily asked herself, why didn't she perceive it then? Such subtle differences then and glaring incongruities now.

Emily turned away from the door, kept her back to the wall and walked against the walls as slowly as she could until she came upon the open galley of the kitchen and had no more wall to hug. She then advanced toward the center of the room keeping her eyes up toward the balcony on the figure as she approached her.

"You sneak. You underhanded, dirty little sneak. You were so nosy. I knew you took those financials. That stupid Ida. I told her to deliver those directly to me or Rudyard. When you kept asking for them, I realized you had to be the one who took them when they weren't in the drawer. You have just about messed up everything I've set up," Rochelle said. She came down the stairs to trap Emily in the circular room. "I hate it when anything messes up my plans.

"I'm not going to let it happen though. No one knows what you've got. They couldn't begin to figure it out. Ida and I worked out those statements, so that she and I were the only ones who knew where that money was. Even Chad can't decipher them completely, and, believe you me, he's tried. Wherever you've deep-sixed those papers, they'll stay there. You are gone. You are history."

Emily licked her dry lips and squeaked out of her even drier throat, "I know about Ida and Ralph. I know how they got too close to the truth."

"No, chicky. You don't know." Rochelle had eased herself down the staircase, so Emily had to keep her eyes on Rochelle's gun. In so doing, Emily had to turn away from the door because Rochelle had placed herself in front of Emily with her back to the front door. Even though it was still ajar, Emily wouldn't be able to escape out of it because Rochelle blocked her path.

This time Emily's voice was strong, "Yes, Rochelle, I know about them. I know why you shot them. I know Ralph found out about stealing the drugs from the hospital; I know about the money laundering. I can even guess how it's done. However, I can't figure out how you got Blythe in on this."

"You can buy anybody," she sneered. "I bet I could even buy you, but I don't want to. I just want you out of the way. Blythe was a convenience, you're not. I hate those stupid kids of mine. They are a damned pain in the ass."

Emily interrupted. "Then, why? Why'd you have them? You could've chosen not to."

Rochelle shook her head at the stupidity of Emily's question. "It was easier to keep Geoffrey on the hook. I needed him as my cover. Make him think he's a man because he fathered a couple kids and then kick him out of my bed. If there are kids around, I can use them as leverage; he won't want to get a divorce because the mother of his children might take away his kids. Kids are annoying. Always having to do stuff for them, and they're always asking questions. The boy's dumb. He can't read; he walks around with his head on his chest. What a wimpy kid. The girl is okay; she's smart. But, the boy, can't stand him. If I hadn't come up with my latest brilliance, I was going to ship him off to boarding school. Would've done it earlier, but the girl likes having him. If he's around, I don't have to do much with her. Now, with Blythe around to deal with all that family shit my job is easier. I'll keep her around as long as she's useful. I hate playing happy housewife. Then, one day, bang, she's gone." She snorted a laugh. "Blythe wanted kids so much, she'd take anybody's. She'd even lose her identity to have kids. It was perfect. Even Geoffrey, that prick, doesn't even know his own wife is not his own wife."

She started laughing hysterically at that. As tears of laughter coursed down her face she said, "Can you imagine? He'll go on for years and not know he's got a different woman sitting at his dining table? Serves him right, him and his stupid family. They think they are the answer to all the world's problems. That's another thing. With Blythe around, I don't have to sit on those boards and do all that charity work for those hopeless people. She does all that wife-of-a-successful-man shit.

"I got this brilliant idea when I understood it takes two of me to run my business, one to cover and one to work. Just a little nip and tuck here and there on another body, and I can do anything I need to keep my business going. Blythe and I are the same body build. Plastic surgery can do amazing things. It's as good as being in two places at once." She laughed harshly. "I am so brilliant. If any of those career women want to see a woman succeed without a glass ceiling to stop them, they should see my operation. I hold the power. Nobody touches me."

Rochelle, using the gun to direct Emily to start walking toward her, paused before she declared. "I am wonderful. Do you hear? WOOOON DER FUL. You sat in that meeting and rode all over Rudyard for his attitude about women. You dumb cluck. Don't you see that's how to get ahead? I played that dumb role with Rudyard, and, now, I control everything. I control the money; I control those men. All because I played him for the sucker he is. You should take a lesson from me, girl. Don't get on your high horse; use it to your advantage. Those two assholes are scared to death of me and will do anything I say." Again, Rochelle laughed at her own huge joke. Emily glanced around with her eyes, but Rochelle straightened the weapon in her grip.

Just as quickly as it roiled up, the laughter died, and her tone was menacing. "No one messes up my operation. Not Ralph. Not Ida. And certainly not you. Ralph was going to tell the cops about Joan stealing those drugs for the clinic. So I invited him to leave this world just a little ahead of his time."

"Why so obvious? You were so obvious about where you put Ralph."

"Me? That wasn't me. Stupid Chad did that. Should have shot him for that. It was an invitation to the police to come and get Chad. What a dope! He did it because he thought it'd scare the others if they knew Ralph was gone. Stupid, stupid Chad. He didn't do it with Ida; hid her real good. Threatened him with his life if he made some boob mistake like that again. May still have to get rid of him. Made him hide her good, not like Ralph.

"Ida, what a bore. She told Rudyard she wasn't going to keep the books any longer. Can you imagine? She actually thought she could leave my organization with that kind of information. If she told someone what was going on, I could be out in the open. I can't operate that way. What a dope she was. They're all dopes—except Blythe. I don't have to worry about Blythe, not as long as she thinks she's protecting those kids. That's the only use they've ever been to me, an insurance policy. Such a business deal."

She moved the gun toward the door to show Emily where to go. "I want you out there. We've got a drive to take. You will walk out the front door first, and I will walk behind you. We're taking Blythe's car; I'm dumping you in it. Blythe is gone, blown off the face of the earth as far as anyone is concerned. If they ever put together it's Blythe's car, and they will, they'll think she did you in, but they won't be able to find her. You and your goody two shoes attitude. They'll think you were playing Jane Addams and trying to rescue a poor, homeless person.

"Are you understanding now how smart I am? I have virtually eliminated Blythe Oberstein, yet I can pin a murder on her, and they'll never find her. Even when she's under their own noses. They'll never find her. She knows it, too. She knows she no longer exists; she is a non-person. I can get rid of her, and no one will even care. No home, no identity, no person. She is, basically, well, she's my slave. Give her those kids, and she's my slave. Now, that's power.

"Move."

Emily prolonged the walk as much as possible as they withdrew out the door. She had left a message for Bob Washburn to return her call, and Miriam knew to tell him it was important. Miriam didn't know she was in danger, though; she hoped Bob would realize the danger. All Miriam was aware of was the car lying in a heap at the bottom of Bluebird Hill. What a grand mess. And where was Blythe? Hope against hope, could she have gone for help? Or had hysterics muddled her rationality? If she had the presence of mind to go for help, would it come on time?

The soft drizzle that was enveloping the two women as they stepped onto the porch reminded Emily of Ida and the watery environment in which her body had been lodged. Emily dreaded the thought and supposed that was to be her fate also. At least, she wouldn't feel the fish and bacteria eating away her water-swollen skin. Nor would she be fearful of a foreign environment. How could she be afraid? She'd be dead.

Dead. The word burned a neon agony into her brain. No Jojo and Lulie to watch grow up. No David to help with his business. No Louisa to shower motherly worry over her adult daughter. She strained to hear the sirens she fervently hoped were on their way, but there was nothing. Why should there be? The police were just going to examine her car and file a report; it wasn't like she had called in a need for a rifle team. She desperately scanned the area around her for clues she could leave like Hansel had done with breadcrumbs. As if to torment Emily, the rain began to drive harder and pelted the two women causing Emily to give up the thought of leaving clues because she realized just as birds ate Hansel's signs, the rain would probably wash away her clues.

Where was Bob? She needed help so desperately. Where was Bob?

Bob wasn't going to be available for some time. He and Detective Yoshiwara had just arrested Chad Woodley. Chad Woodley wasn't going to divulge information for some time. He had just asked for his lawyer. Rudyard Millup wasn't going to wait around to see what tale Chad and his lawyer were going to create, not after Shannon called to tell him of Chad's arrest. He had just arrived at the Oakland airport to board a plane to Mexico. All this was occurring because Emily had told Joan to give Bob information regarding Chad's, Joan's and Thomas's roles in stealing drugs from County Hospital. Joan's responsibility was laudable; her timing was lamentable.

Emily's unscheduled appointment with a hit-woman was going to be kept.

CHAPTER 39

Rochelle anticipated Emily's stalling when she said, "We've got all the time in the world, so you can stall as much as you wish, bitch. Houses in this neighborhood aren't near enough to each other for people to get curious about us. If they can even see us in this rain, they'll think we're going out to lunch or something because that's what ladies of my social standing do—go to nice, long lunches. They spend their husband's money on their empty lives. Keep moving."

But Emily had stopped their walk down the cobblestone-lined path to the garage. She could feel the gun Rochelle was holding jam into her upper back. She turned slightly to try to face Rochelle and got an angled look at her face. The smirk on Rochelle's face had crept up to her eyes giving them a hard, flinty fix. Realizing there was no chance of reversing Rochelle's resolve to end Emily's life, she turned back to face the front and allow Rochelle to continue her dawdling nudge to Blythe's blue sedan.

"How'd you get into this?" Emily filibustered.

"It's not going to work, you know."

"What's not going to work?"

"The stalling. People, if they realize I'm going to shoot them, try all kinds of things to put it off. It doesn't work. But my story is interesting; I'll tell it to you. You're a fairly sharp woman; you'll probably like hearing how I bested the world. I have everything I want, power and money. It only takes two things to make life—money and power. I've got them both. A woman who's the best in her field. That should appeal to you. Too bad I can't write an autobiography. It'd be a bestseller. People love violence, and I could give it to them in spades. I'm one of the best hit men in the business. I could make millions with my story. Then, I wouldn't have to be married to that rich prick, Geoffrey. But if I wrote the story, I couldn't do the job I love. So I'll keep Blythe married to Geoffrey as long as I need. It's not a bad identity. In fact, it's such a genius thing to do. No one knows. Well, you do, but you're going to be gone, so it doesn't matter. So, you want to hear my story? Here goes.

"Enjoy it because it's the last entertainment you're going to have. I used my network. I've spent years networking and making my contacts. I like guns, and I always have. I know everything about rifles, shotguns and handguns, and I know how to use almost all of them. I am an expert. I know it all. That's the one thing that dirt-poor excuse of a father gave me, knowledge of guns. I could shoot anything—cans, targets, cars, animals, people—from the time I was six years old. Plus I'm smart. I'm so smart I've managed to avoid any record of my existence. I know how to organize and manage. Just like any business.

"Disguises, fringe people, hey, it's a big country. You wouldn't even recognize the real me. Hell, there are times I almost forget the real me. Plastic surgery, money—I can lose myself real easy anytime I want." She laughed her nasty, harsh guffaw.

"Who would imagine the wife of Geoffrey Emory doing my job? It was absolutely perfect. What a goof. I hate that stuffed shirt. Always wants me to do things for the well-being of the community. That's how I met Rudyard and, then, Chad. Rudyard always has some scam going, and when he met Chad through his work with the homeless, it was a natural fit. That Chad has been milking those start-from-scratch bleeding heart agencies for years. Rudyard is a pompous fart. Put the two of those sociopaths together, and they were making the big bucks."

Sociopaths. If they're sociopaths, you, Rochelle, are a true psychopath, thought Emily. After Blythe, whom else would Rochelle kill? Who else would get in her way?

Emily stopped slightly; Rochelle jammed the gun harder into her back. "Keep moving."

"Ida?" Emily asked dully.

"Ida," mocked Rochelle. "I should have known. Even before I trained her, I should have known. Stupid old maid. Thought that once she had Rudyard's name, she'd have a fairy tale life. I told her no one lives happily ever after. Almost got her trained. Showed her how to skim Rudyard's money; showed her where to stash it; showed her when to blackmail him. But he still ignored her. She could've walked away at any time, but, no, she said she loved him. Loved him. Weak old prune. Love's not an answer; not a reason for doing anything."

The dullness of her frustration gave Emily no impetus of ideas to stop Rochelle and her one-woman killing bent. If anything, Emily would soon be leveled to ineffectiveness because her situation was inalterably pessimistic. She could feel the tears of despair edge themselves into her consciousness. Those same tears that so often wipe away the downheartedness of a situation and enable one to progress to solutions to seemingly unsolvable predicaments were not going to allow her to see an auspicious conclusion to this waterloo. If she yielded to the tears, she would lose any grip on her present state. Instead of giving her renewed strength, tears, at this juncture, would display a weakness that Rochelle would use to scornfully insult her. Maintenance of dignity at the thought of a bullet in the back of her head was difficult enough now. Crying now would only dissolve her into a puddle of dithering nerves.

The slow walk to her hearse dampened Emily's spirit, just as the cloud cover that produced the rain that jabbed icily at their faces dampened the sounds of the environment. The quiet was as deafening as the gloom was blinding. Emily's death march was almost at an end when they heard the low roll of distant thunder.

CHAPTER 40

Both women started at the thunder. It is a noise alien to the California coast and, because of that, always a surprise when it rumbles. Thunderstorms in Pleasant Creek are as rare as earthquakes in Florida. The women looked to their right, but, as they did, Rochelle clutched the gun harder and pushed it into Emily's back. Emily fleetingly wondered if there would be enough bruises on her back to make a coroner suspicious as to how they came to be. As the women shot their gazes to the front, furious panting consumed their attention. Looking again to their right they saw the massive broadness of wet fur and teeth gritted in fierce wrath bound out of the hedges behind the cobblestones. With the low, angry growl earlier mistaken for thunder, the creature leapt between Emily and Rochelle separating the two women and slamming Rochelle's right forearm against her body.

Rochelle, split timing so critical to her profession, reacted with alacrity in squeezing the trigger of the weapon she held. Emily, surprised at the sudden lurch from the bushes, gasped and fell onto her left side as the huge dog catapulted her body into the space separating the two women. The bullet from the fired handgun ricocheted off one of the cobblestones lining the pathway to hit Rochelle in the chest. Pulling at her arm in a vicious clamp, the dog tackled her in midfall. Emily scrambled off the wet pavement and hustled to Rochelle.

"Byte, away. Down!" she commanded as she pushed the flat of her hand in midair. "Down."

Reluctantly Byte dropped Rochelle's arm, went down on all fours and issued a soft, intense snarl from deep within her body. Ears perked, eyes engrossed in Emily's slightest move, nose quivering at the smell of human emotions, and body readied to spring, Byte scrutinized the scene before her. The bloody patch that threatened to blanket the chest of Rochelle's rain cape materialized only as a watermarked, pink abstract. Raindrops squelched the vivacity of the red blood and flowed off Rochelle's body in muddy red rivulets. The splashing pools into which the rain accumulated injected the only liveliness into the scene of death.

Emily held Rochelle's head and said, "Hang on. I'll get help. I'll go in the house and get help."

Rochelle's eye slits tried to focus on Emily, and her mouth worked into a smirk. "I hate dogs," she sneered quietly. "Used to have dreams about them. I could control humans, but not dogs. I hate…"

"Life. Rochelle. You hate life." Emily finished Rochelle's statement as she died.

Emily laid Rochelle's head onto the pavement. Shoulders slumped and head down, she moved closer to Byte still on all fours and guarded in her watchfulness of Emily. Emily sat on a row of cobblestones, hunched over and released Byte with the word, "Come." Byte sauntered over to her mistress, raked Emily's face with her tongue and sat as closely as she could without climbing onto her lap.

Gazing into the dog's eyes, she said, "You got out, didn't you? You think you're smarter than me, don't you? You knew it was dangerous; I didn't think it would be. I'm not sure what I thought."

Byte raked her face again in response. Emily reached out one arm to wrap around Byte's back and gathered the dog even closer to her. There they sat in a rain, now gently warming, watching Rochelle's body lose completely any semblance of life it had had. It was one of the few times Emily could recall where the rain made her sad.

Emily and Byte forlornly continued in their still life watching Rochelle's body stiffen as death and cold continued its work on her body. The rain splashed the puddles around the body in exclamation points. In their vigil, woman and dog were impervious to the drenching. Byte pricked her ears and turned them like small satellite dishes. Emily continued looking at the body.

"Come on, Byte. Let's go get some help. This isn't helping anyone while we stay here."

The rustle of bushes sounded like a taffeta petticoat as Blythe slowly broached the distance between the hedge lining the driveway and the stones on which Emily and Byte roosted.

"Where were you?" asked Emily tonelessly.

Hesitation marred Blythe's explanation. "I don't know. Down there, I guess. There's a wild area out there. I guess I headed there. I didn't know where I was going." She stood off to Emily's left behind her.

"Did you see what happened?"

"Some."

"You couldn't come to help?"

"I didn't think she'd hurt you," Blythe said.

Emily threw her head in Blythe's direction and said through clenched teeth, "You didn't think she'd hurt me? Aren't you the same woman who was so hysterical because she realized who fired the bullet on the freeway? You knew then she was a killer. That's why you were crying; you were afraid. She was going to kill you, wasn't she?"

"No, she was going to kill you. She was going to scare me."

"And you're telling me now that you didn't think she'd hurt me? You warned me in the parking lot. That's who you were warning me against, isn't it? I thought you were telling me Rudyard would make it unpleasant for me on the board, but you were telling me about Rochelle. And you couldn't come and help?"

"I just didn't realize…" Blythe trailed off lamely.

"You've got to be kidding," Emily finished with a derisive snort. Byte jumped into a protective stance as Blythe approached her mistress.

Blythe, mud splotches staining her wet lime green and orange jumpsuit, tried to hold Emily's wintry eyes with her own imploring ones.

"I didn't live with her. I didn't know. No one knew. She didn't live here. She only came when no one was home. They couldn't know there were two of us. She made threats, but I didn't think they were that serious. I mean, I wasn't sure about Ralph. It could've been anything. She just hinted at her killing him."

"Do you want to explain how you can take over this woman's identity, including her body, and think no one knows?"

"Please, Emily, please. Listen to me. Please, for the sake of my kids. They need me." She groveled all but kneeling before Emily.

"Your kids? What do you mean your kids?" Emily spat out.

"Listen to me!" Blythe screamed. "Just listen. How can you sit there and not try to understand what those children need? You, who have your children on a pedestal above the angels? How can you not understand what I have to tell you? Give me a chance. Your kids and you have each other, and that's all each of you needs. That's what these kids need, too. I love them. No one needs to know I'm not their natural mother. I can be like her, only better and love them more. You love your kids; why can't you let my kids have a mother who loves them as much as you love yours?"

Invoking her own children in her entreaty struck Emily's Achilles heel and diluted her distaste for Blythe.

Blythe sensing Emily would capitulate pressed on. "Look, Rochelle came to me and told me she needed help because she couldn't be all the things she needed to be for her kids. She told me about Scott not reading; she told me how Samantha was more of a mother than she was.

She asked if I'd help her. I've always wanted kids. I wanted them more than anything else in the world. It was no secret; that was one of the first things I told you when I met you. My marriage was bad, and not having kids was even worse. I'd do anything to have some kids, so I said I'd do it."

"But why didn't you just become a nanny or something normal? You went through plastic surgery to look just like her. Why?"

"She said she didn't want to disrupt them by making them think their mother had given up. She wanted them to think she was being a better mother, that she had changed for the better. If I looked like her, they wouldn't know any change had occurred.

"It made sense to me. People are always going through plastic surgery— for lots of different reasons. The surgery wasn't so bad. Look I get kids and a nice life." Blythe said with quiet doubt and eyes averted from Emily.

"You weren't worried about the consequences? What was Rochelle going to do to you when she didn't need you?"

"She'd always need me. As long as the kids needed me, she'd always need me."

"And when they didn't?"

"But they always would. I'd make sure of it."

"Oh, brother," said Emily as she rolled her eyes. "Didn't you think for even one minute that was peculiar? No one goes to a caretaker and makes them look identical to someone else. Didn't you think she might be hiding something? Didn't you think she would want some pay-off that you couldn't deliver?"

"What do you mean?" Blythe asked blankly.

"You haven't a clue, have you? We just talked about your suspicions regarding Rochelle's profession, as she called it."

"I don't know what you're talking about."

"Blythe…"

"I told you before. There is no Blythe. That woman is gone. She could be dead. Call me Rochelle. Blythe is dead," commanded Blythe as she glanced at the dead body at the feet of the women.

Surprised, Emily said, "She killed Ida and Ralph. Don't you see?"

"No, that's impossible," Blythe said questioningly as she looked at the dead body. "No, that's a terrible thing to say."

"Blythe."

"Rochelle. I said, Rochelle."

"Rochelle, who do you think shot at us on the highway? That was Roche…her." Emily pointed to the body.

She started to agree. "Ye…" and then changed her mind and said, "No, I don't know what you're talking about. I don't think you know what you're talking about."

Emily looked at the woman now dubbed Rochelle stubbornly holding firm that she knew nothing of the deaths, looked at her dripping platinum hair, looked at the torn jumpsuit, looked at the sodden, orange leather shoes so loaded with mud they looked like rocks on her feet. She was guarding her ignorance of Ida and Ralph's deaths as firmly as Byte was guarding Emily.

"Please, Emily. We'll go away. Blythe's gone."

She whispered the last plea. "Don't tell anyone."

Don't tell anyone. Again, there's that phrase again. Emily was becoming a reliquary for dead secrets. How many more situations was she not to tell? How much could she forget? How much would mesh together, so that all she could remember was one large, complicated lie?

"Do you know what you're asking?" Emily questioned.

"Yes," she answered firmly. "I'm asking you to save a family."

"How can you possibly hope to pull something as insane as this off? You have three, or more, other people involved."

"I can pull it off. People lose themselves all the time. The children want a good mother so badly, they'll not question where she comes from.

Geoffrey isn't home enough to notice changes in his wife. I can pull it off. I promise. Don't tell anyone."

"Geoffrey," Emily said thoughtfully. "How can a husband not know who his wife is? Plastic surgery can do a lot, but it can't change your whole body. He'll know in the bedroom, if you ever get back to it."

Rochelle's face reddened. "He doesn't know. He hasn't been in her bedroom for years. She hated him so much she threw him out. That's one reason he travels. There's no marriage. The feeling must be mutual because when he's home, he only talks to the children. Don't you see, maybe I can make a difference for the whole family–him, too. Maybe it will work. He loves those kids; I see it when he's with them. She made it so hard for him to show love to those kids. She lied to the kids about their father and told them how bad he is, and how much he dislikes them. Said the reason he traveled was to get away from them. The real reason he traveled was to stay away from her. Please understand. I can rescue them all. I can make this a good family. Those kids deserve parents who love them. Help me. Please."

"What about Rudyard and Chad? They'll know."

"They're not much of a threat."

"How do you know?" asked Emily.

"She said so. She made sure they never knew exactly who shot Ralph and Ida. She scammed them as much as they scammed the public. She hinted to them I was the one who arranged for Ralph and Ida to be shot; I was the one with the connections. Sometimes she'd make them think Bo was the one with the connections. She was a master at making people believe lies about other people."

"I thought you didn't know about the operation."

"You're right. I don't."

With that she turned to go back to the house.

"Where are you going, Rochelle?" asked Emily.

Rochelle slowly turned and said, "I'm going into the house to get cleaned up. Then, I'm calling the police."

"They're on their way."

"How do you know? Did you call them?"

"Awhile ago. Before I came up here. Roche…, no, Blythe intentionally ran into me and wrecked my car. It's a mess. I called them then."

"Then, instead of calling the police, I am going to get in my car and drive away. Then I will drive back into the house when they're here."

"Why?"

"So I can tell them I know nothing about this. They'll think I've been away," Rochelle answered.

Emily acknowledged Rochelle's plan with a slight nod.

"What will you tell them?" Rochelle asked cautiously.

"I'll think of something," replied Emily dully.

CHAPTER 41

The detectives' car splashed up high banks of water as it charged through puddles up the hill and braked short of the garage door. Detective Washburn spilled his height out the passenger's seat of the car. Byte again placed herself in front of Emily as the detectives approached her.

To the dog, he said holding out a downward fist, "It's okay, Byte." To Emily, he said, "What happened?"

"First tell me. Couldn't you have come sooner?"

Bob stared at Emily, then surveyed the surrounds and sighed. "Looks like you needed help. Maybe lots of it. I couldn't get here, and I'm sorry." Emily breathed in, put her palm up and moved it side-to-side as if she could erase the past few hours. "No, it's okay. Everything worked out, I guess."

"Just so you know, Emily, so you know we're not holding out on you. We arrested Chad Woodley."

"Anyone else?"

Bob smiled slightly. "Not going to let me off easy, are you? You know, the reason we could arrest Chad was because of the bargain you struck with Joan Chavez. She's talking with the district attorney now."

Emily nodded. "Great."

There was a pause. Emily repeated, "Anyone else?"

"Pretty close. Guess the secretary, what's her name…"

"Shannon."

"Guess Shannon alerted Rudyard to Chad's arrest. She didn't mean to, but she needed to know what was going on when the police took him from the office. He's probably at the station, now."

"So what happened, Mrs. Kristich?" asked Detective Yoshiwara.

As Byte relaxed, Emily related the story of the wrecked van at the bottom of the hill.

"Who's that?" Bob Washburn asked pointing to the body.

"I'm not sure. I think it might be Blythe Oberstein, a woman who said she was homeless."

"She's dead."

"Yes."

"Do you know how?"

Emily looked a long time at Bob Washburn and his partner before saying, "Byte got out of Miriam's house, and I had to chase her up here. Just as I came up the hill, I thought I saw her raise her hand. It had a gun in it. I couldn't stop her.

"I guess she shot herself," Emily said without conviction.

"You guess?"

"Right. She shot herself," she said unequivocally.

"Why?"

"I don't know. She was homeless. Maybe it got to her."

"Right," Bob said doubtfully, "maybe it did."

Emily looked away from Bob's eyes first. Again he asked, "What happened, Emily? How did she shoot herself?"

As Detective Washburn went to examine the dead body more thoroughly, the new Rochelle drove up in her Rolls.

Her hair was tucked into a rain hat, and she wore a long raincoat.

"Oh, my gosh!" She feigned coy surprise.

"What is Blythe Oberstein doing here? She isn't dead, is she?" she said to no one in particular.

"It looks like a suicide," said Bob Washburn.

Rochelle had the courtesy to look gravely distressed while she said, "Poor thing."

"Do you know this woman, ma'am?" asked the accompanying detective.

Detective Washburn leaned against the pillar of the house and watched Rochelle's response. When Emily glanced at him, he glared at her until she dropped her eyes.

"Oh yes. She sat on a board of directors with me. Well, Emily, too. Only Emily didn't know her as well as I did. She was so pathetic. Wasn't she just the saddest thing you ever saw, Emily?"

Emily looked at Rochelle and turned away.

Rochelle continued at a fast clip, "She was homeless and always telling me how she wanted to be just like me. She said I had everything to make me happy. She'd be happy with just a little bit of it. Poor thing. She just kept telling me how she wanted to be me. Sometimes she even tried to dress like me.

"A few times she actually came to my house. I had to chase her out. One time I actually had to threaten to call the police. It was like she was a stalker or something. Poor, pathetic Blythe. It's good we have such organizations as Sustain and Shelter, isn't it, Emily? They can help these poor people who have nothing—just like Blythe. Poor thing."

Emily continued to look at the ground; Bob looked at Emily as Rochelle prattled on about poor, pathetic Blythe.

As if a new thought had occurred to her, Rochelle said, "Oh dear. Do you suppose that's why she killed herself here? Oh, how sad. She wanted to be so much like me that she killed herself on my front porch." Rochelle manufactured a few tears to punctuate the sobriety of the occasion.

"I don't know, ma'am. We'll have a crew out here shortly. We'll get it cleaned up," promised Detective Yoshiwara.

"When you finish whatever you have to do, release the body to me if you find no family, and I'll take care of the funeral." Rochelle dabbed delicately at her eyes with her fingers. Having composed her broken emotions, she drove into her garage and, presumably, went into her house. Bob's companion detective and patrolmen attended to the scene surrounding Blythe's body, but Bob continued to watch Emily absent-mindedly rubbing Byte's ears. Upon Emily's command, the dog and her master turned to go down the hill.

Bob Washburn caught up with her, grabbed her arm, and turned her to look at him. Emily gazed toward him but not directly into his eyes.

"If I ran fingerprints on this body, would I find this to be Blythe Oberstein?"

Emily slowly shook her head, "Probably not."

"I wouldn't think so. Tell me why you wouldn't think so."

"I would think she wouldn't have any fingerprints on file. She said she never worked, so fingerprints wouldn't be available. If she's homeless…I don't know, Bob. She has gloves on now. That means you're not going to find fingerprints on the gun."

Bob rested his chin in his hand, thought a few minutes and then asked, "When Chad was arrested, he didn't give us much of a story. He asked for his attorney. We expected that; that's procedure. But he said some interesting off-the-wall things, you know, trying to throw the blame on Rudyard, anyone he could. Ida's name was mentioned. Much of it was disjointed; we'll sort through it. But the strange thing he said was that the same person killed the three people we know about. Said it was a person connected with Sustain and Shelter."

"Did he have proof? Did he know who it was?"

"He didn't give names, but he said he didn't kill anybody."

"You believe him? You don't think he was the murderer? Maybe Rudyard is. Are you going to arrest him for murder?"

"No, fraud. Chad even threw out Rochelle Emory's name as the contract killer."

"Guess their scamming days are over, you think?"

"Perhaps. Depends on how much evidence we can build against them. You know that. Depends on how good their attorneys are. Do you have anymore to add? Did this woman say anything to you? Did Rochelle say anything to you?"

Save a family. Don't tell anyone. When Ralph Watkins died, even Bob had said it, don't tell anyone. If I don't tell anyone, do I save a family? Emily looked away from Bob and thought before she said, "You just saw Rochelle Emory, Bob. Does she look like a woman who kills people for a living? She's got a family; she's got a husband who has big bucks. Why would she kill three people? Why would she launder money? She doesn't need that. Raising two kids is a lot of work. She wouldn't have time to kill and launder money. Why would she do that?"

"I don't know. You tell me."

Emily thought some more. The rain had stopped, but she was cold. Bob saw her try to stifle her shivering.

"Come in the car. We can turn on some heat. The coroner's van from the sheriff's office just drove up. They'll be busy for a while. Come on, you can warm up." He guided her into the detectives' car and put the thermostat at blast-furnace level.

"So what do you think?" Bob asked when Emily could talk through her blue lips without a shivery voice.

She took a deep breath and dived into a hastily thought out, but plausible, she hoped, explanation. "Okay, Bob. Here's what I know and here's what I think I know. When Byte got out of Miriam's garage, and I chased her up here, Blythe was standing in the driveway of Rochelle's house. I'm pretty sure she was the one who rammed my car. Did you see my car at the bottom of the hill?"

Emily waited for Bob's acknowledgement before proceeding. It gave her time to warm up and think.

"I couldn't understand that. Why would she crash my car? Then you're telling me about a hit woman. Do you think she was trying to kill me? Maybe she was trying to get me out of the way. Rudyard and Chad must've thought I was learning too much about Sustain and Shelter. Perhaps that's why…Emily trailed off. "Perhaps that's why she seemed to be pointing her gun at me. Yes, that's exactly what happened. Bob, she was going to shoot me. That's why Byte…of course, that's why Byte ran at her. She must've sensed what was happening. When Byte knocked Blythe off balance, the gun went off. It ricocheted off a rock. That's what happened. Your crime scene investigators can confirm that, can't they?"

Bob slowly nodded his head as he turned down the heat in the car. "Okay, Emily, you've explained everything beautifully. I can even buy into it. Now, do you want to tell me why Chad was yammering on about Rochelle Emory being a killer?"

One more hurdle. Save a family. If muddling though this half-truth were going to save a family, why did she feel so deceitful when talking to Bob? The irony was that honesty, which should be the best policy, wasn't going to make her feel any more virtuous. So she plunged into the pool of muddied truth one more time.

"Don't you think, Bob, that's why she tried to hang around Rochelle? Maybe by aligning herself with Rochelle, she could adopt her identity and make Chad think Rochelle was the murderer. I mean, you saw her. Look how closely they resemble each other. You heard Rochelle say how Blythe was a stalker. Maybe the times she, Blythe, came in contact with Chad, she looked enough like her that fooled them. Then, when she came in contact with all of us, like at a board meeting, she took on her own identity? I don't know, Bob. I mean, that's all I can figure out." Emily looked askance at Bob.

"You mean you want me to believe she played Rochelle when some people were looking? She played Blythe when other people were looking?" Bob leaned back in his seat as Emily quietly nodded. She reached out and turned the heat down even more. Was she sweating the truth, or was she sweating with the increased temperature?

"Bob, you know it couldn't be Rochelle who killed those people."

"How do you know?"

"Rochelle was in the car with us when Miriam was shot on the freeway. How could she be shooting people if she were being shot at? Emily's voice was elated at this bit of proof she had just fished out of the pool of half-truths.

Swimming around in this muddy pool of truth, however, was clouding Emily's understanding of the story she was proposing to Bob. She had to remember that Blythe was actually playing Rochelle in the car when Miriam was shot. Now, explaining that the real Rochelle was the one who fired those shots at the pretend Rochelle was going to be hard to keep straight. What Emily wouldn't give to have a flow chart in front of her. She sweated a little more.

As if it would help order his thoughts, Bob shook his head. He sighed and said, "Your explanations are creative. We'll see what results the investigators come up with. If that bullet did ricochet and kill Blythe, then there's not a whole lot we more we can investigate.

"You owe me one, Emily."

Emily looked into his honest eyes and said somberly, "Yes, I do. I owe you a big one. If you don't mind, could I owe you one more?"

Bob nodded silently.

"When you've finished here, could you take Byte and me to my mother's office? Like everything else you've done for me, I'd greatly appreciate this."

CHAPTER 42

"Dolly, is it okay to bring Byte in the office," Emily asked the office manager at Community Action Group after she and Bob had greeted the woman.

Dolly waved off Emily's question. "My heavens, yes. That dog is better mannered than some of the clients we've had in here."

As Dolly greeted Byte, Genevieve strolled through the waiting area and parked herself in front of Bob. "Well, hello, stranger," she drawled out. She smiled brightly enough to put California into another rolling blackout. "Haven't seen you for too long." Placing her hands on his arm, she guided him into her office.

Dolly shook her head. "Actually, the dog has better manners than some of the employees in here.

"Your mother is just finishing with a client, and, then, her appointments are done for the day. If that's who you're looking for."

Emily smiled. "You're psychic. What shall I do about Bob? Think Gen will let loose of him? Anytime soon?"

"Her husband just left a message to say he's on his way to pick her up. She'll let loose then. Shouldn't be too long."

However, it was Louisa, having walked passed Genevieve's office as she escorted her client out of her own office, who rescued Bob. Louisa stepped into the office, interlinked her arm with Bob's and said, "Did Genevieve pull you in off the streets, or did you walk in on your own?"

"I'm playing knight errant for your daughter. She needs you, I think."

"Something to do with Sustain and Shelter?"

Bob shrugged. "She'll let you know."

Genevieve changed her glare directed at Louisa to scrutiny of the conversation Bob and she were having. "Sustain and Shelter? Isn't that what Emily was asking us about at lunch? Something about Ida. Ida McIvey. What's happened? Tell me what's happened. I'm hearing too much about this group. Something's going on. What is it?"

Bob turned to Genevieve. "Ida McIvey is dead. She was the body found in the river earlier this fall."

"Oh." Genevieve sat down quickly and in silence.

Louisa and Bob left her office, retrieved Emily and Byte and led them into Louisa's office.

Closing the door, Louisa put her arm around her daughter's shoulders, looked at her and said, "But you knew about Ida, so that's not why Bob brought you here. You suspected that was Ida in the river. What really happened?"

Emily leaned her head against her mother's shoulder and said to Bob, "You tell her."

As the group stood in the center of the room, Bob related Emily's story. "Now, I'm going back to City Hall, so I can finish my day before midnight. Louisa, I might catch you later, but I will definitely call tonight."

"Good. I'll be waiting." To Emily, she said, "We need to pick up the girls at school, right?"

"There's a carpool, but if you have time, I'd appreciate going to get them."

Louisa pulled away from her daughter and gazed at Emily.

"What else, Em?"

Emily grimaced. "What do you mean?"

"There's more to the story. Bob doesn't know all of it, does he?"

"Answer me this, Mom. Is this your social work intuition or your mother intuition?"

Louisa smiled knowingly and shrugged slightly. "Don't know. What's the rest of the story? Do you want to tell me?"

Emily thought and, finally, answered. "Yes and no."

Louisa nodded.

"You know, Mom, that age old problem. When a lie helps someone, is it good or bad to keep it? If it helps more than one person, is it good or bad? If one person knows about it, and the other person will never care, is it worth it to keep it? Don't tell anyone; save a family."

Again, Louisa nodded. "Guess only you'll know. You and God."

"Yeah. God and me. That's got some weight to it."

Emily and Louisa didn't wait for Jojo and Lulie to come to the car; they met them at their classrooms with the promise of ice cream. Telling the girls that Mom had an accident, and Gramma was going to be their chauffeur for the afternoon covered a multitude of explanations. The ice cream finished off any questions they may have had.

As the four of them headed toward Gramma's car, Emily saw Rochelle, or Blythe, maybe it'd just be easier to call her Mrs. Emory, get out of her Rolls and greet Samantha and Scott. With a beaming smile, she leaned down and grabbed both children in an octopus hug. Only with the protest of the children did she finally release them.

Don't tell. Save a family.

CHAPTER 43

Just before Thanksgiving Miriam picked up Emily for their Tuesday luncheon. Instead of tooting the horn and waiting for her in the car as she usually did, Miriam pushed into Emily's house, excitedly flourished a newspaper from inside her raincoat and shoved it under Emily's nose.

"Did you see this? Did you look at the San Francisco paper this past Sunday? Look at the 'Style Section'. Did you see it?"

"No, I only got through the 'Book Review' section. Too much homework for Lulie. What're you talking about?"

"Look, there's a picture of Rochelle and Geoffrey. It has to be the same people, the ones who lived at the top of our hill?"

Grabbing the paper Emily said, "Let me see that." She scrutinized the picture. Geoffrey hadn't changed much, but Rochelle had dark hair upswept into a twist and wore a strapless, glittering long evening gown. Both wore bright, society news smiles. The caption lined out both their names, Rochelle and Geoffrey Emory.

"Sure looks like them," mused Emily.

"Did you know they had moved to San Francisco? I didn't know that. One day they're in that big old house, the next they're gone. Even the kids were surprised when they went to school, and Samantha and Scott were gone."

"No, I didn't know," Emily said absently as she continued her study of the newspaper.

Miriam said tentatively, "I heard a strange story about them. Ramona said she heard there was a suicide up there. She claimed a homeless person shot herself up there. Do you know anything about that? It was around the time your van was hit. Did you ever find out anything about who hit it?"

"I could never identify the car. I didn't even have a license plate number."

"Had you heard about the suicide? Do you know anything about it?"

Don't tell anyone. Don't tell anyone what you know. Kill the secret; make the secret die. Dead secrets shouldn't be resurrected. Kill a secret, save a family. After a pause she looked up at Miriam, "No, I don't know anything about it. But it makes sense they would go to San Francisco. What better place to hide from the rumor mill than where your husband's family is top dog? People gossip about you anyway, and no one knows what to believe, so even if the story is true, they'll figure it's grossly overblown."

"What's Bob Washburn say about all this?"

"What do you mean?"

"Well, all this Sustain and Shelter stuff."

"I didn't think we were discussing Sustain and Shelter."

"Sure, we were. Rochelle was on Sustain and Shelter, so we were discussing it."

"Not really. All Bob cares about is that he did his job and put those scumbags, Rudyard and Chad, out of circulation. Bob's just out to do a job. I get the feeling he wouldn't find this as interesting as you and I would because it doesn't have anything to do with solving the crime.

"Speaking of which," Emily continued, "come with me to the next meeting of Sustain and Shelter. You can see if you want to be on the Board of Directors."

"What do you mean? I thought with the arrest of Rudyard and Chad that that place would have been boarded up and closed," said Miriam.

"Yeah, you're right. But Joan Chavez and Thomas Oakhurst think it can continue. They did do a bunch of good for the homeless at that clinic, you know. They want to keep it going. They figure they've got a nice budget with which to keep it going. Joan has the time, now, because she lost her job at County Hospital. She still has to deal with the Board of Medical Examiners to see if she can keep her nursing license, but she has all that community service she needs to put in time for. Sustain and Shelter might be able to continue. Let's find out."

"And working together will be good for Thomas and Joan's staying together?" Miriam asked.

"Something like that," agreed Emily. "Come to it, please. Just to see what it would be like."

Lips set to form the word, no, Miriam looked at her friend and said, "I'll think about it."

Christmas came early for Emily that year. The Friday after Thanksgiving, David, Louisa, Bob, Jojo and Lulie simultaneously got out of their chairs between finishing dinner and eating dessert. As Lulie giggled, David produced a scarf he had absconded from Emily's drawer, bound her eyes and said, "You must trust us. We will lead you to a great treasure."

Emily sensed Jojo trying to quiet her sister's muffled giggles as David and Louisa guided her out the kitchen into the garage.

"Okay, Lulie, I'll lift you up, and you may remove the blindfold. Keep your eyes shut, Emily, until Jojo tells you to open them." Emily could feel Louisa tightly holding in her excitement as she turned her daughter to face the garage door.

Emily smelled it even before Jojo let her open her eyes, but she was still caught off guard by her own surprise. Parked in the spot normally occupied by her rental car ("Just until we get the van repaired," David had said.) was a gold SUV complete with showroom aroma. Tan leather interior, compact disc player, back speakers, six cylinder engine began the list of extras designed by Detroit to enhance one's life in one's home away from home.

As their mother gaped in astonishment, Jojo and Lulie squealed in delight at the surprise they had carried off. Louisa and Bob, arm slung around Louisa's shoulder, stood next to the van broadly smiling. Producing a camera from her pocket, Louisa recorded the event in pictures.

Emily's "ohing" and "ahing" was accompanied by David's laughing with her delight as he explained, "There was no way to fix the old van. The insurance company totaled that as soon as they saw it. We had to search around for this one because I wanted it to be perfect for you. That's why it took so long to get it. I told the broker he had to find one with everything on it."

He paused. Then he said, "There's just one thing we couldn't arrange very well."

"What's that?" Emily said as she threw her arms around his neck.

"A dog seatbelt."

Byte, who had been sniffing the exterior of the van, looked at the family and snorted.